CW01501668

THREADS OF SHADOW

The Wendlelow Mysteries

By P. A. Sheldon

ALSO FROM P. A. SHELDON.

The Wendlelow Mysteries
Fireside Horror.

Selected Collections
Pocket Horror.

THREADS OF SHADOW
Copyright @ 2025 by P. A. Sheldon. All rights
reserved. Printed in the United Kingdom. No part of this
book may be used or reproduced in any manner
whatsoever without written permission from the author,
except in the case of brief quotations embodied in
critical articles and reviews.

This is a work of fiction. Names, characters,
businesses, places, events, locales, and incidents are
either the products of the author's imagination or used in
a fictitious manner. Any resemblance to actual persons,
living or dead, or actual events is purely coincidental.
P. A. Sheldon 2025.

All quotations included here fall under the fair use or
public domain guidelines of copyright law.

FIRST EDITION

Original front cover and images courtesy of
Tangra.link.

ISBN: 9798323992898

For Karen,
with all my love.

Contents

About This Book

Threads of Shadow is a sequel to my first book, Fireside Horror, published in 2024. Like its predecessor, it is what I have come to think of as a novel told in short stories. That is to say, all the tales in this book are linked together to tell one larger narrative. The stories are set in the same timeline as *Fireside Horror*, as such some characters, who may have died or disappeared by the end of that book, may make an appearance here. I have dated each tale so anyone who is interested can see where it fits in the overall time line of *The Wendlelow Mysteries*, although understanding this is really not essential to your enjoyment of the book.

The Wendlelow Mysteries will be a trilogy of books, outlining the fate of that troubled Shropshire town and its unfortunate inhabitants.

Thank you for buying a copy of my book, my friend. I hope you have as much fun reading it as I had writing it.

Henry Swain

November 1898

An explosion of stars obscured Nolan's vision as his head was thrust against the wall. This was followed by an inevitable dull throb in the back of his skull. Feebly he tried to break the grip on his collar, but it was hopeless – easier for a mouse to free itself from a cat's jaw than to escape this vice-like hold.

Nolan Perkins had been at Toadstone School for only a couple of months, but he hated it and knew he would continue to hate it for the length of his tenure. He wished he had been tutored at home like his older sister Dorothy. If his father could afford the fees to this prestigious Shropshire boarding school, surely he could afford to hire another home tutor. He knew his sister detested Miss Bramble, her teacher, who she described as, *a tyrant in petticoats*, and would moan on an almost daily basis about the woman, but surely that was better than the hell to which he was currently subjected.

Yes, he could have been home-schooled, but his father, who was an important aide in Queen Victoria's government, was a proud man and wanted to be able to boast to his colleagues in Parliament that his only son went to one of the best schools money could buy. Even if that meant Nolan had to suffer endless taunts and beatings at the hands of his peers.

His father was no despot, and no doubt had Nolan asked, he would have removed him from the school. But Nolan felt ashamed, ashamed at his own physical weakness, ashamed of having to look his father in the eye and admit to his failings, and so he remained silent, dreamed of what might be, and wallowed in his misery.

Nolan was small for his age. Though not particularly sporty, he did enjoy a good game of tennis. But what was worse, and had drawn the most attention from the bullying miscreants attending the school, was his stutter, which was only aggravated by the frustration it caused. All these factors made him a prime target for the average schoolyard tough, who viewed weakness and difference with the eye of a ruthless predator.

"Are you listening to me?" barked his nemesis, shaking him again like a terrier with a rat.

"Y-yes," Nolan stammered.

"My algebra – finish it tonight, you little swot, or I'll drown you in the pond!"

"All right," Nolan managed to gasp; the grip on his collar really was rather tight and was causing him to see dark spots before his eyes.

"Good. I'll leave it on your bed in our dorm." His tormentor let go his hold, and Nolan slowly slid down the wall to rest, legs spread out before him on the gravel.

Casper Trenchton was a tough schoolyard scrapper and the bane of Nolan's existence. Casper and his two muscle-bound cronies were thugs in smart trousers and immaculately pressed school jackets. He watched them walk away, hatred burning his eyes.

"You really should stand up to that boy, Perky." The speaker was Horace Tipperon, an unnaturally tall, gangly boy, with large protuberant eyes and a relaxed attitude to the world at large. He leaned against the wall a few metres from where Nolan sat in disgrace.

"Some fr-fr-friend you are," Nolan muttered bitterly, running a hand through his brown hair.

"My dear boy, I am the best friend you could ever have," Horace said, "but there's no way I'm taking a beating for you."

"And j-j-just how am I supposed to st-stand up to him?" Nolan asked, slowly getting to his feet and brushing himself off. "He's nearly t-twice my size, all muscle, and he's got no bloody n-neck."

Together, they walked away from the secluded area where Nolan had been waylaid and out onto the playing fields. It was late November, all about the grounds the oaks and alders, so vibrant and colourful just a few weeks earlier, were starting to look forlorn and bedraggled, as the cold autumn winds made way for winter by snatching the leaves from their branches and scattering them about Toadstone's considerable grounds.

It was late in the day and behind them the large school stood stark against the pale sunlight, its red bricks and large arched windows dominating the surrounding countryside, its multitude of soaring chimneys conquering the sky like the towers of a medieval castle.

The centrepiece of the building was a large clock tower that stood over the main school entrance. The great white clock face stared down at the students, like a sinister, black-flecked eye.

"I'm not saying you should give him a thrashing – clearly that ain't gonna happen, old bean. Just don't… don't make it so damn easy for him. Throw a punch or two – make him work for it. Perhaps then he'll go elsewhere and find easier pickings."

"He'd murder me!" Nolan snapped back.

"He ain't got the nerve to put you in the infirmary – if that happened, questions might be asked and he could very well find himself expelled. Then he'd have to face his father's wrath, and that would amount to murder, from what I hear," Horace laughed. "I don't suppose it helps that you're so damn smart for your age, or he'd probably be trying to get some other poor sod in his own year to do his stupid work."

It was, reflected Nolan, a black day when Casper had been moved into their dorm room. It had happened after Casper and his friends had been dragged in front of the headmaster following the notorious *Badger and Bear* public house incident in the local village.

His whole gang had been split up amongst the junior dorms, an insane idea to Nolan's mind, for now their bad influence was infecting the younger pupils. But clearly the school's masters thought the idea had merit, though quite why was beyond him. He had come to believe that had they not been placed in such close proximity, Casper would never have taken notice of him.

Overhead rooks beat their wings against the grey sky, calling out to anyone who cared to listen as they made their way back to their nests in a particularly venerable alder tree that grew towards the edge of the school grounds.

"Going back to Henry's tree," Horace said cryptically.

"Henry's tree?" Nolan asked.

"You don't know the story of Henry Swain?"

"No," Nolan said, "should I?"

Horace paused for a while, watching the last of the rooks settle in the tree's grey boughs, with an excited look on his face. "It's a good story Perky, a ghost story, but I think I'll save it for the evening, when our dorm is together, just before lights out. That's the best time for a story like that," he said excitedly.

*

Casper leaned against the Rugby goal posts, talking with his friends Ewan, the second son of Lord Baughan, and George Pelton, the eldest son of a cabinet minister. He felt happy here in the company of good friends, far happier than he ever did at home.

When he was not at Toadstone, he lived with his father in a manor deep in the Herefordshire countryside, he spent his free time scrambling up trees, hunting for bird eggs, scrapping with local boys and occasionally playing cricket.

But unlike a great many of his peers Casper's home also held a great deal of misery, so much in fact that he learned to prefer his school life. Casper's mother had died of consumption when he was very young and his few cherished memories of her were of a pretty but sickly woman who, though never short of affection for her large boy, seldom had the energy to join him in his childish play.

But it was not just the lack of a mother's influence that made Casper's home so unbearable, oh no, the true source of his misery was his father. The honourable Major Trenchton, respected soldier, landowner, and bane of his son's life.

Major Trenchton was a man to whom the words, fatherly affection, were nothing more than a collection of meaningless syllables. Nothing his son attempted or achieved was good enough for him. Casper knew he could never impress his father with his intellectual achievements which were, to be fair, very limited.

Indeed, his father had been heard to say that Casper waged a constant war between the thick walls of his skull and education. Almost, without question, his skull was victorious, holding back any invading knowledge.

But what Casper lacked in academic achievements he more than made up for in sporting accomplishments. Rugby and cricket were second nature to him and he had received accolades for his abilities. However, trophies and praise counted for nought to his father.

As if this were not bad enough, Major Trenchton had a temper, one that could flare up like dry grass beneath a relentless summer sun, explode for the most innocuous of reasons, and woe betide any man or woman who was too close at such moments. Casper had been on the receiving end of his father's tempers more often than he could remember. They usually left him bruised and bloodied and in one extreme case, two years previously, with a broken finger. So it was that Casper had learned to dread his returns home.

He lived in fear, fear of disappointment, and fear of his cruel parent with his unpredictable moods. Even as he grew taller and stronger, he still quailed before his father's blows, held by the fear that had been instilled into him throughout his childhood, rendering him incapable of lifting a hand in his defence.

*

Horace was a natural storyteller, he knew it, and loved the attention it brought him. True to his word, he revealed nothing of his tale, just cryptically telling the other boys whom they shared their dorm with that he knew a great ghost story which he would tell them later, promising it was a real humdinger!

The dormitory slept twelve boys, all of whom, with the exception of Casper, were the same age as Nolan. There was little in the way of decoration – just beds and a stone fireplace.

A large window looked out over the grounds and beyond to the fields and woodlands that surrounded the school. Somewhere in the distant gloom glistening lights betrayed the whereabouts of the small village of

Toadstone, whose inn had been Casper and his cronies' downfall.

It would have been a very sparse place to live, but each boy brought with him a little bit of home, a small portrait of his family or maybe a well-thumbed novel. All about the dorm were collections of workbooks piled in a higgledy-piggledy manner, seemingly with no care or order.

Horace sat in the window seat; behind shone the autumn moon, its pale light giving him a silvery outline against the frosty glass. At his insistence, the oil lamps had been dimmed to provide better ambience.

"Can't tell a ghost story in a bright room – it'd be like dancing a jig to a funeral dirge," he announced in his usual airy manner.

And so all the boys crowded about Horace, an air of expectancy permeating the room, and despite declaring a lack of interest in the whole thing, even the normally bitter and resentful Casper could be seen to lean forward, the better to catch Horace's every word. For what boy can resist a macabre tale, skilfully told on a dark and windy evening? And all there knew that few told stories as well as Horace Tipperton.

"Henry Swain," Horace explained, "was one of the school's previous headmasters, a cold, ruthless old gentleman, who had run the place more like a military prison than a centre of learning. It had not been a happy school under his tenure; punishments were meted out seemingly at random and for the most dubious of reasons.

"This made the pupils fearful, for they knew that it was not enough merely to follow the rules and be mindful in their lessons; simply being in the wrong place at the wrong time could find you on the receiving end of the old tyrant's cane! It was said that you need only walk past Master Swain on a day when he was in a bad mood, and you would find yourself unable to sit comfortably for a week."

This much of the tale was enough to give most of the boys a cold shudder, for whom amongst them had not known someone who had felt the sharp whack of birch wood on tender skin, seen the terrible welts it left on fellow students' hands, or watched, wincing as a comrade had lowered himself painfully into a chair at the start of a lesson?

"The old villain was said to have derived great pleasure from these punishments. He loathed the weak, and always targeted children who were unwilling or unable to stand up for themselves. These unfortunates could be dragged to his office at a moment's notice, where alone with this tormenting figure they would suffer terrible thrashings, often coming away with ugly bruises or bad lacerations.

"Henry Swain was a most cunning and dastardly individual, but he knew on which side his bread was buttered, and so he was careful never to target children whom he felt had someone powerful or influential behind them.

"But there were worse allegations levelled at the former Headmaster than merely the casual abuse of his charges. It was rumoured that he was a dabbler in the shadowy arts and that at certain potent nights of the year he had been seen around a local standing stone, known as *The Toadstone*, for its squat batrachian appearance, dancing, chanting and, well, perhaps the less said on this matter the better!

"One might ask about the other masters at the school. How could such bright and well-educated men miss these vile crimes being perpetrated, as they were, beneath their very noses?

"No doubt some of the tutors were simply too self-absorbed to notice anything amiss, after all, children were children. If occasionally one or two had bruises visible on their hands or arms, well, boys were known for their rough and tumble antics.

"It is also possible that other, more observant masters could have chosen to ignore their suspicions. Headmaster Swain, for all his faults, ran an efficient school and one where the students left with good prospects. He also had important friends in high places and it didn't do for the chickens to ruffle the feathers of the rooster, particularly when he had the ear of the farmer.

"This awful state of affairs continued for many years, the hairs on the old villain's head turned grey, and many students came and went through Toadstone's black iron gates, until one day, the inevitable scandal erupted.

"School legend, so carefully handed down from boy to boy, does not record the name of the child who brought about the Headmaster's downfall. But doubtless a determined adult could find it by rifling through the relevant archives.

"Whatever his name, the child committed suicide, throwing himself from the clock tower, unable to face another brutal encounter with the merciless Headmaster.

"This alone would not have been enough to doom Swain. But the child had sent a letter to his father, a final pathetic message, revealing everything: One midsummer night Headmaster Swain had swept the boy from his room while his fellow students looked on, too fearful of the old man to raise a hand to help him.

"The terrified boy had been dragged to The Toadstone, a place where ghastly things happened… a place all the students avoided. There, he was left a shuddering husk of his former self. The headmaster ignored him, and addressed the night in a strange language that no decent folk would dare utter. After a moment, something answered back, something joined them... something the boy could never bring himself to describe.

"Doctor Swain had believed that the boy's father possessed little influence, and his initial complaints had fallen on deaf ears. He had not, however, counted on the child's uncle, a prominent politician. Letters were written to governors, newspapers were contacted, other victims slowly came forward and gradually the web began to tighten about Doctor Swain.

"In early November of the same year, he took his own life, rather than face the disgrace of a public inquiry, hanging himself from the great alder tree that even then dominated the school's grounds. It was said that it was foggy that day, so the body hung for many hours before it was finally discovered. By that time the rooks had already made a bloody meal of the wicked old man's eyes."

By now the whole room was silent and a crowd of young faces stared expectantly at Horace, waiting for him to deliver the grisly finale that must surely follow as inevitably as the rising sun follows the dark of night. And Horace, knowing he had his audience captivated, delivered it with relish.

"And now every thirteen years on the anniversary of his death, the ghost of Henry Swain wanders the corridors of Toadstone. The rooks precede him, warning of his coming. He waits till the night is at its blackest, looking for a victim, a weak individual, one incapable of standing up to those who terrorise him.

"And while the whole school slumbers, he slips into the unfortunate's room, moving slowly toward his victim, savouring every moment, as a wolf might savour a slab of bloody meat until finally, he stands over the unlucky boy, raises his spectral hands then plunges them down into the sleeper's mind."

"The next morning when his roommates awaken they find him lying there, a gibbering wreck, his mind broken, destined for the asylum – there to while away the remainder of his miserable days, in a padded cell, subject to the cruel caprices of modern medicine."

Then Horace revealed the most terrible fact; for he had it on good authority that it had been thirteen years since the spectral headmaster had claimed his last victim, which meant, sometime this month he would walk the halls again!

An uncomfortable silence fell about the room, with many glancing about warily into the shadows as if expecting the school shade to leap from them at any moment. Horace smiled, pleased with the effect of his story.

It was Casper who spoke first. "Perky had better look out then. Mind you, I hear you can pay the Bedlam guards sixpence to see the raving lunatics gibbering away, it's supposed to be quite amusing, so at least we will all be able to visit you," he said giving Nolan a spiteful look.

"H-how do you kn-know all this?" asked Nolan, trying to ignore Casper's comment. He was a deeply superstitious boy and the story had terrified him. He hoped Horace would laugh it all off, tell them it was made up, a prank to put the willies up them.

He was sadly disappointed.

"An old family friend came to this school," Horace replied sincerely. "In his day the story was common knowledge, he even knew the names of some of the boys who had encountered old Swain and been shipped off to the mad house. He did tell me them," he said, and then added dismissively, "but I can't remember who they were."

*

The following morning Nolan sat alone in the dormitory staring out of the large window toward the alder tree, the very tree where the dastardly headmaster had taken his life at the end of a hemp rope. He tried to imagine his body swinging, puppet-like in the breeze.

As he stared, he thought he could make out a shape standing in the shadow of the great trunk. At first it was vague, hard to discern, but as he watched he became convinced it was the shape of a man, tall, thin, pale, with white wispy hair that should have blown in the morning wind, in the same way the autumn leaves flew so carelessly, but instead hung lank and still, down to his shoulders.

As he watched, he could have sworn he saw the figure appear and disappear, flickering like a dying candle flame. Although it was too far to be certain, he felt sure that whoever was out there was staring directly up at his window. Sweat coated his body as he looked on. But then, faster than you could conjugate *amo*, the figure vanished and the candle flame extinguished.

Nolan blinked and rubbed at his eyes, he was exhausted, having barely slept a wink the previous evening, after Horace had told his horrific tale.

Since the other boys taunted him constantly, he felt he had abundant reason to worry – as if the tale were a warning of some dire fate that awaited in the oh-so-near future.

Nolan had lived with the supernatural all his life, his family home was reputed to be the haunt of a woman in grey. He had even seen her sometimes, on the main stairs on wild winter evenings. The wailing of the wind would announce her arrival.

The story went that she was a servant who had been wronged by one of the house's previous owners. He had been her lover but had abandoned her after he discovered she was with child. In despair she had thrown herself to her death from the upstairs balcony.

The first time Nolan encountered her, was on a December night when he was much younger. After bidding his parents good night, he shuffled down the hallway to his room but was stopped in his tracks by a grey wraith drifting down the main stairs. He ran back to his parents, sobbing. Over the years, he saw her a couple more times, and even though he was older, she still caused him heart-wrenching terror. Generally, he made it a point to remain in his room on stormy evenings.

Nolan had no illusions about himself – he knew he was weak. He had heard the other boys describe him as puny when his back was turned. He was always the last to be picked when it came to selecting teams for sports. So he was horribly certain that when Henry Swain walked the lamp-lit corridors this year, he would be coming for him.

In his mind, the cold-hearted old master tormented him until, like a weakened branch in an unrelenting gale, his sanity snapped! He considered running, fleeing the school, but he knew if he caught the train home he would only be sent back again by his parents and he had nowhere else to go. He felt he had just one chance; he had to find his strength, he had to prove he was not weak and in doing so turn the vengeful spectre's gaze on some other unfortunate.

But how?

He thought he had the answer, he had to stand up to Casper… to fight if need be. To Nolan this train of thought was almost as terrifying as Horace's bogeyman, but he was convinced that it was the only option open to him. He had no wish to just attack Casper without provocation, to do so would require a courage he didn't think he had, he would need to devise a plan to force Casper into an encounter.

Such a plan did not take long to formulate; he would mess up Casper's algebra homework, make a right pig's ear of it. Casper would have no choice then but to confront him or risk losing face before his peers.

*

Doctor Crumpton was a man who liked to make examples of boys, especially belligerent or stupid ones who, in spite of all of his efforts, refused to learn even the simplest mathematical principles. And now, he had a boy before him who he considered to be both stupid, and belligerent: Casper Trenchton.

The master was a man of middling height, with a head of patchy brown hair and a high-pitched voice. He was thin, bespectacled, and looked for all the world like a scarecrow in a school master's gown. But to the boys who studied beneath him, he was a despot, a classroom Napoleon, dispensing punishment with an eagerness that would have made a hanging judge proud.

These punishments were always accompanied by a lecture about the idleness of today's youth, their inability to grasp even the most basic mathematical formulae, how he, in his day, had applied himself with diligence, and how it would well become his charges to do the same.

His favourite means of apprehending a wayward child was to firmly grip the miscreant's ear between thumb and forefinger, and apply a forceful twist, a method guaranteed to extract a cry of pain and immediately get the boy's undivided attention.

Casper stood at the master's side, enduring just such a grip. He had been hauled from his seat within moments of the man glancing at his homework; it was an almost comical sight, for Casper was slightly taller than the master and far sturdier in physique.

Yet the thin man held the stocky youth firmly, ranting about the terrible quality of his work and occasionally giving Casper's ear another twist, causing him to yelp like a scolded pup, which in turn caused a great many of his peers to snigger. Serving to further antagonise the master.

Casper for his part was seething. Seething at the master for his heavy-handed treatment and barbed insults about his lack of intellect. Seething at his classmates for witnessing his humiliation. But mostly, seething at Nolan Perkins.

Perkins, that skinny little toad, he had done this on purpose; Casper was certain of it. He'd listened with horror to Doctor Crumpton's explanation of all that was wrong with his work, knowing that the mistakes were deliberate, intended to make him look the fool. Everyone knew Nolan was smart. Casper had heard the boy bragging about how good he was at algebra just a few days before, and that was why he had approached him.

He knew he should have been more careful, even a cursory examination would have shown him that the work was littered with errors. But Casper had just snatched the paper from the little prig without even glancing at it.

But why should he have checked it? He remembered being terrified of the older boys as a first-year, and he knew Nolan was afraid of him. He could only wonder what the boy hoped to achieve by crossing him, even some of the older boys feared him. At first, he had attempted to put them at ease by being friendly – but over time these attempts eventually gave way to contempt and he started to enjoy the feeling of power he could exercise over them.

When the humiliating lesson had finally come to an end, Casper stormed out of the class, seething with rage.

"And don't forget, boy, I want that work redone, and properly this time!" Doctor Crumpton shouted from the classroom door.

"Three bags full, sir," muttered Casper under his breath, well aware that his face had turned a bright crimson.

He immediately collected his two friends, Ewan and George, and went in search of Nolan, determined to scare the boy into doing his work properly this time. Toadstone was a fairly large school, so Casper knew there were plenty of places for a pipsqueak like Perkins to hide, and hide he must, for surely he knew his act of mathematical sabotage would not go unanswered.

So, after checking all the places a boy might choose to conceal himself – the toilets, the wall behind the kitchens, not to mention other places too numerous to list – he was surprised to see Nolan standing on the playing field, in full view, as if it were any normal day and he wasn't about to cop a piece of Casper's mind, and very possibly the full force of his fist.

Why wasn't he hiding? Perhaps he thought some well-meaning individual would come to his aid? He'd learn he was wrong; no blighter would step up to help him, of that Casper was certain. They all had too much sense than to involve themselves in his business.

As he approached, he saw Nolan was chatting with that lanky streak of nothing Tipperton. He would definitely get no aid from that quarter, Tipperton was the biggest windbag he had ever met. Nolan seemed to be talking with a casual ease, as though he had no worries in the world, and Casper started to wonder if Perkins was not as smart as he had believed. Perhaps he really had done the best he could with his work and the mistakes were genuine.

He quickly dismissed the idea. The only thing that bag of bones had going for him was his brain, and he had overheard several of the masters saying how clever he was. Clenching his fists he stormed over to where Nolan and Horace stood, his two brawny friends close on his heels, like faithful hounds.

"Oi, Perkins, you little prig, I want a word with you!" he shouted. The younger boy stiffened and slowly he turned to face him. Casper could tell he was scared; his usually pasty face was paler than ever, and he was clenching and unclenching his fists.

"Yes, wh-what do you want?" he asked.

"You know exactly what I want, you little scut," Casper spat venomously.

"Problem with the algebra, old thing?" Horace asked, a smirk on his face. Casper chose to ignore him, but his comment confirmed his suspicions. It was as he had thought, the mistakes with the work were deliberate and worse still, Perkins had been bragging about them to his stupid gangly friend.

This could not go unanswered!

He became aware of a crowd of boys gathering about them, drawn to the unfolding drama as a flock of ravens were drawn to the bloody corpse of a lamb. They sensed a fight brewing, or at least a beating, for all knew Perkins did not stand a chance against him.

He knew that with his peers watching, he'd have to assert dominance immediately.

"You'll do it again, properly this time," he demanded.

Perkins was silent for a moment, as if bracing himself. "No," he said firmly, and without a hint of a stammer.

There was a murmur from the surrounding crowd, then suddenly rooks broke cover from the alder tree behind Nolan, they looked like a black undulating cloud as they wheeled about in the wolf-grey sky, before winging their way over the surrounding farmland.

"You think you have a choice, you little twerp? You're doing it," Casper snapped.

"N-no, I'm not," Nolan said; but Casper noticed, with a little satisfaction, that despite his belligerence, he suddenly looked terrified.

Casper was however growing frustrated. The skinny boy was creating a problem; on the one hand, he had no wish to do the algebra assignment or be seen to back down. On the other, the crowd of boys was getting larger, sensing the brewing of a fight. If he gave Perkins the beating he deserved, the noise they made was likely to draw one or more of the prefects out of the school to investigate. If he was caught fighting this soon after the Badger and Bear incident, he could very well be expelled.

No, he would not back down now, he felt certain that with just a bit more intimidation, the pipsqueak's resolve would shatter. So, flexing his shoulders, he took a step closer.

"You will do it, or I'll wring your scrawny neck," he snarled in what he hoped was his most trouser-wetting voice.

The fist that struck Casper forced him to take a step back, feeding the hungry crowd, causing them to jeer. It was not that Nolan had been able to put much force behind the blow, or even that it had connected with a particularly sensitive part of the body; indeed, Nolan had deliberately aimed the blow at Casper's shoulder, so as to warn him off without actually hurting him too much. It was just that it came as a surprise, and instinct had made him step away.

Cursing his unintended retreat, Casper raised his fists; he had no choice now, he had to strike back. He didn't want to. If he was caught fighting and it got back to his father… But he was certain one good blow would break Nolan's morale and either see him running for safety, or else pleading to do all his work for the remainder of the term.

So, he flicked a fist forward, hitting the smaller boy on the upper arm with all the force he could muster, he saw Nolan stagger back, wincing, but his opponent quickly recovered, springing forward with an uncanny speed that took Casper by surprise. He tried to dodge the wild incoming blow, swinging himself to one side, but the boy's fist connected with his lip.

Nolan was stick-thin and whilst this meant the blow lacked power, it also meant that he had bony knuckles, and these seemed designed to stab painfully into Casper's flesh, making the blow hurt more than it deserved to. Worst still, Casper came away from the exchange with a bloody lip and a dreadful sense of humiliation.

*

Nolan stared in horror at the blood running down his opponent's face, this was getting seriously out of hand. He had hoped that a few punches to the arm would be enough to end this whole horrible incident, that when Casper realised he was willing to fight back, he would back down and search for easier pickings. He had clearly misjudged the larger boy and now he had actually hurt him!

Nolan was not sure how that had happened, he had been aiming for Casper's arm but at some point his opponent had moved, and to his horror, he had actually caught him on the face!

He knew he was in trouble now, there was no way Casper would let that blow go unpunished. Pride would ensure he had to bloody Nolan at least as much, if not more so. He could run, he should run, but that would merely postpone the inevitable beating. Besides, he had some pride himself; he had struck first, he had instigated this fight, so he couldn't shame himself by fleeing from it now.

He watched in horrified fascination at the change of intensity on Casper's blood-dripping face. He had been angry before, a rumbling volcano threatening to blow. Now he was furious and the volcano was in full eruption.

"You little …" he hissed between his teeth and charged at him, Nolan didn't even get a chance to throw another punch, Casper bulled into him with a force that felt like a runaway train. Nolan was knocked off his feet and landed with a skull-blinding thud on his back. The crowd of surrounding boys seemed to go wild, with out-of-control cheering and jeering.

Casper followed him down.

Nolan found he was pinned, one arm trapped beneath the larger boy's leg, the other held by a large beefy hand, whilst Casper sat heavily on his chest. This left his opponent with one arm free, which he raised threateningly, it lingered there for a moment, like the sword of Damocles, then was brought down, once, twice. Nolan's world went grey, his head awash with pain. His vision cleared enough for him to see Casper raise his fist a third time, he saw the look of hatred on his opponent's face and knew with a terrible certainty that he was powerless before him.

He closed his eyes.

*

The dormitory room was silent; most of the occupants were in a deep restful sleep. The only light came from the dying fire in the grate, its small orange flames illuminating the coal scuttle that sat on the hearth. Outside, a cold wind persistently rattled the window panes. Nolan lay in his bed, miserable, sheets pulled up to his chin, an impending sense of doom coursing cruelly through his body.

It had been two days since his fight with Casper; the encounter had left him with a cut lip, bruised cheek, and a black eye – what Horace described as, "a real shiner."

He had been full of praise for his friend, saying how it had shown real vim and guts to stand up to Casper. It didn't feel gutsy or courageous to Nolan, just painful, and stupid. He had spent the remainder of that afternoon with Casper outside the headmaster's office. Neither boy had spoken a word, each dreading the moment they would be called through that imposing dark oak doorway.

Bizarrely, it had been Nolan who had come off the worst. Several boys had been prepared to say that he had thrown the first punch, perhaps because they were innately truthful, or more likely because they feared Casper's reprisal if they didn't.

So, it was Nolan who had received the sharp edge of the cane, followed by a stern letter to his parents outlining his regrettable behaviour. Not that Casper had escaped completely; he also had a letter dispatched to his father, informing him of his various misdemeanours, this had seemed to distress the large boy considerably.

Nolan had harboured a small hope that the incident would see Casper removed from his dormitory, but this was not to be. Instead, they had been firmly told that any more fighting would see them receive a caning they would never forget and that they had best start acting like grown-ups and put their differences behind them.

So, Casper remained, though he had made a point of completely ignoring Nolan over the last couple of days, and that was, Nolan supposed, a small mercy.

But what was really eating at Nolan was the sense of failure. His punches had not forced Casper into retreat, as he had hoped they might. Instead, his nemesis had stood and fought back, and Nolan had been roundly beaten, so proving that he was the weakest boy in the school. If the prefects had not come over to see what the commotion was about, it was likely that he would have been knocked senseless. As it was, Casper had only landed a few punches before being hauled off him.

Since then he felt constantly ill at ease, as if awaiting some unpleasant event to transpire. He knew he wasn't imagining this. Over the past couple of days, he had dreamed of rooks flying to his window and pecking at the pane, as though wanting to be let in. In the night sky behind them, Nolan could see the silhouette of a man, floating in the moonlight.

He knew who that man was, and knew also that he waited... waited for the night he would be released into the school like a biblical curse.

Free to wander the halls.

Free to hunt down his victim.

Free to hunt Nolan down!

Somewhere far off in Toadstone's deeper recesses he thought he heard a door slam; he sat up in bed, rigid. No one should be about at this hour. Nolan held his breath, listening intently for the slightest sound.

In the grate, the remains of the fire hissed, nearly causing him to cry out in surprise. In a bed opposite, Casper groaned and shifted in his sleep; another boy coughed then fell silently back into his oblivious rest. Nolan's eyes stared at his roommates enviously. He was tired, so tired; he only wanted to sleep. To rest his frantic mind, but the churning anxiety would not allow him to fall into that glorious abyss, would not grant him even that small mercy.

There was a sudden rapping noise at the window. The heavy curtains were drawn, but in his restless mind, he imagined the cruel beak of a rook, steadily testing the strength of the glass, rap, rap, rap.

He tried to calm himself by regulating his breathing – tried to convince himself that he was overreacting, that he was allowing irrational fears and a fevered imagination to get the better of him. But Horace's tale of terror had sunk too deep within him, and his recent dreams were too vivid to allow him to just set the fears aside.

Then he heard the sound he'd been dreading – the creak of floorboards made by someone approaching down the corridor... slowly.

The footsteps stopped outside his door.

For a while, all was silent again.

Nolan released a ragged breath, allowing himself to relax a little; it was just the sound of the old floorboards reacting to the cold weather. Nothing more.

There was another rap upon the window and Nolan spun to look once more in the direction of the curtains. Again, he imagined the rook tapping at the frosty pane, like a herald announcing the coming of the school's phantom, but without slipping out of bed and drawing back the curtains, he could not be certain what made the sound.

He looked slowly back towards the doorway, deciding as he did so that he would try settling back down, try to clear his mind and get some much-needed rest. Instead, he froze, in absolute terror, a terror so bone-chilling that he found he was unable to move or speak!

Inside the room, stood before the closed door, was the shadowy figure of a man, only faintly visible in the dying firelight's orange glow. He was tall, with skin like old leather drawn tightly over his skull, and wispy hair that seemed to float about his head like fine silk in a summer breeze. A morose mouth split the face in half and his head lolled slightly to the right, a testament to the time he had hung from the noose. Black eyeless sockets stared at him, remorseless and cold.

The figure seemed to blink in and out of existence as if unsure whether it really belonged in this reality. With each flicker, he appeared just a little bit closer to Nolan's bed, seeming to stare intensely into the young boy's very soul with that pit-like gaze.

He stopped within arm's length and, for a while, just remained there unmoving, whilst all about, Nolan's roommates slept in blissful ignorance unaware of the horror that moved among them.

Nolan wanted to cry out, to shout and bawl, anything to draw someone to his aid, but his voice caught in his throat and all he could manage was a wheezy croak.

Neither could he move, for his limbs were stiff and unresponsive.

Before him, the figure flickered again; this time he raised a hand to point at Nolan, the long fingernails blackened and crusted with grave dirt. The horror in Nolan's mind reached a pitch and he felt his bladder loosen and a warm wet sensation run down his right leg. Then there was another flicker, and the apparition had lowered his arm and turned to face the foot of his bed.

Flicker, he appeared in the middle of the room, the firelight clearly visible through his ghostly form.

Flicker, now he stood with his back to Nolan, seeming to tower over the bed of another sleeper.

Confused, Nolan watched, more desperate than ever to cry out, but now in warning, to rouse the sleeper from his dreams, to give him a chance to run or fight. But still, his voice remained a prisoner in his throat, desperate to escape but held by a force so primal and ancient that all attempts to free it were hopeless.

Flicker, the figure raised his hands in the air, long nails pointing down towards the sleeper's head. He glanced over his shoulder at Nolan, that black eyeless face smiled, and Nolan's world went dark.

*

The spectre turned from Nolan's unconscious form, poised for a moment, then plunged his fingers down. Like ethereal lances, they pierced the mind of Casper Trenchton; the boy's body went rigid, his eyes shot open and his mouth widened as if to scream, but no sound came forth. After a few agonising moments, his horrified eyes took on a vacant cast, and a trickle of saliva dribbled down the side of his mouth.

*

31

He was found that way in the morning, and quickly and quietly removed from the school. Some of the students said that Casper recovered, though he was never really himself again, but whether that was true or not, he never returned to Toadstone.

As to what had put him in that state, well, on that subject, there were more rumours than there were bricks in the venerable school building, and only a terrified Nolan knew the truth of it.

Fallen Leaves

October 1901

I am scared, Molly, really scared, more scared than I have ever been in my entire life. I want to run, but the door is locked. There's always the window, but we're too high up and I don't think I could climb down. Besides, it's dark out, and I know what wanders in that darkness.

The night should not scare me, I am eleven, a big girl. But it does.

I could open the window and scream for help, but the vicarage is half a mile from the village – no one would hear, no one would come. I wish Daddy had never left. I wish he was here now, but I am alone, alone with him.

I told Daddy I didn't want him to go, but he said it was an important duty, that there were people in the city who needed him just as much as the people of Babbinsmoor. I begged him to take me with him, but he said the lodgings the church was providing were too small, that I would be happier here, that Miss Preece would take good care of me. Besides, he would not be gone for long – a couple of months only.

When Miss Preece first joined us, not long after Mummy died, Daddy introduced her as a housekeeper and tutor who was coming to live with us.

I liked Miss Preece, she was like a new Mummy – young, very pretty and clever as well. I want to grow up to be just like her! Daddy seems to like her too. He is always doing things for her, and sometimes I see them walking together in the vicarage grounds, laughing. At times like that, Molly, I wondered if she might really become my Mummy one day.

Miss Preece was very busy when Daddy left, looking after me and keeping the vicarage clean. I helped as much as I could, but even so, there was a lot to do.

Fortunately, we have old Ned. He is a sort of handyman who tends the garden, fixes broken things, and helps out in a lot of other really important ways. He also tells the most wonderful stories – about the people he met and the places he saw when he was in the army. He is very old and lives in a sort of hut just outside the vicarage grounds.

To call it a hut makes it sound horrid, but it really is quite nice, and he keeps it clean and tidy. He told me that cleanliness is a virtue the army instils in a man, and that cleanliness is next to godliness, and that I should try to keep my bedroom just as tidy as he keeps his cosy little home.

I suppose the vicarage grounds are quite large when compared to the little cottage gardens in the village. Old Ned told me that they are over an acre and take quite a lot of looking after. The vicarage is surrounded by woodland, but I am not supposed to wander about in the woods on my own, especially in the summer.

I don't know why I am telling you all these details, Molly – you have been here as long as me – but somehow it helps to set everything out. It tidies my mind and, in a small way, helps to relax me.

We have a little vegetable garden round the back of the house and a lovely lawn out the front. This time of year, it is very hard to keep it clean, as the leaves from the trees cover it almost daily – something Ned is always grumbling about. I suppose the most impressive thing in our garden is the old English oak tree. It dominates the back lawn, casting much-needed shade in the summer months.

At this time of year, the leaves are copper, yellow and russet – really rather pretty. Some mornings I like to kick my way through them. They make an exciting rustling noise, and there is something pleasant about the earthy smell that rises from them. It is not its size or leafage that makes this grandfather of trees stand out, but the odd pattern on its trunk, the way the bark is raised in places to form interesting shapes and pictures: spirals, animals and strange figures, almost human, but with certain animalistic features like horns or hooves.

Ned says that a very ancient people decorated the tree with copper wire, twisting it about the trunk to form all the fabulous pictures, and that over the centuries the bark has grown over the wire, leaving the raised patterns we see today!

Daddy had been gone just over a week when he sent the telegram. Miss Preece read it to us after dinner. It was short, simply saying his brother Roger would be arriving in two days, and that he would be staying with us for about a week or so. This caused a buzz of excitement – I had met Uncle Roger, but it had been when I was very young. Mummy had still been alive at the time, and I could not really remember him.

Neither Miss Preece nor old Ned had ever met him before, and I imagine they were as nervous about making a good impression on him as I was. We all gathered in the parlour after dinner and discussed the best ways to make him feel welcome, and how to prepare the house and grounds for his arrival. The following day was spent tidying the house and preparing the back bedroom for our guest. I was more than happy to help, remembering what Ned had said about the importance of tidiness. I did not want my uncle to think we were messy people!

I had heard many stories about my uncle from Daddy. He was a missionary and had spent many years abroad, visiting exciting places and meeting interesting people. I thought he sounded like the most wonderful person and could not wait to meet him and hear all his fascinating stories. I was certain he'd have plenty to tell.

I worked so hard that I was exhausted by bedtime. I said my prayers and climbed into bed, but as tired as I was, I could not sleep. I kept trying to imagine what my uncle would be like. I pictured him as a big man with a large beard. Because he had worked abroad, I kept thinking of him as one of those explorer fellows you see in adventure books – wearing a domed hat and beige clothes, his face tanned and possessing a deep, booming voice like the sergeant majors in Ned's tales of army life – but when he finally arrived the next day, I discovered he was nothing like that at all!

It was early afternoon when he drew up in a small horse-drawn trap he had hired from the village. He paid the driver, climbed out onto the gravel path and looked about approvingly. I had been watching excitedly, sitting in a downstairs window. As soon as he pulled up, I ran outside calling, "Uncle Roger! Uncle Roger!" He stared at me for a moment, clearly confused, and I had to remind myself that I had been very small when last he saw me.

He was shorter and thinner than Daddy, wearing a dark suit and a top hat. He possessed a small beard that reminded me of one of the Billy Goats Gruff from my storybook. He didn't have Daddy's kind face – instead, he looked very stern, as if someone had been naughty and he was about to give them a jolly good telling-off. I gave him a big hug, and when I pulled away, he wore a broad smile.

Whilst Ned took his belongings to his bedroom, Miss Preece and I took him to the morning room, where we served him drinks and sandwiches.

We talked, and he told us about his life abroad, the people he had met and the fabulous things he had seen. He then explained how he had been lodging in the city when he bumped into Daddy, and how happy they had been to see each other... how Daddy had insisted that he stay at the vicarage for a while and catch up with his family.

I told him everything about myself. At first, he was very interested, but after a while the smile drained from his face and he interrupted me, asking Miss Preece if he might be forgiven if he retired to his room for a rest.

I was very disappointed, Molly. I had planned a tour of our home and was looking forward to guiding my uncle around. Besides, I had a great many things I still wanted to tell him – and even more to ask! I told Miss Preece that I wanted to knock on his bedroom door, but she said the polite thing for me to do was to let him rest. He would come out when he was ready, and I could talk to him then. So, I decided I would sit on the landing by his door and patiently read a book – that way, I would be ready the second he came out.

I couldn't really concentrate on the book, though. I read the words, but I did not seem to take them in, and after five pages I realised I did not know what was going on – my mind was on other things. Besides, I could have sworn that I could hear someone pacing about in my uncle's room. If he wasn't sleeping, why did he not come out? We had so much catching-up to do.

After an hour I gave up waiting and wandered off to find Miss Preece. She was preparing the meal for that evening, and I did what I could to help. When Uncle

Roger finally came down, he wore his broad smile like a fine hat and eagerly accepted my invitation to show him around.

I took him all about the house, taking extra pride in my room, which I had worked so hard to keep tidy. He asked a lot of questions about our home's past. Who had owned it previously? Were there any interesting stories connected to the place? Questions I did not know the answers to, so I told him that Ned knew all about that sort of thing, having grown up in the nearby village, and that he should speak to him.

Uncle Roger's interest grew when we got outside into the grounds. As we walked around the house I pointed out the flower beds and told him how pretty they were in the summer. I showed him the vegetable garden – now bare after we had harvested our small crop – telling him of all the things I had helped Ned grow there.

He was most interested in our ancient tree. For a while he just stared at it in wonder, craning his neck to the topmost branches, then walking around it, tracing the patterns on its trunk with his fingers. I was filled with a sudden pride that this great old thing should belong to us, and that my uncle should be so impressed with it. When he turned to look at me his smile had gone, and there was a look on his face, one I did not understand and certainly did not like. It made his eyes seem cold, and for one moment I was a little scared, but then the look passed, to be replaced once more with that broad smile.

Uncle Roger was very entertaining at the meal that evening; he told a great many silly stories that had Miss Preece and me in fits of giggles. He even offered to help do the washing-up – something Daddy never does. After dinner, Daddy usually retires to his study to work, leaving the horrid, greasy plates to Miss Preece and me.

Of course, Miss Preece turned down my uncle's offer – it wouldn't be right to have a guest toiling away in the kitchen like a potboy – and so, whilst we worked, he went for another walk about the grounds. We had just finished putting away the last of the plates when Ned stumped in the side door. He seemed very grumpy, and he soon told us why!

Apparently, he had run into my uncle, and there'd been something of a to-do. Ned was quite vocal about what had happened. He had been wandering the garden, smoking a pipe and deciding what chores most needed doing the following day, when he encountered Uncle Roger, daydreaming beneath the big old oak and kicking at the piles of leaves that had built up around it.

Feeling a bit embarrassed that our guest should see this part of the grounds in such a mess, Ned had offered an apology, promising that all the dead foliage would be cleared away the following day. At this, my uncle had become rather sharp, telling him to leave it as it was.

Not happy with my uncle's tone, Ned had retorted that Reverend Harrington liked the leaves gathered up regularly, and he had already been forced to neglect it for too long, what with all the other tasks he had been doing. To this, my uncle said that Reverend Harrington was not here, and in his absence, Ned would do as he said.

"Giving me orders like he owns the place!" a red-faced Ned had seethed. "I don't like him, he's a…"

It was at this point that Uncle Roger had walked back in, and a nasty silence fell over the kitchen. I felt terribly guilty, as though it had been me saying rotten things about my uncle. He looked at each of us in turn, staring straight into our eyes. It felt as though he were peering into my mind, as if my eyes were windows that he might look into and see my innermost thoughts. I quickly looked down at my shoes.

For what seemed like an eternity, he controlled that silence, before finally breaking it by announcing that he was retiring for the night. Instructing Miss Preece to bring him up a warm drink in twenty minutes, he strode from the room, firmly pulling the door shut behind him. After that, I did not see him again for the rest of the evening!

The next morning was a wonderfully bright day, and warm for the time of year. At breakfast, Uncle Roger was in very high spirits, and when Miss Preece announced that she intended to walk to the village shop to fetch some supplies, my uncle very graciously offered to accompany her. I offered to go too, but my uncle was very dismissive of this idea, telling me that I would only get in the way – as if I hadn't helped Miss Preece shop dozens of times before!

So I watched the two of them from the doorstep, making their way down the path. Miss Preece looked very pretty, Molly. She was wearing her best dress and hat – the one she always wears when she goes to the village or to church – and carrying her wicker shopping basket. My uncle was dressed in a dark suit, hands clasped behind his back. Just before they reached a curve in the path that would take them out of sight behind a thick mass of trees, Miss Preece turned and waved to me. I waved back, then they were gone.

It was the last time I ever saw her!

Ned was too busy with his jobs to have any time for me, so I spent a boring morning wandering about the house and gardens, waiting for Uncle Roger and Miss Preece to return. They were gone an awfully long time; midday came and went and there was no sign of them. I became hungry and made myself something to eat, then I walked down to the lane and stood looking for them, but the afternoon started to grow chilly, and so I went back inside. Ned came in and built a fire in the sitting-room grate.

"Summer's gone and the chill is starting to settle in, little one," he announced. This made me a little sad.

Despite the warm fire, I decided I would not waste my afternoon sitting around. Instead, I wandered up into Daddy's room. I knew he kept a precious collection of photographs in a shoebox under his bed. Some of the pictures were of mummy, and whenever I was alone and feeling a bit fed up, I would creep in and look at them. It was a special thing I did. Sometimes, I would talk to the images, telling Mummy all about the things that were upsetting me. I liked to imagine that, somewhere, she was listening to me, and even though she couldn't reply, I could feel her sympathy reaching out to me.

There were not many photographs of her – just five. My favourite was the one taken on her wedding day. She looked very pretty in her wedding dress, and I only hoped that when I was older, I would look just as pretty, and the man at my side would be just as handsome.

I had looked at this particular photo many times, but I really had eyes only for my mother, largely ignoring the other people with them. My father was there, obviously, looking proud and happy, a flower tucked into his buttonhole. A much older man and woman stood to their left, and to their right stood a woman about Mummy's age. She wore a big hat and was short and a little plump. By her stood a man, probably the youngest of the group. He, too, was short, a little overweight, and wore thick spectacles.

I paused for a second; there was something wrong with this picture, something that unsettled me. This photo showed Daddy's closest family, taken just after they had come out of church. The older couple were Grandmama and Grandpapa, the short plump woman was Aunty Sybil – but where was Uncle Roger? He had been the best man at Mummy and Daddy's wedding. If this photo was of Daddy's closest family, why wasn't he in it? And who was the short, spectacled man who stood with them?

I think it was about three o'clock when Uncle Roger finally returned. He was alone and carrying Miss Preece's basket, which was full of goods.

He gathered Ned and me into the kitchen and explained that while they had been shopping in the village, Miss Preece had received an urgent telegram calling her back to her family to help tend to a sick relative. He went on to say that she apologised for leaving without saying goodbye and was hoping to be back within a week.

"We will make the best of it," said Uncle Roger eagerly. "I expect that between the three of us, we will be able to rustle up a bit of food and keep the place ticking over nicely." He favoured me with that charming, broad grin. I tried my best to smile back, but I felt strangely empty.

I looked at Ned. He had been watching my uncle silently all this time, never speaking, and I was suddenly aware that he was the only person I really knew. Daddy was away, Miss Preece had gone, and my uncle still felt like a stranger. In truth, though it was horrid to admit at the time, I was not even sure if I liked him. He seemed nice, but at times it was like he was playing a game of pretend, or acting on stage before an audience he was desperate to impress.

"She hasn't taken any clothes with her," Ned suddenly spoke up.

"What?" My uncle seemed momentarily uncertain.

"You said she'd gone to help out at a relative's, gone to stay there, but she's left all her things here."

My uncle's smile broadened. "Dear chap, the relative is her mother. I did ask if she wanted me to forward anything on to her, but she told me she had plenty of belongings at her parents' home."

"Is that so?" The two men stared at each other for a few moments, then Ned silently turned and walked out the back door.

That night I sat up in bed alone, praying Miss Preece's mummy would get better quickly so she could return home to us. Sleep would not come. I found myself jumping at every noise, and sounds that were once just the quiet melody of the night now seemed to rage in my ears, making hideous images in my mind. The wind blowing through the trees became some nameless beast calling out to the night, and the creaking of settling floorboards had me imagining shadowy horrors creeping through the rectory's halls.

I lay there for a long time, desperate for sleep. I gradually managed to convince myself that creaking floorboards were just creaking floorboards, and the wind merely the wind, only for new troubles to seize me. I worried about Miss Preece's mother. How sick must she be if she needed her daughter at her side? How would we cope without her here?

Daddy always told me to count sheep to help me drift off, so I imagined myself in a green field, shepherd's staff in hand, a long line of white woolly lambs stretched off into the distance. One by one they would bleat, then jump over a low wooden fence. I must have sent hundreds of them over into the next pasture, but I felt no sleepier than when I first began. I finally decided that I was too thirsty to sleep and so crept out of my room and quietly made my way downstairs to the kitchen.

It was very cold downstairs, unusually so, and I soon discovered why – the kitchen door had been left ajar. I suddenly became aware of how still the house was; there was no sense of life in it at all. I crept out of the open door, my bare feet cold on the gravel path. I knew my uncle was out here somewhere. I glanced to the right and saw him by the light of the moon, so I moved silently to the corner of the house to watch.

He stood before the old oak, dressed very strangely, in a robe that almost resembled a lady's dressing gown. It was hard to make out the colour, but it was a dark shade and covered in strange patterns in shiny thread. His head was bowed as if in prayer, his arms raised. I could hear him muttering something beneath his breath, in a language I did not understand. In front of him lay what looked like a bundle of rags.

His voice grew louder, and I started to get scared. I should have run back into the house or to old Ned's place, but I was terrified that he would hear me.

The wind began to rise, blowing the fallen leaves about, gusting them into the air. As I watched, the leaves began to spin like a dervish, forming a vaguely human shape, but gigantic in size – easily twice that of my uncle.

He dropped to his knees before this awful thing, raising his voice in a way that reminded me of Daddy in church on Sunday, when he was delivering a passionate sermon to his congregation. I desperately fought back the urge to scream, not wanting to find out what would happen if I were discovered!

This tornado of debris reached down and, with massive hands, gathered up the pile of rags that lay before my uncle. I saw it draw them to its chest, saw a white face amongst the rags, dimly illuminated by the moonlight. The monstrous thing threw back its head, howling to the sky – the noise of a summer storm tearing through a woodland canopy.

I turned and ran back into the house, pounding up the stairs, heedless of the noise, slamming my bedroom door behind me. I fell sobbing onto the bed. The pale face I had seen had been dead – and terribly familiar!

*

The next morning, I crept downstairs. I was terrified but determined to find Ned and tell him what I had seen in the night. But, to my dismay, Uncle Roger was waiting for me in the hall. He said he had prepared breakfast and, taking me firmly by the arm, guided me to the kitchen table. We ate in silence, the food like ashes in my mouth.

Eventually, my uncle spoke. "I think it is best if you stay indoors today, young lady. It's getting colder outside, and Miss Preece would not be happy with me if I let you wander about and catch a chill."

I did not answer but just stared at my plate.

"Now don't look so down – tonight will be Halloween. We can have a nice, warm bonfire outside and have a little party. Wouldn't that be fine?"

"We normally have a bonfire on the fifth of November, not Halloween. Daddy doesn't like Halloween," I said boldly.

"Well, I do," my uncle replied firmly. "It's a very important time of year. People forget how important it is. If you are a good girl and do as you are told, I may introduce you to someone very special!"

My uncle spent the remainder of the day in his room, so I was free to wander about the house. I wanted to speak with Ned, to tell him my suspicions, but both the front and the side door were locked, and I was unable to find the keys. The windows were also securely fastened. I was a prisoner in my own home!

I spent the whole morning sitting on the window cushions in my room, looking out into the garden, and hoping to see that friendly, sun-browned face. If I did, I wondered if I'd have the courage to call out to him, to bang on the glass. I was scared of what my uncle would do, you see, Molly, if he caught me.

It was not until later that afternoon that Ned appeared, walking from the woods that surrounded the grounds, a hatchet in his hand. I raised my hand to bang on the glass – I wanted to shout and scream, I wanted him to break down the door and take me away from here before something else terrible could happen, to take me to Daddy, where I would be safe. But I couldn't do it – I was too scared.

All I could do was watch.

Ned approached the front door. I heard his familiar, loud knock and listened as my uncle made his way downstairs, muttering in an annoyed voice.

I waited a few moments, then crept onto the landing.

I could hear my uncle talking to Ned. Both men sounded annoyed. I listened really hard, but I couldn't tell what they were saying.

I screwed my hands into fists.

I wanted to run downstairs, ignore my uncle, speak to Ned – yell and scream at him until he understood how scared I was.

But fear had me glued to the landing.

I tried to find my courage – I breathed slowly – that had always helped me whenever I was upset or agitated about something.

Downstairs, the tone of the conversation had shifted, and I was somehow aware that this meant it was coming to an end.

I breathed deeply, closing my eyes. I relaxed my hands.

A brief moment of calm stole over me.

Then I did it!

Without thinking, I ran faster than I ever had across the landing and down the stairs, jumping the last four steps.

I shouted out something – I can't remember what – screamed it. My uncle turned towards me, a look of anger on his face. Through a gap in the door, I saw Ned's shocked expression.

My uncle reacted quickly, slamming the door shut – but he was not quite quick enough. Ned wedged one of his sturdily booted feet between the door and the frame, then pushed hard with his shoulder. He might be old, but a lifetime of hard work had made him strong. My uncle staggered back, almost falling over, and I dashed over to Ned, throwing my arms around his waist.

"Ned, he locked me in – he won't let me leave. I'm scared. I think he's done something horrid to Miss Preece." I sobbed the last part out.

My uncle very quickly regained his composure. "Now that is very silly. You know very well that Miss Preece is away caring for a relative. I am sorry about this, Ned, I did not wish to worry you – but as you can see, my niece is not well. A sad affliction of the mind, making her prone to delusions. I am regret to say, she has had this problem for some time, which is why my brother sent me here, to help care for her. The poor fellow is beside himself – he has been trying to keep her illness quiet!"

I stared at him in shock, hardly believing the awful things he was saying. He spoke with such confidence and authority that I became possessed with the dreadful idea that Ned might actually believe him.

For a few tense moments, we all stood in silence.

Then Ned raised his hatchet and pointed its sharp head at my uncle's chest. "I've known this little girl nearly all her life," he said. "There ain't a damn thing wrong with her head. I should know – I've seen enough minds broken by war. She's a good girl, not prone to fancies, and definitely not a liar. You, on the other hand – I don't know." He put a reassuring arm about my shoulder and I buried my head into his earthy-smelling jacket.

"Go pack some clothes, young 'un. I'm taking you to your father."

I dashed back upstairs, grabbed a bag from my cupboard and started to throw belongings in. I put on a warm coat and hurried back down.

By the time I returned, my uncle had vanished.

Ned led me down the garden path and into the little wooded lane that meandered its way to Babbinsmoor. Behind us, we could hear my uncle's voice from somewhere in the garden. It sounded panicked, as though he were desperately calling out to someone for help.

We quickened our pace.

I took hold of Ned's hand and squeezed it tightly.

"The man's touched in the head," muttered Ned, glancing back uneasily.

"I don't think he's my uncle at all. I don't think Daddy even knows he's here! Daddy would never send anyone so horrid to live with us," I said, and then went on to tell him about the previous night: of my uncle's activities beneath the old oak, of the strange thing whose very body seemed to be made of fallen leaves, of the pile of rags and that familiar dead face.

"I'll have the police down here just as soon as you're safe, and if he's hurt Miss Preece – well, he'll be glad I did fetch 'em, for if I get my hands on him I'll rip his…" He stopped and took a deep breath, then gave me an apologetic look. "Never liked him," he went on, "too full of himself, coming here, bossing folk about like he owns the place. Too obsessed with that bloody tree. I should've cut it down a long time ago, never could abide the thing!"

I had not realised that Ned disliked our old oak, but as he talked I began to understand why. I had always thought it a rather quaint relic of our rude forefathers, but from what Ned told me now, it was anything but. The tree, he explained, was old, some said hundreds, even thousands of years old.

"It's long drawn the attention of a certain kind of person," he said, "the kind that dabbles in things best left untouched. It was said to have been marked by the ancient folk, folk that inhabited the land before the arrival of men. Some called them fairy folk, but they ain't nothing like the pretty, butterfly-winged, flower-capped creatures that are in your storybooks.

"These were a very ancient, deformed folk, who hold nothing but bitterness and hatred towards the sons and daughters of man. A Saxon lord had driven them from the land and imprisoned them in a hidden kingdom beneath the earth. Their king was a terrible antlered lord. Still, some of his kind found ways to haunt the villages, byways, or the lonely cottages of men. Some very wicked folk even used spells and magic to try to contact this fairy king and his kin, no doubt believing their efforts would see them rewarded. They could be seen on certain auspicious nights, gathered at old stone circles, or other such places of power, working their wickedness.

"Our old tree had been one such place, drawing evil magicians with their rites and spells, a place of power, a place where these monstrous beings could be called forth. Perhaps that was why church elders had the vicarage built there – so that men like your father could act as keepers, turning away people who might otherwise work their meddlesome tricks beneath its boughs."

A cold wind blew at us through the trees. It carried the scent of leaf mould, a decaying smell that made me want to be sick. Ned quickened his steps, and I had to hurry to keep up with him.

"I'd no idea that he'd locked you in the house," Ned said, sounding apologetic. The breeze increased, causing leaves to dance about our feet. "He'd sent me to clear dead brush from the woods around the property. I thought it was an odd task, but truth be told, I didn't want to question it. I was glad to be as far away from that man as possible. Something about him raised my hackles. But I should never have left you, though. I promised your father that I'd watch you like you were my own. Please forgive me."

Almost as soon as Ned finished talking, the wind rose, howling, buffeting us in the back. It was so strong that it caused us to stagger. I may very well have fallen, Molly, had Ned not kept a firm grip upon my hand. It blew around us, seeming to come from many different directions at once. The dead leaves were whipped up from where they lay on the path, blown from out of the surrounding woodland, even ripped from the very trees themselves.

They spun violently in the air, gathering together in an impossibly complex vortex, forming a shape that to me was horribly familiar, a body made of dancing russet, towering over us. It had no discernible features, being little more than a vague shape, but somehow this made it all the more alien and terrible, and I saw that not only did leaves play about within its form, but also sticks and small sharp stones.

Ned stopped and stared at it in shock, only occasionally moving when a particularly strong gust caught him unawares. I felt his grip tighten on my hand and he raised his axe. Then the thing thrust an arm-like appendage toward him. I screamed and pulled free, throwing myself aside, but not before it had brushed my arm. The flying debris tore my sleeve to flinders, scratching me and leaving a painful, bloody mess.

I staggered to my feet and ran blindly back the way we had come. Behind me I heard Ned crying out in pain. I should have stopped, Molly. I should have gone back to help him – he had tried to help me – but I left him, left him with that thing.

Ahead I saw Uncle Roger striding down the lane towards me. I turned and darted into the woods, stumbling, scrabbling through the twigs and the dirt. I paused a moment to look behind, leaning and panting against a tree, but saw no one following.

I started out again, this time in a direction that I hoped would lead to the village. If I could get there, I would go straight to the police constable's cottage and tell him everything.

But, within a few moments, that ghostly wind had risen again, and the dead leaves, dirt, and twigs spun before me, forcing me back, as if I were a stray sheep before a shepherd's hound.

It was like a strange nightmare, Molly. Every time I tried to alter my direction the wind would rise, and the thing would set me back on the path of its choosing. But there was no waking from this nightmare, no comfy bed for sanctuary, and you were not there to cuddle and squeeze. There was only the fear, the thing, and the knowledge that I was being driven back to the vicarage.

I saw my uncle before I saw the house. He stepped from behind a tree, grabbing my bad arm and squeezing it with such force that I cried out and sobbed.

He was angry, dragging me behind him. When I tried to resist he hit me in the face, saying such terrible things and making such awful threats, that my legs went weak with fear and I collapsed to the earth. But he merely hauled me to my feet and struck me again, reminding me that tonight was Halloween, saying it was an important occasion and that I should be grateful for the honour that was to be bestowed upon me.

By the time we reached the house I was almost relieved. I wanted to go to my room, to curl up in my bed, to just be left alone.

And so here I am. I have pulled the covers over my head. You are here, Molly, as you have always been since I was tiny, my raggedy little lady. You have always listened to me and never judged, whatever I told you. It is warm underneath the covers and if I block out all thoughts from my mind I can imagine, for a few moments, that I am safely cocooned away from the world, like a butterfly, awaiting a time of my choosing to appear.

But there is one thing that breaks this illusion, my uncle. Sometimes I hear him moving about the house. There are bangs and exclamations and other sounds that I don't want to dwell on. I have no idea what he is doing and I am trying really hard not to care, but every time he makes a noise, a creeping dread twists my stomach.

I hear him now, Molly. He is walking down the hallway towards our door. I sneak a peek from beneath the covers.

Night has cast its veil, it is so dark!

I pull the sheets back over my head.

I hear him stop outside my door.

I know he is coming. I should have barred the door, I should have pushed the dresser against it. Perhaps I still could, but fear keeps me frozen.

I wish Daddy were here.

I wish Mummy was still alive.

Slowly, I hear the bedroom door open.

The Faeries' Feast

February 1902

C asper Trenchton had been advised to keep a diary by his nerve specialist, who said it would help to alleviate the feelings of melancholy and distress – those relentless spectres that so haunted his life.

But Casper had never had the greatest interest in writing, which to him seemed more like an unpleasant chore than a way to relax and distract his troubled mind. So, although he attempted it, he had found the process so frustrating and unfulfilling that ultimately he had given up on the exercise after less than a week.

Sleep did not come easily to Casper, not since that terrible night years before at his boarding school. Something had happened to him that night, something that had broken his mind. And yet, whatever it was that had seen him committed to the asylum on and off for so many years, he could not – mercifully – remember it.

Many was the night he found himself pacing his room, mind racing with unfounded fears, his stomach so twisted with nerves that he could barely stand up straight, pulling at his hair in agitation, praying for rest.

Why was it he could only find sleep in the daylight hours?

Naturally, his father, a proud, critical, military man, was greatly ashamed of him – they hardly ever spoke now. Following Casper's release after his recent episode, he had been sent to stay at Llangorse Fawr in southern Powys with the family of his father's recently deceased friend, Lord Alfred Baughan.

How well he remembered that day, standing before his father, withering beneath his disappointment. It was as though Casper's problems were a personal affront aimed solely at the man. He had said he would not have him about the home, said he was humiliated by him, that he brought shame upon the Trenchton name. Perhaps his father sending him away was for the best. Casper did not believe that time spent in his company was very conducive to his recovery.

The new Lord Baughan was Rhodri, Lord Alfred's eldest son, a handsome fellow with dark hair, dark eyes and fine cheek bones. He was a careful man who took his new duties seriously.

His younger brother, Ewan, was an old friend of Casper's from his days at Toadstone School and one of the few people to stay in contact with him since his troubles had started. His was a friendship that Casper valued highly.

But it was Jane, the youngest member of the Baughan family, that had shown him the greatest kindness on this visit. She tended to his every need, as though he were a sickly puppy, showing him a kindness that was otherwise sadly lacking in his life.

How she had changed from the little girl Casper remembered meeting on his youthful visits to Llangorse Fawr with Ewan, during those glorious long-ago summer holidays. The awkward, skinny girl had been replaced by a lovely young woman. The family resemblance was strong, with her black hair and deep dark eyes.

Casper found himself very drawn to her and also uncomfortably aware that a broken man like himself could never hope to win her affection. And yet, they spent a lot of time in each other's company. She had taken to calling him 'Casp', in what he thought of as a fond way.

Llangorse Fawr was a grim old pile, a fortress of a home, with crenellations on the roof, a heavy, iron-studded oak door, and many arrow loop windows that peered suspiciously out at the carefully tended gardens – as if the house itself expected an intruder to emerge from behind the box bushes or among the rose beds.

To the south of the house was the lake of Llangorse, called by the locals Llyn Syfaddon. Jane had told him that it was the largest lake in all of Wales, and Casper believed her. It was a great stretch of water, a mile long. To its east arose the scenic Black Mountains, which were visible from his room, and which he derived much pleasure from looking upon, enjoying the way the clouds swirled about their peaks, like the steam from a giant kettle, and the way the sunlight played upon the contours of their slopes.

Jane had told him the lake was a source of many unusual stories. It was supposed to be the home of a monster, some kind of great serpent, which locals still claim to see to this day. It was also said that the lake was once the site of a town that had been drowned – the act of a vengeful god for some unholy misdemeanour committed by its populace.

Perhaps the strangest of the tales was about the fairy feasts that were said to take place in the area. Locals believe the lake to be a portal to the realm of the Tylwyth Teg – the land of the mythic folk, and it was said that on certain nights, their lights could be seen over and around the waters. Often, the following day, sheep were found dead, their bodies eaten and marked in strange ways.

These events still occurred. As recently as this morning, a local farmer had blamed the death of a sheep on the fair ones' nocturnal antics. This had caused quite a headache for the new Lord Baughan, as the tenant farmer demanded that he deal with the problem. How poor Rhodri was expected to apprehend supernatural creatures was quite beyond him.

In truth, Casper believed the villains to be more human in nature, and if that was so, then at least it would be possible to bring them to justice.

*

Lord Rhodri Baughan paced the library, a troubled expression marring his face. This was the third death in two weeks and the local farmers were angry, scared, and looking to him for answers. But what answers could he hope to provide? Sheep deaths of this nature had been occurring in the area for many years. His father had investigated them, as had his grandfather, and no doubt many previous generations of his kinsfolk. But if there was a family who believed they could slaughter their neighbour's sheep for a bit of free meat, they had never yet been uncovered.

"You did the right thing, Rod," Ewan said, "asking them to leave the body untouched."

The superstitious locals had always quickly burnt the bodies of any sheep that they thought to have been killed during a Fairies' Feast, believing it brought ill fortune to delay this action or dispose of them in any other way.

So, this had meant that by the time he arrived at the site, the body was gone, and with it any potential evidence left by the perpetrator. After the last death, Rhodri had it put about the district that he wanted any cremation delayed until he had a chance to view the remains.

Finally, this very morning, a farmhand had arrived to report another death, informing him that the beast's owner, a Mr Jones, had left the unfortunate creature undisturbed, awaiting his arrival.

"At last, a chance for you to see a victim first-hand," said Casper Trenchton. He had been here two weeks and had been a quiet guest. When he was not in Ewan or Jane's company, he was either walking the estate or could be heard pacing his room with an agitated step.

He was a large man. Rhodri thought he resembled a rugby player whose team had suffered a terrible defeat. There may be times when he resembled a rugby player whose team had just lifted a trophy, but Rhodri had never seen it.

His sister, Jane, an intrigued gleam in her eyes, stood next to Casper. Now that Casper had arrived, there was a little excitement in her life, and she doted on him. He was her new project.

"I shall ride out with you," she announced.

"No," said Rhodri. He was prepared for this, being aware of the descriptions of the carnage. He had no wish to expose his sister to that. His father and mother never would have forgiven him.

"I need you here, Jane," he continued. "It may be that one of our ancestors wrote about these killings – maybe something we can use. Please try to find it for me." He did not believe that such clues existed, or they would have been found long ago. But if he wanted co-operation, he had to give Jane something to do. "Besides, you must stay to see to the needs of our guest."

"I can help you look through the books," Casper offered.

Jane was frustrated but was raised to believe that arguments should be kept behind closed doors and never aired in front of guests. So, to Rhodri's relief, she held her tongue.

"Thank you, Casper," she said, smiling at the giant man and patting his arm affectionately, "that is very kind.

You are a true gentleman." She gave Rhodri a look that suggested he was anything but.

"We should be leaving soon," Ewan said. "Those clouds are dark; the weather could turn for the worse."

"Then Casp, we shall light the fire and have a cosy time here in the library with our books," Jane announced. "I think warm drinks should be the order of the day, and maybe even a few of cook's delightful biscuits."

*

Rhodri and Ewan rode together. Close to their left, the waters of Llyn Syfaddon lapped against the shore; to their right, in the distance, they could make out the silhouettes of the Black Mountains, rising from the earth like the spine of a giant beast, feathered with pines.

A perpetual drizzle, accompanied by a cold northerly wind, meant they could never truly enjoy the ride. Their horses were sluggish; great gouts of steam billowed from their nostrils with every step they took, bringing to Rhodri's mind the stories of dragons he had so loved as a child.

"There is worse to come," Ewan complained. "Those clouds behind us are as black as the pit. We will get a proper drenching before we see a warm fire again."

"It can't be helped," Rhodri replied. "This is more important than a warm fire; it's gone on far too long."

"True," Ewan agreed.

They rode along quietly for a little while, but unlike Rhodri, Ewan was not a man who could suffer silence when in the company of another. He saw silence as a void that must be filled with chatter, be that jokes, anecdotes, or reminiscences.

"Did I ever tell you about the time I saw the monster?" he asked, nodding in the direction of Llyn Syfaddon's wind-tousled waters.

Rhodri looked over at his brother. He was hunched against the bad weather, as if trying to fold in on himself and thus preserve some warmth and comfort. He had a faraway look in his eye.

"No, you never did. I'm certain I would have remembered a story like that," Rhodri said. He could not believe that the talkative Ewan would ever have kept something like this to himself, and wondered if his brother was about to fill the hated silence with a load of old pigs' swill.

"I was much younger. It was the summer. You were away – I don't remember where, probably school. Mother had taken me out for a walk along the lake. It wasn't like today; the weather was glorious – too hot, if you can imagine such a thing. I wanted to paddle in the water to cool down, but you know what Mother was like." At this he laughed. "She had brought a picnic with her; it was very fine. Jam sandwiches, pork pies, and cake. I shall never forget it." His eyes twinkled as he remembered the tasty delights. "Mother had just turned to speak with the maid who accompanied us, telling her to pack away the things. I don't remember the woman's name, she isn't with us now, and it was so long ago."

"It was probably Georgina. Mother used to take her everywhere with her," Rhodri said. "Nice woman, used to let me take pastries from the kitchen."

"Well, whoever it was, it is not important now," Ewan continued. "What is important is that they were both distracted. I got up and walked to the edge of the lake. The waters were still, like a mill pond – the perfect conditions for skimming stones. And so I did, and I got a sixer too! I remember that stone dancing along the water. I thought it would go on forever, skip across the whole lake and come to rest on the far shore, but of course it didn't.

"I looked up at the sky, so blue, hardly a cloud to be seen. Bless me, even now I can picture it, a flock of ducks taking flight, causing me to jump. They were so noisy, the beating of their wings, their quacking, I wondered if something had spooked them.

"Then, looking out over the lake, I saw it – a great grey shape moving in the water. I only glimpsed it for a moment, but I know it was there." He said this last part with great conviction, almost as if he were trying to convince himself the event was real. Then he fell silent.

"So, what did it look like?" Rhodri asked, intrigued but still unsure whether or not his brother was making the whole thing up. There was something about the younger man's demeanour that made him think he was not.

"Truthfully? Slightly disappointing. I had always imagined a great serpent with spines, a huge horned head, a mouth full of vicious, sharp teeth. And I suppose it might have been like that, but all I saw was a part of it, a huge grey, smooth shape that rolled in the water before vanishing from view. It happened so quickly, but it was big, bigger than anything that should be in that lake. I never saw it again, not then, or any day since."

Ewan fell silent. Rhodri had heard tales of a monster; the locals were fond of talking about it when in their cups at the local alehouse, but he had never seen anything, and to his knowledge neither had his father.

"Perhaps it is your monster killing all the sheep," Rhodri joked.

Ewan laughed.

They were met by a man on foot, a miserable-looking fellow with a flat cap and a dense, unmanaged beard. Rhodri recognised him as a farmhand who worked for Mr Jones, but he could not remember the fellow's name. He led them away from the lake, through a gate and into a system of fields. Ahead, Mr Jones stood alone by the fallen ewe. The rest of the flock was squeezed up against a dry stone wall, putting as much distance as possible between themselves and their fallen comrade.

"Greetings, Mr Jones. Thank you for leaving the body untouched," Rhodri said, dismounting and passing his reins to the farmhand.

"M'lord," the man said, pulling his forelock. "They've been like that since I got here – won't come near this part of the field." Rhodri and the farmer walked over to the dead animal, followed by Ewan.

"She was found this way by Mostyn over there," he nodded in the direction of the silent farmhand. "Just after dawn. I sent for you straight away. Untouched, as you asked."

"You did the right thing," Rhodri said.

"One of Mr Griffith's shepherds reported lights on the lake last night. From the look of her, I'd say the Tylwyth Teg have been about their business again."

"You really think the Fair Folk are to blame, then?" Rhodri asked doubtfully.

"Yes, M'lord. That ain't the work of no beast. There ain't no rhyme nor reason to why any human would do such a thing."

Rhodri crouched down by the fallen animal.

The unfortunate beast bore terrible wounds, and yet, no blood stained either its dirty white fleece or the ground about it. When Rhodri made this observation to the farmer, his only reply was, "'Tis always that way."

There were three blackened holes in the creature's side, but most of the damage was to the beast's face. It looked as though a mad surgeon had set about his work with an intense vigour; whole portions of skin and tissue had been cut away, exposing the pale skull. The lips, eyes, and tongue had been removed with a sinister care. One of its front legs, the left, had been amputated at the knee, though there was no sign of the missing appendage.

"Your father paid for a veterinary physician to perform a necropsy on a few animals, M'lord," Mr Jones said.

"The reports were all the same, many of the internal organs gone."

"But not this animal. Other than the face, I don't see any wounds large enough to allow someone to remove any innards."

"Oh, they're gone all right, M'lord. Look at the beast, like a deflated football."

It was true; the area where the creature's stomach should have been seemed to have collapsed in on itself.

"So how were they removed?" asked Ewan. His face had taken on a greyish tinge, he looked as though he might be sick at any moment.

"There weren't no large cuts on the ones your father had examined either, but still much of the innards were gone, M'lord," Mr Jones said. "The ways of the Fair Folk are not to be understood by the likes of us. They takes them bits they savour."

Rhodri massaged his temple with his fingertips. He looked about him, searching for tracks, some indication of where the killers had approached from and where they might have taken the sheep to butcher it. But the ground kept its secrets well.

From the north, there was a flash, a great inverted tree of light that lit up the sky, followed by a dull rumble of thunder. As if this were a cue, the rain intensified.

Mr Jones rested a hand on Rhodri's arm. "There's one more thing you ought to see, M'lord, the place where the Tylwyth Teg held their banquet."

*

Casper and Jane sat in the library. In the grate, a fire burned merrily away, warming the room with its russet glow, causing shadows to leap along the book-lined walls. Outside, the weather had worsened; the rain fell more heavily, it could be heard hammering on the large window, the wind whistled through the branches of the estate's trees, causing them to dance about like wild performers.

Casper was very glad to be indoors; he certainly did not envy Rhodri or Ewan. He suspected that now even Jane was glad she had not accompanied them, despite the fact that she had spent much of their time together complaining about being excluded from the outing.

As promised, she had instructed the servants to bring them tea and biscuits. Now they sat, the warm drinks further helping to keep the cold at bay. They had spent a fruitless hour searching through the shelves looking for something to cast a light on the mystery. Casper suspected that there was nothing to find. He understood that this was just a pointless job, meant to keep Jane busy.

He suspected Jane knew this too, though it only served to make her more determined to find something.

As soon as the young woman had finished her drink, she rose from her seat and went back to the bookshelves.

"There must be something here, Casp," she said, the frustration evident in her tone. "It's been going on so long, someone must surely have written about it?"

She looked over at him in an appealing way, "Oh please don't just sit there like a perfect hound, come and help me!"

Of course, I will. I think I would do anything for you. I would follow you blindly into a burning building, poor broken fool that I am, thought Casper.

Reluctantly, he left the comfort of his warm seat and made his way over to where she stood. Plucking a book at random from the shelves, he flicked his way through the pages, pretending to study the text.

"This section of the library seems to contain some notes and journals from the last century," Jane stated.

Casper risked a look at her. She was tapping her finger against her lips, a very serious expression on her face. He quickly went back to pretending to study his book, worried she might notice him staring.

"Here is a journal of my great-grandmother's." She had picked out an old leather-bound volume which she carried over to her seat by the fire. Sitting down, she proceeded to riffle through the pages.

As she did so, something fell to the floor.

A collection of envelopes.

Casper walked over to join her, bringing his unstudied book with him. He too sat down; his chair still held some of his body warmth and he settled into it with satisfaction.

"They are copies of letters," Jane had picked up one of the envelopes and was examining the contents, "written by my aunt to a friend in a town called Wendlelow, somewhere in England." She sat in silence for a while reading through the letters, and gradually a smile spread across her face. "Here Casp, she talks about the Fairy Feast."

When she had finished reading the letter, she passed it excitely to Casper.

Dearest M

Llangorse Fawr is so lonely without you! I miss you and our rides about the estate, and our evenings reading, talking, and playing cards.

Father is well, though he is still as moody as ever and it is best not to engage him in conversation too early in the morning or too late at night. But this you know well. Duncan is still away at university and by all accounts is doing well; he is due to return in the summer months and I look forward to his company.

I have decided to make a copy of my letters, which I will keep. You know how poorly my memory serves me, and I should hate to repeat myself in one of these missives.

The thought that you may find my letters repetitive and tiresome to read is a great worry.

In any case, there should be nothing tiresome about this letter, for I have news to relate that has greatly shaken the district and that I am certain you will find most interesting.

You will remember the many stories that surround our lake, the stories of fearsome monsters that dwell there, of lost sunken villages, and of course the Tylwyth Teg. It is said that there is a great cave at the lake's deepest part, and that this cave is an entrance to the realm of the Fair Folk. Every so often they leave these enchanted lands to roam about ours in their great chariots of light, and sometimes, just sometimes, they hold a great banquet by the lake.

Such an event occurred recently. Just two nights ago the lights of the twilight folk were reportedly seen by local farmers and shepherds above Llyn Syfadden. The following morning two sheep were found dead, said to be devoured in that strange manner so typical of the little people.

Father is terribly distressed. The local population looks to him for answers. If it is a human culprit, then it is possible he will be able to apprehend them. But I sometimes wonder, what if the legends are true? How can he ever hope to hold the Tylwyth Teg to account for their mischief? He cannot simply ride into the lake, visit their Kingdom and demand compensation for the slain animals.

Still, there is hope he may yet catch the culprit in the act.

It has been a great many years since the last of these unnatural sheep deaths occurred, but when they previously did, they continued for several weeks. It is my father's hope that he will catch the perpetrators in the act.

He and a group of men intend to patrol the area over the coming evenings.

The loyal Bulstrode, my little black spaniel, is nosing at my leg, wagging his tail and staring up at me like a Christian. It is clear the poor fellow desires a walk, so I will finish this letter here and oblige him.

Your dearest friend,
Anna.

"It is certainly interesting but it really doesn't shed any new light on the matter," Casper said, handing the letter back to Jane.

"There are more letters; let us see if my great-grandmother has anything else to say on the matter." She opened another and started to read it; after no short time her eyes widened, and she slowly lowered the paper to her lap.

"Oh, Casp – she saw one! She writes here she saw one of the Fair Folk!"

*

When Rhodri and Ewan finally returned, they went straight to their rooms to change into dry clothes. By the time Rhodri reached the library, Ewan was already there, warming his hands before the fireplace.

"Move up, Ewan," Rhodri said. "You're not the only one to take a chill today."

Outside, the weather had done what Rhodri considered to be impossible, and got even worse. The rain bore down, a steady drumbeat, a damp percussion to the rhythm of their lives.

"Casper, be a hero, and pour us both a brandy, will you?" Ewan asked.

Dutifully, his friend obliged. The brandy was most welcome and warmed Rhodri's insides in a way that the fire could never hope to do. He sipped it slowly, relishing its taste.

"We found something, Rod," Jane said. "A letter written by our great-grandmother. In it, she speaks of a fairy feast that occurred when she was a young woman."

"Tell me more!" Rhodri said. He was at a loss as to how to deal with the unfolding events, and wondered if this newly discovered letter might show him a path through this forest of mystery.

"Oh no, first you and Ewan must tell me about your adventures," Jane demanded, stubbornly crossing her arms.

And so, Rhodri told her all that had passed that morning, being sure to censor some of the more unpleasant aspects of the unfortunate animal's fate.

For her part – once she had finished listening to Rhodri's story – Jane went on to explain all she had learned from their great-grandmother's first letter.

They sat for a while, thoughtful, silent, until a gust of wind blew a sheet of rain against the window, bringing all four of them out of their contemplation.

Rhodri glanced out of the window. The clouds were now so dark that an unnatural dusk had settled over the countryside.

Casper was the first to speak. "I'm thinking your great-grandmother's father had the right idea, sending out patrols. Indeed, I don't see what else you can do."

"I think Casp's right," Ewan agreed. "It looks like we are going to have a few sleepless nights."

Rhodri nodded his agreement. "I can gather men from the village to help. We can split up to cover a larger area. Three groups, each led by one of us." He nodded towards Ewan and Casper.

"I shall not be left behind," Jane said indignantly.

But both Ewan and Rhodri shook their heads.

"It could be dangerous; I suspect sheep rustlers." Rhodri would not lower his dignity and give any credence to the local superstitions. "Such men could be desperate, and if they are armed, you could get hurt."

"Yes, it's out of the question. What would Father have said, if he thought we were putting you in danger?" Ewan added.

To Rhodri's surprise, his sister did not argue, though she did spare her brothers a dark look. "Fine," she said coldly, "but you must do something for me."

"What?" Rhodri said.

"Lady Hanoria Addington has been writing for some time, asking to visit Llangorse Fawr. She is a historian, or folklorist, or some such thing – writes for a ladies' magazine. She has heard about some of the legends of our lake and thinks they would make a great article."

Rhodri sighed. "Surely she does not need to visit to do that. Could you not simply put the stories in a letter?"

"No. Her niece, Miss Elspeth McGinnity, will be with her. She is an accomplished artist and will make sketches to complement the article. The price of my... capitulation to your frankly unfair demands is an invitation for this pair."

Rhodri saw the determined look on his younger sister's face, and she had mentioned Lady Hanoria's desire to visit before. But he had always felt that guests were a distraction to the smooth running of day-to-day estate business. But the arrival of these two ladies would be company for Jane, so it was a small price to pay for ensuring her cooperation and safety.

"I agree," he said, after a moment's pause.

"Good, I will go and write the letter now, and you can deliver it to the post office when you visit the village later." So saying, the young woman swept out of the room.

*

By the evening the rainstorm had passed. In fact, the sky was now nearly cloudless, the stars clearly visible. During the afternoon he had ridden to the village and the outlying farms, explaining his plan and asking for volunteers. The results of this labour were before him now. Fourteen men, eight mounted, six on foot, all carrying shotguns.

For his part, Rhodri, sitting atop his horse, carried his Webley service revolver in a holster at his side, a relic from his days in the military, while Ewan, also mounted, carried his favourite shotgun, breech broken, tucked under one arm. Casper was on foot, gun resting on his shoulder.

Rhodri had divided the men into three groups. He would lead four mounted men south along the banks of the lake, in the direction he had taken that morning. His brother would lead four riders northward, to patrol the ground there. Whilst Casper's and his men would be on foot, heading east towards the mountains.

They were in Llangorse Fawr's courtyard, lanterns and torches providing a warm illumination. Jane was leaning against the doorframe, watching with interest. Rhodri nodded to his sister, but she merely sniffed and looked away from him. She might have complied with his demands, but she was most certainly not happy with them. Well, that was fine with him, just so long as he knew she was safe.

Rhodri led his men along the banks of the lake. They rode slowly; the ground was uneven, and none of them wanted to risk their mounts stumbling and injuring themselves. He looked back to the hall, its glowing windows the only part of it now visible in the night. No doubt, Jane watched from one of those upper windows.

From her vantage point they must be nothing more than giant fireflies, drifting through the landscape.

He thought back to the morning, to the odd things he had seen. Mr Evans had burned the carcass of the sheep that afternoon, but the sight of that mutilated corpse still lingered in his mind. Whoever had committed the crime, be they animal, man, or... elf, it was strange that they had left so much good meat untouched.

And then there was the area where the farmer believed they had held their banquet; it was a big circle of flattened grass. Rhodri did not share the man's conviction because there was nothing there to suggest the remains of a great feast, no scraps, no bones, no wool. And the flattened grass was too orderly. It had a discernible spiral design. If there had been a large number of people dining here, then the ground would certainly look more chaotic.

He was quickly drawn away from his thoughts by an exclamation from one of the men, who was pointing at the lake. Beneath the surface at the centre, there was a glow as strong as a lighthouse beam. As Rhodri watched, it grew larger and brighter.

"The gates to the realms of the Tylwyth Teg have opened," exclaimed one of the older men.

There was a sudden eruption of water, an unsettling humming sensation, and a great circular light hung above them for a few moments.

Nobody moved, even the horses stood their ground, unflinching. As they watched it streak northwards, back the way they had come.

Dumbfounded, they sat in silence, watching the light disappear behind the treeline. "Well I'll be a squirrel's sister," one of the men muttered. "'Tis one of the Fair Folks' chariots."

Rhodri stared at the distant treeline in disbelief, then, coming to his senses, he put his whistle to his lips, blew hard upon it, turned his horse, and careless of any danger galloped after the light, his men following close behind.

With one hand he clutched the reins, with the other he held the lantern high, desperately trying to illuminate the ground before his mount, but it was to no avail. The light bobbed uncontrollably before him.

Ahead, the treeline grew bigger; beyond that lay Llangorse Fawr. He knew they had little hope of catching the light, it was simply too fast, and was considering calling a halt to the mad ride when, once more, it came into view, this time from the east. It was like a falling star, getting larger, then once again it vanished from view behind the woods before them.

"Whoa." Rhodri reined in his horse and his men followed suit. The glow illuminated the tops of the branches.

Just what was he leading his men towards?

Up until now, he had never believed that the perpetrators could really be Fair Folk. He had been convinced they hunted a very human foe. But now he knew that could not be the case. His world had tilted very sharply, and things like monsters swimming in the depths of local lakes did not seem quite so silly. He found that now, after the initial rush of the chase, he was not so certain he wanted to confront whatever lay ahead.

The riders milled about uneasily.

A sudden scream restored their purpose.

It came from up ahead in a tangle of foliage.

A woman's scream.

A scream of abject terror.

Once more they set forth at a heedless gallop, riding amongst the pillars of the trees.

At one point a horse tripped, throwing its rider, but no one stopped to help their fallen companion.

They were drawn onwards toward the desperate cries.

Rhodri's horse broke into the glade first and came skidding to a fearful halt, unwilling to go any farther. Rhodri stared in disbelief at the scene before him.

His sister lay prostrate, one arm curled around the trunk of an oak tree. A metal cable was wrapped around her legs and abdomen, one end climbing high above her into the overhead canopy. The end closest to him rose from her body like a cobra preparing to strike, its head a bright red light, its gaze burning in his direction, swaying, daring him to come closer.

Rhodri drew his pistol but was unwilling to fire in case he should accidentally hit his sister. He watched in disbelief as the cable shook, trying to dislodge the woman's grip. Some of the men, those armed with hand weapons, dismounted, abandoning their skittish horses, but were unwilling to advance farther, that red-eyed cobra holding them in place.

Then there was a roar.

Casper came charging into the glade. In moments, his powerful strides had brought him to Jane's side. Realising it was too dangerous to fire, he gripped his shotgun by the barrel, wielding it like a club, and with all the strength he could summon, brought the butt crashing down upon the metal appendage. There was a sharp clang, and the weapon flew from his grasp.

Jane, a look of terror on her face, cried out Casper's name in desperation. The giant man threw himself onto the metal cable, using his hands, and all the strength in his mighty arms to try to tear it from the woman's body.

Then it flexed – just like a muscle.

A ripple ran down its length, a wave that sent Casper flying back through the air to land senseless against a tree.

At the same time, this dramatic movement dislodged Jane's grip from the trunk.

She was lifted into the air, her horrified expression burning itself into Rhodri's soul.

Moments later she was gone.

*

Casper sat dejectedly on the side of the bed; it had been three weeks since Jane's disappearance. No more lights had been seen since that night, no more animals had been mutilated. He clenched and unclenched his fists, a vacant expression in his eyes, his mind elsewhere, reliving that night, reliving his failure.

He had not been able to save her, all his strength, all his determination, all his rage had not been enough, and what was worse, it was his fault she was there.

She had come to him that day, after she had finished writing her letter to Lady Addington, waiting until her brothers had ridden off to find volunteers. She had never intended to follow her brother's directions and stay in the safety of the hall; she told Casper of her plan. She intended to walk out to the little wood at the end of the estate. She had asked him to meet her there. She would patrol with him. At first he had protested, saying it was not safe, that her brother, when he discovered the deception, would hold him responsible.

She had responded, saying she was safer in the company of armed men than ever she would be at the hall with just a few servants about her. He could tell Rhodri he knew nothing of her plan, that he had discovered her roaming about on her own and felt it safer to keep her with him.

There would be no trouble for him.

And of course, fool that he was, he had gone along with her request; he could never have refused her anything.

Rhodri blamed himself for what had happened that night; he said he had been frozen with indecision, that if he had been quicker and more decisive, she would still be with them. The man was distraught, and Casper was too much of a coward to tell him that it was he who was really to blame.

Lady Addington and Miss Elspeth McGinnity had arrived two days ago, their invitation completely forgotten in the chaotic swirl of days following that terrible night. They had pulled up in a pony and trap, completely unaware of their hostess's fate. To his credit, Rhodri had been the consummate gentleman, not blinking an eye at their arrival, and quickly ensured that the servants prepared rooms for them, and that a good meal was laid out that evening.

In Casper's eyes, their arrival had been good for the house, providing it with some energy and purpose, following weeks of misery. It had been particularly good for Rhodri, who seemed to have made a connection with Lady Addington's pretty, red-haired niece. The young woman, greatly moved by Lord Baughan's grief, had spent much time in his company, helping to distract him from his sorrows.

He had seen them this morning, after breakfast, walking out of the front door together, Rhodri with his dark hair and sun-brushed skin, his shoulders down, and the young assistant's hair in one long plait, flashing in the morning light. She had been talking, and he could only imagine the words of comfort she spoke, as they strode away together, arm in arm.

To Casper's mind, there was one thing above all others that was to blame for Jane's death: her great-grandmother's letters, and one letter in particular, that final one that had so excited her, the one she had concealed from Rhodri and Ewan, the one that had made her so determined to walk out alone that night.

The piece of correspondence where that old-time relative claimed to have seen one of the Fair Folk. After she had disappeared, Casper had read and reread the thing, hoping it might provide some illumination into the darkness surrounding the terrible events. He would have surprised his old tutors – who despaired of him and his lack of academic prowess, his inability to commit even the shortest Shakespeare sonnet to memory – at the way he could recite that thing almost word for word.

Dearest M.

I have such exciting news I can hardly believe what I am to write.
I have seen one.
One of the Fair Folk.
It happened last night whilst I was out walking.
It had been a busy day. In the morning a great many people had visited the Hall, local men, eager to assist my father in his nocturnal search for the individuals responsible for the sheep deaths. He was also joined by other titled landowners, drawn to the adventure of the hunt. They filled the hall's lower levels, laughing, drinking and frankly being a little coarse.
They had ridden out just after taking a light lunch, like a regiment of light cavalry. Many carried guns, some of the noblemen, who had served in the army, carried pistols and swords. One old farmer even carried a lance – the relic of a continental war.
It seemed to me that the people of the area had declared war on the Tylwyth Teg. I pictured the Fairy horde coming out to meet them, with its beautiful banners and strange alien armour. I imagined they would carry enchanted swords and spears made of bronze – for it is known that the beautiful folk cannot abide the touch of iron – perhaps some of their soldiers would be lifted on gossamer wings and, carrying bows, rain down flint-tipped arrows on my father and his unfortunate men.
Then the victorious Fair Folk would march onwards to claim the spoils of war. Maybe they would come here, to

this very hall, and capture me and the servants, carrying us away into the Fairy realm, where I would be forced to marry some wild Elvish prince.

I smiled at my dangerous and romantic imaginings. Of course, none of those terrible things happened, I simply watched my father and his men ride away until, eventually, they disappeared into a thicket of trees. I did not see them again until later that evening.

I spent a frightfully boring afternoon wandering about the Llangorse Fawr, reading in the library, my only company the loyal Bulstrode. Gradually the shadows about the estate lengthened, the evening was drawing in, dusk had crept upon me.

I looked out the window, hoping to see my father return. But of him and his men there was no sign.

Something drew my attention though, a glow beyond the woodland at the edge of the estate, it was a surprisingly clean glow, by this I mean there was no evidence of smoke, no sign of burning. It was a pale illumination as pure as the light of the moon and stars.

Intrigued, I pulled on my warmest coat, and with Bulstrode at my heels I made my way outside, I carried a small table lamp with me. Walking slowly in the direction of the woods, I never once let my gaze drift from that beautifully illuminated skyline. Bulstrode seemed on edge, his hackles were raised, and where once he might have roamed ahead, in search of any errant squirrels that might need encouraging back into their trees, today he stayed close to me, padding along at my side, a silent floppy-eared protector. I was starting to feel nervous, no woodland looks inviting in the evening, at night they are things best viewed from a distance, magical places for whimsical ponderings, not areas to be physically explored. They are the domain of poachers, and wild nocturnal animals. To keep up my spirits I sang Bulstrode a song.

Do your ears hang low?
Do they wobble to and fro?
Can you tie them in a knot?
Can you tie them in a bow?
Can you swing them over your shoulder,
Like a regimental soldier?
Do your ears hang low?

If Bulstrode was in any way moved by my little ditty, he did not show it, never even glancing in my direction, indeed his ears hung very low, as did his whole body – by now his usual sprightly trot had been replaced with slow, cautious movements.

Taking a deep breath, I passed through the tree line, turning up my lamp to provide its best illumination, Bulstrode leading, I moved amongst the trees, eyes scouring the darkness ahead. Eventually, the perfect light I had seen earlier began to filter through the foliage ahead of me.

It was then I saw movement.

Ahead I made out a small shape, not much larger than a child, thin and with an unusually large head. It was at this moment that Bulstrode froze in place, staring intently in its direction, and I do declare that had the thing ahead made any sudden movement, or noise, I most certainly would have turned tail and run just as fast as my legs would carry me. Not stopping until several inches of solid oaken door separated me from the outside world.

But I held my nerve, I do not know how.

Perhaps it was that driving curiosity that is said to have claimed the lives of so many cats, pushing me onwards. I walked as stealthily as I was able, circling about so as to come at it from the side.

Thankfully it did not see me.

What kind of fairy this being was, I could not say, I am certain I have never read of its like before. It was neither gnome, pixie nor dwarf. It wore what I took to be a tight military outfit that clung to its body like a second skin, the short sleeves revealed long arms of a sickly grey colour, mottled with the occasional dark stain. Its hands had only three obscenely long fingers and no thumbs.

But it was its large head that troubles my dreams, for this was not the head of a handsome Faerie prince. This was the hideous visage of a thing from hell. The head rested atop a thin puny neck, and had the same grey mottled skin that I had seen on its arms. There was no visible nose, just two vertical slits. It had a small lipless mouth, but worst of all were its eyes, they were much too large for its head, oval shaped, pitch black, soulless.

A strange humming filled the air, not far from this horrid creature was its chariot, a glowing thing made of some strange metal, it hovered not far off the ground, in shape it was like an upturned saucer with a dome at its centre, I could see no beast of burden to lead it. I took a single step forward, drawn to its beautiful strangeness, but this movement drew the attention of the being, and it looked about searchingly. At this, abject terror replaced my courage and I fled, dragging Bulstrode with me.

Never once looking behind me.

They had discovered Jane's body two weeks ago; a shepherd had found it in a field not far from where Mr Evans had found his dead ewe. Casper had not seen her body, had no wish to look upon the mutilated corpse of the woman he loved. It had been Rhodri and Ewan who had ridden out to identify her. But he knew the stories. He had heard what the housewives whispered to each other when they met in the village store, what the old men in their cups said at the local taverns.

That the Tylwyth Teg had feasted on her.

Let Sleeping Dogs Lie

June 1906

Wendlelow University had stood at the edge of that old, troubled town for many centuries, its large playing fields backed onto the wooded Shropshire hills which eventually gave way to their more rugged Welsh cousins.

Its spires and parapets dominated Wendlelow's skyline, a fortress of knowledge, a castle of learning; it had attracted some of the finest scholars of the ages.

Its museums and collections housed many old treasures: books, artefacts and pictures, some of them of great value and interest, some, sadly, less so.

Professor Matthew Wainwright, the curator of Wendlelow's treasure, was a middle-aged man, bespectacled, with a receding hairline, of which he was very self-conscious.

Matthew had only just assumed the role of curator; the previous occupant had moved to pastures new at a university further south.

He, like so many people who find themselves in a new, longed-for position, was keen to leave his mark, to show not only the good professors who had appointed him – but also his rival applicants – that he was the right man for the job.

As is typical with most newly installed people, Matthew decided to achieve this goal by changing things – in particular, the system of categorising and storing the vast number of artefacts, documents, and antiquities that the university had acquired.

It mattered not that the current system – in use for over one hundred and fifty years – worked perfectly well; some men believe they can always improve upon things, and Matthew was just such a man.

The problem was that the task he had set himself, and the small team who assisted him, was a gargantuan one, and so, whilst the professors who had raised him to his current position were impressed with his new plans, those who worked beneath him, and were thus expected to implement them, were most certainly not.

The two men in question were Mr Rogers and Mr Todhumer. They had been employees of the university for a great many years, and had, up until now at least, enjoyed a relatively quiet, unhurried existence.

Matthew Wainwright changed all that.

From a life of quiet ponderings, drinking tea, and perusing various dealers' catalogues – for items which they felt would expand the university's collection in the most satisfying of ways – they now found themselves lifting, carrying and documenting untenable quantities of old and valuable things.

Truth be told, Wendlelow University probably did not need three men to curate its collection; it is doubtful it needed two, since extra work could have been taken on by eager students. But it was a wealthy establishment, and as such the previous curators had been given an ample budget, with which they had not only purchased many valuable things but had also put to good use hiring outside help, thus lessening any burden on themselves, and ensuring more time for quiet contemplation.

But Matthew Wainwright was not a quiet man, prone to periods of contemplative silence; he was one of the world's doers and now, so it seemed, were poor Mr Rogers, and poor Mr Todhumer.

"Where's His Highness want this then?" asked Mr Todhumer, waving a small early-Georgian mezzotint.

Mr Rogers looked at him unhappily. "I know where I'd like to put it," he grumbled.

This comment received a smirk from Mr Todhumer.

"No, I think that one's for display," Mr Rogers said, then added, "Look smart, His Lordship's back."

Matthew had just come down the stairs, a self-satisfied smile upon his face. "Ahh, Rogers, Todhumer, hard at it I see, good men, just the thing. At this rate, we will have it all re-categorised in just a few months, as well as having the new display set up in the university museum."

"Aye, Professor Wainwright," both men muttered in a decidedly unenthusiastic way.

Matthew proceeded to walk about examining shelves and occasionally tutting to himself. Matthew was one of this world's great tutters. He believed that a well-delivered tut could speak volumes. At the moment, his tuts were intended to say, the grime down here is awful, and not at all what one expects to find in a great university.

Mr Todhumer and Mr Rogers made no reply, so he translated his tut. "The dust here is most dreadful! It makes me wonder when last any of these things saw the light of day. For instance, what on earth is in these? They aren't labelled."

He strode to the pile of wooden crates stacked against the wall and began moving them away so that they could be inspected more easily.

"I say, Rogers, Todhumer, come and look at this," Matthew said, in an excited voice, after he had finished moving them aside.

Both men looked at each other and shrugged unenthusiastically. An excitable Professor Wainwright probably meant a Professor Wainwright with a job for them to do – never a desirable turn of events.

Slowly, they made their way to where he was standing.

"Just look at this," Matthew declared.

"It's a door," said Mr Todhumer, in a flat voice.

"Yes, but I mean to say, I didn't even know it was here, my predecessor never spoke of it."

"He probably didn't know it was there either. Them boxes have never been moved, not in our time," Mr Rogers said.

"Oh, confound it. The thing's locked," complained Matthew, imagining what treasures lay within. "There must be a key somewhere."

"Probably best to leave it be," said Mr Todhumer, who unlike the good professor did not see a room of hidden treasures – just a door, leading to more hard graft!

"Aye sir, let sleeping dogs lie," seconded Mr Rogers.

*

But Professor Matthew Wainwright did not leave it be, he was not a man who was capable of leaving it be, and as for sleeping dogs, it was likely he would have given them a sharp poke with his toe, had he discovered any dozing near him.

When a mystery presented itself, he had to solve it, and the locked door was a riddle that nagged at him day and night.

He spent days rifling through drawers looking for – and trying – any key he could find for the door's lock; relentlessly he interrogated other professors about the college, asking what they knew of this strange portal, or better still, its contents. But it was to no avail. No one had any information and no one really cared enough to help him find it.

Mr Rogers' and Mr Todhumer's attempts to dampen his eagerness – by suggesting that it was merely a forgotten broom cupboard, and therefore of little or no interest – were sadly to no avail.

After a week of fruitless searching, Matthew made the following declaration to his largely unenthusiastic subordinates. "If after one more week, I have failed to find the blasted key to that room, I shall hire a locksmith."

And true to his word, after another week of hopeless searching, this is what he did.

*

So it was that the professor stood, with Mr Rogers and Mr Todhumer, peering cautiously into the gloomy space beyond the newly opened door. It was small; indeed, Mr Rogers' and Mr Todhumer's assumption that it was merely a broom cupboard did not seem far off the mark, for barely two men could enter at any one time, and then with very little room to move.

But there were no brooms or besoms in this cupboard. Nor were there to be found any buckets or mops; indeed, it was largely empty, but for one thing.

A three-by-six-inch wooden box. Eagerly, Matthew knelt down and snatched it up, then carried it upstairs to the better-lit office where he and his companions usually worked.

Carefully, he laid the box on his desk. Mr Rogers and Mr Todhumer, finally interested, crowded in behind him.

The box was made of a dark wood, and a strange symbol had been burned into its lid – it was a triangle set within a circle.

Beneath this, also burned into the box's lid, was a message, clumsily written. It read: *Do Not Open.*

"I've seen those marks before," Mr Todhumer said, "burned into some of the doors in town."

"Aye," Mr Rogers added, "heard there was some sort of story attached to 'em, don't know what it is though."

Both men now regarded the box warily, as if it might contain an angry, venomous serpent.

However, Matthew, who was not a superstitious man, seemed largely unconcerned. "There is no lock, just a catch. It's old, but I think it still works."

He fiddled with something on the front of the box. There was a satisfying click. Mr Rogers and Mr Todhumer quickly took several steps backwards.

Matthew lifted the lid, letting out a gasp. His two companions watched warily as their employer stared down, a look of pleasure on his face. Gradually, as it became clear that he was not going to be brought down by some terrible supernatural wrath, the two men crept forward.

The inside of the box was bare wood. It contained no velvet cushion on which to seat an object of great value, and yet the thing within would have looked very well upon one.

It was a torc, made of gold strands interwoven together to form a stiff neck ring. At one end of the torc was a stag's head, at the other a boar's. They stared at each other, their faces not quite touching.

"Blimey!" Mr Rogers said.

"Stone the crows!" Mr Todhumer added.

Matthew reverently took up the torc and held it up to the window, letting the sunlight play upon its surface. "Wonderful," he whispered.

*

"But why is there no record of it?" Matthew said in frustration. He had spent most of the afternoon looking through ledgers and files to see when and where the item had been purchased, or who may have been so good as to donate it to the university, but to no avail.

"It'll have to go on display, something that nice, sir," Mr Todhumer said.

"You should put it back, sir. Back in the box. Back in that room," Mr Rogers said.

"You know who might be able to help you, sir?" Mr Todhumer said. "That librarian fella, Whiskerbusker."

"You mean Baltus Whiskerfisker." Matthew mused for a moment. "Yes, I suppose he might be able to point me in the direction of a book, one that could tell me something of this thing's history."

"May I, sir?" Mr Todhumer enquired, and held out his hand.

"Certainly." Matthew handed the torc over. Mr Todhumer cradled it in his hands, admiring the workmanship and wondering how much money the thing was worth. Probably more than he'd ever earn, he decided.

He turned around and offered the torc to Mr Rogers, but his colleague merely stepped backwards, holding up the palms of his hands.

"Not for me, Mr Todhumer, no thank you. If it were my decision it would go right back where we found it. It was put there for a reason. That warning was on the box for a reason. And I think you should heed it, sir." This last part was directed to Matthew.

But the professor just smiled. "Now Mr Rogers, don't let all that nonsense worry you. We are grown men, not children, and I for one do not believe this thing is any more dangerous than any of the other items in the museum's display."

Having said this, he took the item back from Mr Todhumer, laying it reverently on his desk. "I think I shall speak to Professor Templeton. He specialises in history;

if anyone will know something about the thing's past, it will be him."

Later, Matthew performed a further exploration of the small room, but it revealed no other hidden objects. However, the strange symbol that had adorned the box was discovered on the inside of the room's door, and this had just added to Mr Rogers' feeling of discomfort.

*

Neither Mr Rogers nor Mr Todhumer resided on the university grounds; instead, they lived in accommodation in town.

So it was, early the next morning, that they arrived at their place of work to find it in a state of great upset. Students wandered about complaining, and the professors seemed all out of sorts; indeed, there was a general unsettled air to the ancient buildings that made up the university.

It did not take the two men long to learn what had happened.

It seemed there had been a great disturbance in the university halls the previous night. It had started after midnight, beginning with the heavy tread of feet upon the floor, as though somebody were bounding up and down the corridors, and at a pace that would have put the university sprinting team to shame!

This was followed by a terrific banging.

It had taken some nerve, but eventually a group of the faculty, with some of the older students in tow, had gone to investigate the origin of this noise.

However, whenever this collection of brave souls thought that they had finally located the source of the sound and crept, candles and lanterns in hand, to confront the ne'er-do-well, they found nothing but an empty room or passage before them.

The noise had continued intermittently until around four o'clock in the morning, when it suddenly just stopped, and the thankful residents of Wendlelow University were able to gather a few precious hours of sleep.

Mr Rogers and Mr Todhumer made their way through a hive of gossip and speculation to the office they shared with Professor Wainwright.

They found their employer in a state of some dismay, and the office itself turned upside-down.

Papers and books lay scattered about the floor. One chair had been placed upside-down on Professor Wainwright's desk, another lay on its side by the window, Five books balanced precariously on it.

The torc had been removed from the locked safe the professor had secured it in the night before, and was now sat on the mantelpiece.

"Blimey!" said Mr Rogers.

"Stone the crows!" exclaimed Mr Todhumer.

It took the three men nearly an hour to set everything straight. All the while, Mr Rogers cast the most suspicious and accusing of glances at the torc.

But it was only when everything had been properly returned to its place that he decided to speak up.

"It's that thing's doing," he announced, pointing an accusing finger at the ancient item. "I tell you now, Professor Wainwright, get rid of it, it's cursed or something."

If Mr Todhumer shared this opinion, he did not speak up, but it is to be noted that he gave their precious find the most dubious of glances.

"Nonsense, man, it's some students up to their pranks. They were messing about all over the college last night. You should have heard the racket they made! They'd best hope I never find out who it was," Matthew growled. "But how did they manage to get at the thing, it was securely locked in the safe?" Both Mr Rogers and Mr Todhumer detected a hint of uncertainty in his voice.

"Now," he continued, "you two, back to the job of reorganising those stacks. I'm off to show my find to Professor Templeton, and maybe get Mr Whiskerfisker's opinion too."

*

Back in the lower levels of the university, Mr Rogers and Mr Todhumer worked in relative silence. Both men were on edge, prone to jump at the slightest noise. The dark corridors that had once been nothing more than a place to while away the day in pursuit of an honest coin now seemed totally different.

Where once shadowy corners had been inviting places to retreat to and have a peaceful natter – while Matthew was busy elsewhere – they now seemed brooding, uninviting places where might dwell things of a sinister nature, things that might pounce.

It was at midday, when both men gladly returned upstairs to their office to eat their lunch and enjoy a cup of tea, that they finally met up with Professor Wainwright once more.

He strode in – just as they were each pouring a second cup – torc in hand, and slumped disappointedly into the chair behind his desk.

Everyone was silent.

Matthew tutted to himself.

Mr Rogers and Mr Todhumer looked at each other.

Matthew tutted again, louder.

"Did you find anything out, sir?" asked Mr Todhumer, because he was beginning to feel it was expected of him.

"You would think," Matthew replied, "that working as we do, in one of England's finest universities, home to some of the country's greatest minds, that I would by now be fully informed of the object's history and origins."

"Nothing useful then, sir," said Mr Todhumer.

"Merely titbits, my good man, intellectual crumbs scattered before me. I spoke to Templeton first. He confirmed it was a torc, a fact I did not need pointed out. He believes he can date it to the first century AD, based on its design and the way it was constructed. Beyond that he was of very little help. He said he might be able to find out more, if I were willing to let him hold onto the thing. But I do not feel ready to relinquish it into the hands of another just yet." At the last part the professor's tone took on a slightly possessive edge, like a child informing his friends he would not be sharing his toys.

"What about Mr Whesterfasker?" asked Mr Todhumer.

"Mr Whiskerfisker was little better. He seemed more interested in the box. Said the marking on it was something called a Witch-brand, a sort of charm to protect against evil, or some such. He believed I would be better off putting the torc back in it, and returning it to where I found it."

"Sensible fellow that Wuskerbasker," Mr Rogers muttered.

"Superstitious nonsense," snapped Matthew. "When he looked at the torc he said it was not crafted by human hands. He spoke of old races that dwelt in the hills before men made their homes here. The man may be a fine librarian, but in this he is totally delusional, a fantasist."

"Nevertheless, sir, it was kept in that box for a reason. Perhaps we should err... leave it in there, when not examining it," Mr Rogers suggested.

Matthew did not reply to Mr Rogers' comments straight away; instead he just looked at the torc, turning it in his hands, a strange, dreamy quality to his eyes. He did not like to put it back in the box; he liked it in sight, where at whim he could easily admire it. His find.

"It is extremely valuable, and must be put on display, not squirreled away in a box," he said, never lifting his gaze. "But still, with students roaming the halls at night, causing mischief, it is probably best not to leave it untended."

"The provost also has a safe in his office," Mr Todhumer said, "Well-known fact."

"That's right," agreed Mr Rogers, "Put it in its box and get it locked away in the provost's safe."

"No need for that," Matthew said calmly, "I can put it in my room where I can keep an eye on it. There is a lock on my door so it shall be quite secure."

"In its box… sir," added Mr Rogers.

"What's that, Mr Rogers?" Matthew said.

"What Mr Rogers means," it was Mr Todhumer who replied, "is, keep it in your room, *in its box*, sir, and I'm inclined to agree, it can't do any harm, can it, and you never know, I mean to say."

"You mean to say what? What is it you mean to say, Mr Todhumer?" The professor sounded annoyed. "Mr Rogers, surely you don't subscribe to that nonsense spouted by Mr Whiskerfisker. This item is no more cursed than my hat, an item which, by the way, I will gladly eat, should I be proven wrong," Matthew said, raising his voice to further emphasise his displeasure at what was being suggested.

Both Mr Rogers and Mr Todhumer shifted uncomfortably; they had never before seen their employer so irritated.

"Not only will I keep the torc in my room, but I will leave its silly box here, in the office, and should I hear any more rubbish about curses, I will throw the damn thing on the fire!"

There was a moment's awkward silence, with all three men doing their very best not to look at each other.

It was Matthew who finally spoke. "Now back to work, the both of you."

*

The following evening was no more peaceful than the previous one. Again, at the midnight hour the university was awoken to the sounds of footsteps in hallways which should, by rights, have been silent at such a time.

This was followed again by much banging and commotion, but where the night before, braver souls had stepped out, light in hand to seek the source of the noise, tonight all doors remained tightly shut, bolts were firmly secured and keys turned in locks.

In their dormitories students huddled together, and the professors, alone in their rooms, did not suffer the oil lamps to burn low.

As the night proceeded, the noises only became louder, until finally there was a strangled scream of such intensity, that many students and professors alike pulled their pillows over their ears.

Then there was silence, and this in and of itself was every bit as unnerving to the restless occupants of the old university as the noises had been. But the silence persisted, until finally the light of the sun drove away the worst of the residents' fears.

*

It was Mr Rogers and Mr Todhumer who alerted the faculty to Professor Wainwright's absence.

At breakfast in halls, a great many of the students and professors had overslept, exhausted by the night's events, and so his presence was not missed there.

But by midday, when he had still not appeared in the office, Mr Rogers and Mr Todhumer became concerned and notified the faculty.

There was an immediate search of the professor's rooms, which, unlike every other in the university, had not been locked that night.

He was found, quite dead, a look of untold horror graven upon his face. He lay upon his bed; about his neck the torc had been placed, but it had been fastened so tightly that not a breath of air could have entered or left his body.

The authorities were immediately notified.

The provost called a council the same day, attended by Mr Todhumer, Mr Rogers, and at their suggestion, Professor Templeton and Baltus Whiskerfisker.

Not much is known of what was said in that conversation. But after a short time, all five men were seen to leave the room carrying an old box with a mark burned into it. The men left town immediately and when they returned, they did so empty-handed.

The following night at the university was peaceful, with both students and professors finding their sleep untroubled.

In time a new curator was selected to replace the unfortunate Matthew Wainwright, and to the delight of Mr Rogers and Mr Todhumer, he proved to be a much more relaxed and contemplative man, one who believed in the traditional organisation of things.

He was most certainly not a man to open strange doors.

P A SHELDON

The Heirloom

The following tale takes place a few years before the mysterious disappearance of Elspeth McGinnity.

From The Journal of Elspeth McGinnity, August 1908

Whatever else one can say of Wendlelow, it is seldom dull.

Oh, I suppose to the metropolitan type, it may seem that way. There are no dance halls and only one music hall. Most of the nocturnal socialising is done in the town's public houses, usually frequented by university students who rub shoulders with hard-working labourers and prosperous merchants.

But I do not judge a place's appeal solely by the quality of its nightlife, as I do not partake in that lifestyle, preferring to stay at home and work on my manuscript.

No, for me the appeal of Wendlelow is in its history, its architecture, and how, at any given time, a seemingly ordinary day can suddenly become eventful.

Yesterday was one such a day.

It began normally enough. I was dictating notes to my assistant, Nolan, on the supposed haunting of a country road that leads from Wendlelow over the border in to Wales. According to my source, a weather-beaten old drover I had encountered at the market a couple of days before, on certain nights of the year it is believed that the ghost of a highwayman gallops down said road, stops at a gate by a field, discharges his pistol, and vanishes in a puff of smoke.

Who the highwayman was, and why he should choose to haunt that stretch of lonely road, and in that manner, the old drover could not say. Still, he claimed many folks had seen the phantom – himself included!

It was as Nolan and I were discussing and documenting this fascinating tale that Martha, my housekeeper and cook, interrupted us. This was very out of character for her; she would never usually disturb me when I am in the middle of my work.

I could tell that something was on her mind, as she had not been her usual bubbly self all day, so I left Nolan to finish writing up the notes and went with her to the parlour to discuss her problem.

Her niece, a certain Rose Upton, was in a state of great distress following the death of her fiancé, a young man called Bill Runnel. Martha felt that I may be able to offer the young woman some assistance.

I must admit that at first I believed Martha wished me to offer her some counsel on bereavement, something I have some experience of since the passing of my husband and daughter.

But I was surprised to learn that this was not the case. According to Martha, her fiancé had died under very mysterious circumstances, and Martha – who understands the channels of my research – felt that I might be in a unique position to offer her assistance.

She would say no more on the matter, and naturally I found my interest piqued. So, I have agreed to pay a visit to the young lady.

*

Under normal circumstances, Rose Upton was probably a very attractive young woman; she possessed thick blonde hair, a small oval face, and a dainty nose. However, misery and distress have a way of draining people, and it had most certainly done this to poor Rose.

The young woman sat hunched in a chair in the small, terraced house she shared with her parents and siblings. She bore the tell-tale signs of a sleepless night, dark rings beneath red eyes, and her nails picked at the back of her hands in a most distressing manner.

Elspeth, who sat opposite her with Martha, could only stare in pity, wondering if she had looked like that after the death of her husband and daughter. That whole episode of her life was now like a vague nightmare, one she did not care to revisit.

"Why don't you tell Mrs McGinnity everything, dear," Martha said encouragingly. "Don't you feel there's nothing you can't say, not to her? She'll hear it all and give you her honest opinion."

Rose gave a sniff and made a concerted effort to compose herself. "Well, Mrs McGinnity, it's like this…"

She went on to tell me how, about eight months ago, Bill, a handsome lad who had run a market stall selling vegetables, had asked her to step out with him.

Rose had been flattered and from that time onward, they had been almost inseparable. After seven months he had asked her for her hand in marriage.

"He did it the proper way, too. Got my pa's permission first, then proposed. It was a Sunday and we'd gone for a stroll to the top of a hill that had a beautiful view of the town and countryside. Then he goes down on one knee, even though it was proper muddy, and gave me this beautiful ring." Rose held out her hand to show Elspeth.

Truth be told, the ring that adorned the woman's finger was rather plain, but Elspeth had no doubt that in Rose's mind it was as beautiful and valuable as any one of the Crown Jewels.

She remembered her own engagement ring, carefully stored in a box in her home, and the very day Rhodri had given it to her. She had first met her husband when she and her aunt, Lady Hanoria Addington, had been invited to stay at Llangorse Fawr, his home in Wales. When she first met him, he had been grieving the loss of his sister – an event he had never fully spoken about. As they spent time together, they had fallen in love, continuing to stay in contact after she returned with her aunt to the woman's home in Warwickshire. Eventually, he had proposed – one of the happiest days of her life. They had a daughter, Kate. Her life's road had seemed laid out before her, and it was one she was more than happy to travel.

Then came the terrible accident on the lake, which left her alone. She was no longer Lady Baughan; that title would pass to the wife of Ewan, the new Lord Baughan. She became Mrs McGinnity, and had left Llangorse Fawr and all its memories to start a new life in Wendlelow.

Rose continued her narrative. "The problem was his old sweetheart, Ivy Weathers. They'd separated a few months before we met. She was a right cowbag, wouldn't leave Bill alone, kept pestering after him. She was foul to me too. The tongue on that woman! You wouldn't believe the things she said. You see he'd split up with her, but she weren't having none of it, oh no," Rose said.

She went on to explain how Ivy would seek them out, just turning up out of the blue when they were walking together. "Just like she knew where to find us, and we seldom took the same walk twice, not once we'd caught on to her antics. Didn't stop her, though. She'd turn up, and start her ranting and threats. 'You're for me, Bill Runnel!' she would say. 'Let this scrawny little pigeon fly.' Scrawny little pigeon, me, like she was something so special herself and then…"

Elspeth endeavoured to listen to the girl's complaints, but found herself wondering why Martha felt she could be of any help to this girl. She had little doubt that being trailed and harassed by your lover's previous sweetheart would be annoying, but quite what it had to do with her was unclear.

"…a witch." Rose finished.

"I'm sorry?" Elspeth said.

"Bill always said she was a witch," Rose said, sounding exasperated, having clearly realised that she had, at least momentarily, lost her audience. "That she threatened to put hexes on people. She had the means to do it too. She had an old family heirloom – one that gave her power. I reckon that was what she used to murder my Bill!"

Apparently it had all started after their engagement. Wendlelow's rumour mill had set to work, grinding up tales and falsehoods, then sending them drifting on the wind. Ivy must have tasted it, and most certainly not found it to her liking.

She confronted Bill at his market stall. There had been an awful argument, culminating in the spitting out of some terrible threats.

"Was Bill concerned? Did Ivy have a large family? A lot of brothers?" Elspeth asked.

"Nah, it was just her and her grandmother, and my Bill never really held much weight with the idea that she had strange powers."

"So, what happened?" Elspeth asked.

"At first not much, but as the days went by, Bill became withdrawn, fretful like, not himself. And my Bill was one to face the day with his shoulders back, and chin held high." Rose shook her head sadly. "I asked him what was wrong, and he told me it was just bad dreams, nothing more. But that last day he was so out of sorts, I begged him to tell me what was really going on."

At this, Rose let out a little sob and sat with her face resting in her hands.

"You tell us in your own time, dear," Martha said reassuringly.

"It weren't dreams, you know, that's what he told me. It were real. I asked him what was real, but he wouldn't say. I told him: 'Go see a doctor,' but he said there weren't a doctor born who could help him with this. Then that night, he died."

At this point, Rose started sobbing uncontrollably.

Martha took over. "It were most odd, Mrs McGinnity. One of the neighbours heard a commotion in the street outside Bill's home. She looks out to see Bill thrashing about like he were being dragged away against his will. But she says Bill were alone. Alone, but surrounded by a lot of wrong-looking shadows."

"In what way, 'wrong-looking'?" Elspeth asked.

"She wouldn't say, but was quite shook up and evasive when I pressed her about them," Martha said.

"She didn't try to get help?" Elspeth asked.

"No, more's the pity. She thought he was drunk, and herself overtired and imagining things," Martha said. Her tone left her opinion of both the neighbour and her decision in no doubt. "He was found the next day in an alleyway. Dead, of course."

"That's terrible. Have the police given their opinion on what happened?" asked Elspeth.

It was Rose who replied. "They said he was attacked, covered in scratches, some of them fresh, some of them up to a week old, all over his body, but out of sight under clothing. But it weren't those 'orrible wounds what done for him, Mrs McGinnity. Oh, no. He were throttled – choked to death, for the only visible scratches were those about his neck!"

Elspeth tapped her nails on the arm of her chair. "To be sure, it's a dreadful story, but I'm not certain what help I can be."

At this, Rose looked desperate. She rolled up the sleeve of her dress to reveal a series of painful scratch marks running up her arm.

"But you must help, you see, I think the same thing is happening to me!"

*

Nolan strode with Elspeth down Wendlelow's narrow cobbled streets. The upper storeys of the houses leaned close together over the lane, like co-conspirators sharing ancient secrets, only allowing thin bars of fine August sunshine to find their way down into the street.

"So, this Ivy threatened Rose too?" he asked.

"Apparently, a few days after Bill's funeral, she came to Rose's door, told her she'd go the same way as her lover, and that she had the means to see it done.

"And that was two weeks ago. She thinks that whatever is going to happen, will happen tonight. The poor girl is beside herself."

"Can you do anything?" Nolan asked. "What form does this curse take?"

"Rose said it started as nightmares, shadows taking frightful shapes, until one in particular, a vile thing she could not bring herself to describe to me, took precedence over the others.

"A week ago, she awoke in the night to find it in her room.

"Standing by her, leering down at her.

"She screamed so hard her voice nearly gave way, indeed, she swears she had a sore throat for nearly two full days after. Her family rushed in to find her thrashing about; her body covered in scratches."

They walked a while longer in silence. Finally, they emerged into the main market area. Here the August sunshine could fully bathe them in all its warmth and glory.

"Ivy doesn't know me," Elspeth continued. "According to Martha, she has often hinted at being in possession of a weird heirloom, with supposed powers, using it to bully her neighbours.

"Perhaps if I were to approach her, tell her about the book on folklore that I'm writing, imply I could include the story of her heirloom in it, well, just maybe I could learn something that might help."

"I don't know, it sounds to me like a job for the police," Nolan said doubtfully.

"What policeman would believe Rose's story? If I had not seen the things I've seen, I would give it no credence."

"But making yourself known to this Ivy could put you in peril."

"Rose gave me her address. She lives on Magpie Lane. We can pay her a visit and make it look like a professional call – you can come with me and take notes. I will appeal to her self-importance, she should not suspect anything untoward," Elspeth said.

Wendlelow was not a large town, and it did not take the two of them long to walk to Ivy Weathers's home.

Whilst Elspeth knocked on the oak door, Nolan examined a strange mark burnt into its wood – a black triangle set within a circle – one of Wendlelow's famous Witch-brands. Supposedly placed on the portals of certain properties centuries ago by a Welsh wizard, they were intended to drive away entities that troubled some of the properties in the town.

He was very familiar with them; Elspeth's front door also possessed such a marking.

Nolan felt the uncomfortable sensation of being watched by hostile eyes. He looked about, but most of

Magpie Lane's residents were about their own business, paying them no heed at all.

All but one man.

He was an odd-looking fellow, completely out of place in this working-class area, dressed as if returning from a visit to the theatre. He wore evening clothes, complete with a short cape, carrying a blackthorn walking stick topped with a golden orb. On his head was a top hat.

It was beyond Nolan's understanding how he appeared to be the only one noticing this man.

But as soon as the man realised he was being watched, he ducked into a side alley.

Nolan was about to mention this well-to-do individual when the front door was opened. Quickly, he made sure his notepad and pencil were visible. Standing there was a young woman, her hair the colour of a raven's feathers, her eyes a sharp grey colour. She was very striking – tall, with a slender figure.

"Yes, what do you want?" she demanded, in a thick Shropshire accent.

"Begging your pardon," Elspeth said. "My name is Elspeth McGinnity. May I ask, are you Ivy Weathers?"

"If I am, what's it to you?" the woman said bluntly.

Elspeth produced her most charming smile; it was the smile she had spent her childhood practising in the mirror, a special smile reserved for special occasions, when she wanted something.

"I'm a writer, Miss Weathers. I collect stories – local folklore, myths and legends. Sometimes I write articles for newspapers and magazines, but at this moment I am working on a book. I have heard it said, by people about the town, that your family has a legend attached to it – something about a magic heirloom – and, to be frank, I wanted to learn a little more about it and, with your permission, use it in my book. Maybe even do an article for a magazine."

"A magazine article?" The woman's tone, which up to that point had been cold, began to thaw somewhat. "I'm Ivy Weathers. I suppose I could give you a little of my time, come in."

Ivy led them into a small room that served as both a kitchen and a general living area. An old woman sat in a chair wrapped in a blanket despite the warm August weather.

"Who's this then?" she asked in a surprisingly strong voice.

"This here is Elspeth McGinnity, and her assistant I assume, I don't know his name."

"It's N-Nolan." Nolan cringed at his stutter, it always happened when he was nervous, and this young woman definitely made him nervous.

"He says it's N-Nolan."

"I heard him, I ain't deaf yet. What are they doing here?"

"Claims she collects stories, writes articles for magazines and the like. Says she wants to write about me and the spinning wheel," Ivy said with a hint of pride in her voice.

"The spinning wheel is it? Well, that tale is well known enough round these parts. Why pester us? Anyone in the street could tell you that story," Grandma Weathers snapped.

"Perhaps not as well-known as you believe," Elspeth said. "Also I thought it best to get the information from the source, rather than listen to misinformed gossip."

"I can see the sense in that," the old woman conceded, "it's an old tale for the telling, and probably many of the young 'uns have forgotten it. Well, Elspeth McGinnity and N-Nolan, there it is."

And so saying, she gestured dramatically to the corner of the room.

It sat there, like some brooding beast, squatting, as if waiting to leap upon an unsuspecting victim. A spinning wheel, but one quite unlike any Nolan had seen before. It was much larger than the usual specimen, and was made of bronze rather than wood. Strange markings adorned the wheel, symbols whose meanings were lost on the young man. It possessed a treadle – a foot pedal used to turn the wheel – but oddly it seemed to lack a bobbin, or any means by which to mount one, so there was no way to wind spun yarn. It was a 'spinning wheel' in name only.

"Very impressive," Nolan said.

"It were a gift," said Ivy proudly.

"Indeed," Elspeth said, nodding to Nolan, a sign that he should start making notes.

"Now, our great-great-grandmother, who I'm named after," (there was a hint of pride in Ivy's voice, as if this were some great personal achievement,) "well she were a real beauty in her youth. Story goes, she was out picking blueberries on Grumple Top – you know, that hill just outside of town? There, she meets someone – a handsome lord, and no mortal lord, neither. No, this were the Lord of the Fair Folk. Now, if you are a story collector as you say, you must have heard of the tale of Lord Wendle and how he drove a Fairy Lord and his host into a mound and imprisoned them there with magic."

"I know that tale," Elspeth said.

"Well, this were the very Lord she met, handsome as the sun on midsummer, and Midsummer were the day they met, as the magical bonds that held him weakened enough for him to roam abroad that day. They became lovers, tragic lovers, destined to meet once a year. Anyway, folks about town learned of their love, and they turned on my great-great-grandmother. See, they feared this Lord. So, they threatened her, said that if she saw him again it'd be the worse for her. Well, my great-great-grandmother, she weren't to be bullied. That next

Midsummer, she goes up to Grumple Top and tells her fairy lover about the threats. So he gave her that there spinning wheel."

"I see," Elspeth said, "and what is supposed to be so special about this spinning wheel?"

Nolan watched her walk over to it; she bent down to better examine the markings that adorned its surface, running her fingers over them.

"Let's just say that whilst we have that there spinning wheel in our home, we're never gonna have to worry about trouble coming a-knocking," Grandma Weathers chuckled.

*

They sat in garden chairs in the rear of Elspeth's home on Blackpaw Road. The property was located on the edge of town and its back looked out over the beautiful Shropshire countryside.

In the distance they could make out Grumple Top, fringed with trees, the tallest hill in the area, and the location of the alleged love trysts between Ivy's relative and the Fairy Lord.

"I suppose if Ivy really is responsible for the death of Bill Runnel, and Rose Upton's current misfortunes, then that spinning wheel must lie behind it," Nolan said.

Elspeth sighed and reclined slightly in her chair, her red hair concealed beneath a wide hat which complemented her white dress. On her lap was a collection of papers, notes written in both his and her hand.

"I have heard that tale before, I'm certain of it," she said as she flicked through the mound of papers. "But I'm certain there is more to it, something Ivy and her grandmother are not telling us."

Isobel, Elspeth's deaf, mute housemaid, came across the lawn carrying two tall glasses of cool lemonade. She smiled at Nolan, who grinned back at her, then placed the drinks on the garden table.

For a few moments, Nolan and Isobel spoke, using the strange hand gestures with which she communicated. What passed between them Elspeth did not know, for she had never taken the time to learn this hand language. But when Isobel walked away she was smiling even more broadly. To be sure, it was an odd friendship that the two shared.

"Here," she said, handing Nolan a pile of papers, "make yourself useful, read these, and see if you can find anything."

They spent the next hour sipping lemonade and shuffling through the extensive pile of notes. Neither spoke a word, so intensely were they focused on the task before them.

Finally, Nolan snapped his fingers. "Eureka, I have it."

Elspeth put down her own papers and leaned over. "May I?"

"Certainly," Nolan handed her the relevant page.

"That is in my hand," she said, "one of my older sets of notes, made before you came to work for me. It is about a conversation I had with a local charlady… yes, and here she tells the story of the Fairy Lord, Alberic, called the Rowan King, taking a local girl to be his lover. I knew I had heard it before."

"Your c-charlady tells a bit more than Ivy and her grandmother did, though," Nolan said.

"She does, indeed," Elspeth said. "Olwyn Cysgod – the shadow wheel – was one of the great treasures of The Rowan King, but such was his love for this mortal girl, and such was his desire to protect her, that he loaned her the wheel. With it, she could spin the very shadows into terrible beasts, ones that might protect her from those who wished her ill. So might she keep this great treasure till her dying day, when it must be returned to the lord's hoard."

"Spinning shadows into monsters? You said Rose talked of shadows," Nolan said eagerly.

"Yes she did. But how does this knowledge help us? Let me think a moment."

And so, they sat in silence again.

It was Nolan who eventually snapped his fingers. "The Witch-brands! Legend says they are supposed to protect against magic and the Fairy Folk. Bring Rose here and she should be safe. Your own front door bears just such a marking!"

*

Rose Upton stood in Elspeth's parlour. Martha had wrapped a comforting arm about her shoulder, whilst Elspeth explained what she had learned that day.

"So, you believe this thing won't disturb me in your house, because of the mark on your door?" Rose did not sound convinced.

"Yes," Elspeth said, "I have had my maid make up the spare bedroom for you, and you are welcome to stay here for as long as you need."

"Thank you, Mrs McGinnity, but... well, I don't mean to sound ungrateful, but that cow Ivy ain't gonna stop. What I mean is, I can't stay here forever."

"Of course not, this is just temporary, until I come up with a better solution. Which I will do," she promised. "This just provides us with more time.

"I will leave you in Martha's capable hands. She has prepared an evening meal. I apologise, but I won't be joining you – I intend to spend some time reading, but Nolan has yet to eat, so he'll keep you company." Elspeth smiled at Nolan, who looked horrified. Socialising with attractive young women was not at the forefront of his skills.

Fortunately, Martha sat with them while they ate, and so the weight of the conversation fell on her capable shoulders.

Eventually, Isobel joined them, taking the seat next to Nolan, and the young man began to feel more comfortable. Indeed, he actually began enjoying himself; Martha was a goldmine of local gossip, and one who was more than willing to spread her fortune with a very generous hand.

It was perhaps an hour later when Elspeth re-joined them; she wore the slightly self-satisfied smile of a cat who has stolen a fried fish from under her owner's nose.

"I think I have it," she announced, as she sat down, "the solution to your problem, Rose – a way to pull the fangs from the wolf."

Rose, who despite Martha's good company had continued to bear a careworn look, perked up slightly upon hearing this.

"It was here all along, in my notes, see," Elspeth jabbed at a sheet of paper she had laid upon the table – the notes she had made of her conversation with the charlady. "See here, this last bit. *And so might she keep this treasure till her dying day, when it must be returned to the lord's hoard.*"

"So, when Ivy Weathers passed, the Spinning Wheel was taken from her and returned to The Rowan King's trove. That means what we saw can't have been the real spinning wheel, then. She must be using some other means to torment Rose," Nolan said.

Elspeth shook her head. "No, that was my initial thought too, but then I remembered the Witch-brand on her door." She turned to Martha. "How long have Ivy's family lived at that address?"

Martha pursed her lips. "As long as I can remember, and probably longer than that. I'd say there have been Weathers in that house for generations."

"I think I see," Nolan said. "The only reason Ivy and her grandmother still have that spinning wheel is because this Rowan King and his agents can't get access to it – the Witch-brand bars their entrance to Ivy's home."

Rose sighed. "Then it's hopeless. She can hold onto the horrible thing till kingdom come."

"Not necessarily," Elspeth said. "Nolan, we have a mallet in the shed and I believe my neighbour, Mr Potter, owns a set of wood chisels. Would you be good enough to see if he is prepared to lend us one?"

*

Elspeth, Martha, and Rose sat quietly in the kitchen. Isobel had gone home for the evening, and Nolan, somewhat reluctantly, had been dispatched on his mission.

The summer sun had finally dipped below the horizon. Martha, who had insisted on staying whilst her niece was in danger, had drawn all the curtains and ensured that the front and back doors were securely locked. Then every available lamp and candle was lit, driving the shadows to the recesses of the room.

They waited. It had taken some time to convince Nolan to leave with the mallet and chisel, and neither he nor Isobel were happy with his allotted task. Yet, it was a task that must be done.

Elspeth walked to the curtains and drew them back.

"Don't!" Rose cried. "It likes to peer in at the windows!"

"It will be fine; it can't get in." Elspeth was intrigued. She squinted into the darkness outside, hoping to catch a glimpse of something, yet nothing stirred in the back garden.

So she went to the front room and peered out the window there. Still nothing – the street outside was silent, a single gas street lamp illuminating the walls and hedges of her neighbours' properties.

It was as she was walking back towards the kitchen that the front door rattled.

At first it was only a slight disturbance, as might be caused by the wind on a restless evening. Elspeth stopped in her tracks and turned, waiting.

It happened again, this time with more force.

She took a step backward, hand on her chest.

Martha emerged from the kitchen, followed by a terrified Rose.

"Is young Master Perkins returned so soon?" Martha asked.

"No," Rose said, an edge of panic in her voice. "It's that thing."

A cannonade of pounding shook the door, threatening to send it flying from its frame.

Elspeth ran to the front window, once more peering tentatively through the curtain, but a bush obscured her view of the front door.

Still, she fancied she could make out something in the night – thin strands of darkness, threads of shadow that trailed away down the street.

How many were there? Two, three, four?

Were they real, or were her eyes playing tricks on her? She couldn't be sure. At times, they seemed so clear, easy to make out, even by the streetlamp's dim illumination. At other times, they became so vague as to be almost invisible to the naked eye. It was at such moments that her rational mind doubted their very existence.

The pounding began anew.

Elspeth hurried back to the hall, where, if anything, the noise was worse. Martha stood with her hands over her ears.

Every blow that rained down was stronger and stronger until it seemed that the door must collapse under them.

"It's going to get in!" screamed Rose.

*

Nolan Perkins stood in the shadows watching Ivy's house. In one hand he clutched the mallet from Elspeth's garden shed; in the other he held the chisel, borrowed from their neighbour, Mr Potter.

When Nolan had approached Mr Potter about borrowing the chisel, the man had asked what he needed it for. Nolan, whose knowledge of carpentry was somewhat limited, had muttered something about an interior door sticking. Mr Potter had not looked convinced, but nevertheless he had kindly agreed to lend him one.

Nolan was not keen on the task that Elspeth had set him. Vandalism was not something high on his list of priorities. He had protested, saying that he had no wish to be involved in criminal activities. But, deep down, he had always known that he would do it.

When he had explained to Isobel what was expected of him, she had become annoyed and had protested through Martha, who understood her hand speech.

But it was to no avail. Once Elspeth's course was set, there was no moving her from it, and Nolan had eventually acquiesced. After all, this seemed to be the only way to put an end to Rose's torment.

And so he stood in an alley, watching the front door of the strange young woman he had first met hours earlier that day, trying to build up enough courage to do what was expected of him. The street was silent; not a single person could be seen or heard.

As he watched, he became aware of something strange. At first it was so subtle he hardly noticed it, but eventually it caught his attention, and once he had seen it, he could not miss it: thin strings, black in colour, hovering about ankle height off the ground, leading from under Ivy's door, trailing down the street only to vanish into the night.

He shuddered, suddenly knowing that he must act now without further delay. People he knew, people he cared about, were in real danger.

He crept forward.

The old door before him had a solid, timeless look to it. The branded mark was at its centre; it had bitten deep. He began to have serious doubts as to whether he could do what was required of him.

Carefully he rested the chisel against the dark mark. With his other hand, he raised the mallet; he paused, many different scenarios running through his head. What if a police constable should come walking down the street, only to catch him in the act?

What if Ivy or her grandmother should reach the front door before he had completed his task?

He glanced down at his shoes. The laces of darkness curled past them. Nolan knew where they were headed, and hated to imagine what it could portend.

He brought the mallet down with all the force he could muster.

His blow was true. Mr Potter's chisel sharp. And yet, though it had bitten deep into the wood, still the brand was visible.

Again, he struck with the mallet.

"I heard you the first time," came the familiar voice of an old woman from within, followed by some inaudible mumbling.

In panic, Nolan struck again and again, scouring the wood.

"Be patient, you'll knock me door in. I'm not as young as I used to be," came the voice.

Finally, he heard the sound of bolts being drawn, and panicking, he turned to run, but in his haste, he stumbled and fell onto the hard cobbles. He looked up to see the door wide open and Grandma Weathers staring down at him in confusion.

"What on earth do you mean by banging away at my door at this hour?"

Nolan said nothing. What could he say? He just stared back.

"Wait a moment, I recognise you." Then she noticed what he was holding.

For a moment, she looked confused.

But only for a moment.

"What you up to?" she hissed and turned to look at her door.

The chisel had done its work.

The Witch-brand was gone.

Her eyes widened in shock.

"What have you done?" she screamed.

But Nolan made no effort to answer. Staggering to his feet, he fled into the night.

*

From The Journal of Elspeth McGinnity, August 1908

For all the beating on my front door, that sturdy oak held firm, and by the time Nolan returned home – looking somewhat out of sorts – the disturbance had completely subsided.

Rose stayed with us for the remainder of the week, but never again were we disturbed, and she says she can finally get a restful night's sleep, no longer harassed by nightmares or the unspeakable thing.

The morning after Nolan's foray into vandalism, Martha walked by the Weathers' home. She reported that, according to the neighbours, the house had been abandoned during the night, and not quietly, either, thank you very much. There was much crashing and banging on their door, and one of the neighbours reported seeing a stranger running off, carrying something in each hand.

Not long after, the old woman and her daughter were seen hurrying away, clutching travel bags. They had not been seen since, though Martha informs me that local gossip says they are staying with relatives over the border in Wales.

Come the morning, their front door was found to be wide open. Martha and several of the more inquisitive neighbours looked in the house, but of Olwyn Cysgod, that terrible bronze spinning wheel, there was no sign, though how and when it was taken, no one seemed to know.

Nolan was on edge for a few days, certain the police would turn up and accuse him of damaging Ivy Weathers' door, but no constable has come calling, and gradually he has come to believe that it is unlikely they ever will.

I never did discover what it was that had laid siege to my home that night. It remained elusive, hidden from my view. And though I have asked Rose repeatedly about the nature and form of the thing spun from shadows that had made her life a living hell over those last few weeks, she would never speak of it.

The Potions of Doctor Mogfadian

September 1922

Casper thanked the Lord for the day he had first met Dr Benedict Mogfadian. The man had turned his life around. Well, perhaps it was better to say that the old fox's medicine had turned his life about, medication that the fellow – always theatrical – referred to as his potions.

For all his adult life, Casper had suffered horrendously with his nerves. He could not remember the event that brought on these troubles, only that it had first occurred one night when he was young and staying at boarding school.

His troubled mind would be most active during the hours of darkness, when he was beset by a constant dread, as though the most terrible, yet undefinable, thing was about to swallow him up and destroy his life.

But this medicine, this potion, this milky white elixir, had changed all that. With it, he had found blessed sleep; his troubles and his sense of despair had receded. It was still there, but it was as if it had been crushed into a tiny ball and pushed into the back of his mind.

After a week of taking this miracle elixir, he actually laughed – a genuine laugh that had rumbled up from his stomach, causing his shoulders to shake. He could not remember the last time he had done that.

When his father had passed, he had left Casper with just two things: an old military sabre, a heavy thing that hung over the fireplace in his room, and a pistol. The latter he had sold, fearful that, in a state of melancholy, he might turn the weapon upon himself.

With his father's death, he had found himself destitute, facing a life on the streets. But the good doctor had brought him more than inner relief – he had offered him a home. "I can use a man with your unique skills," he'd said. Casper wondered what skills he was referring to – he'd never worked very long in any one place, or received any particular training.

But it was not his skills, or lack thereof, that the doctor was interested in, merely his size. For Casper was a large fellow, who most people found intimidating.

And so, he had found employment with the doctor.

His job was that of a general dogsbody: running errands, chaperoning the man's niece when she walked about town and sometimes, if the need arose, to look or act threatening.

Doctor Mogfadian was a man of average height and independent wealth. Casper viewed him as one of life's eccentrics, with a great many affectations. For example, he took great pleasure in wearing dark suits, a top hat, a short, waist-length cape, and carrying a blackthorn walking stick.

He looked for all the world like a stage magician and seemed to enjoy the sense of mystery that his appearance carried with it. He was a man who loved to roll his r's when speaking – something Casper had always found most grating.

The doctor possessed a very high opinion of his own intellect and loved nothing more than to share the bounty of his knowledge with anyone unfortunate enough to find themselves within earshot. When he chose to express himself to his fullest extent, he could lecture his poor victim for upwards of an hour. Casper had been on the receiving end of one of the man's monologues on far too many occasions.

Eccentricities within the Mogfadian family were not confined to the doctor alone. His niece, Julie, a woman a few years younger than Casper, dressed rebelliously, preferring to wear trousers, usually accompanied by a man's shirt and waistcoat.

She had shoulder-length blonde hair, often pushed up and hidden beneath a Breton fiddler's cap. She was a pretty woman, but at times could be much distracted, as if bearing the weight of some hidden problem. Still, she was intelligent and educated, having been taught by her uncle, and frequently assisted the doctor with experiments in his laboratory, in the townhouse they shared in Witchley Street, in the town of Wendlelow.

Casper found her annoying, with her boyish posturing and the way her uncle coddled her. He was forced to accompany her whenever she left the house, and Casper felt a greater part of his time was wasted following the woman around – either to the antiques shop she ran on her uncle's behalf or to the local society meetings she attended on a Wednesday night.

She was supposed to be engaged to a rather powerful man, though Casper had never met the fellow in all the time he had been in the doctor's employ. He sometimes wondered if the fiancé were not a fantasy, made up to discourage unwanted suitors. Doctor Mogfadian relied heavily on the girl for assistance in his various experiments, and Casper could therefore understand why the doctor would be reluctant to lose her to married life.

Casper had been given a room on the upper floor of the doctor's home. He paid no rent but was expected to be at the man's beck and call at any hour – a small price to pay for a place to live, a reasonable wage, and most importantly, access to the fellow's excellent potions.

*

The room was dim and musty-smelling, the walls covered by bookcases on which dwelt a great many volumes. There were other oddities too – stray jars filled with things best left unmentioned, usually preserved in odious, discoloured liquids. A large cabinet dominated one side of the room, filled with jars of different-coloured powders, and bottles of fluids in many bright shades. There was even a cat's skull.

The centre of the room was taken up with a badly scarred and stained table, filled with a collection of fine vials, flasks, and tubes – the latter weaving about and around the table, a nest of glass serpents whose purpose and design boggled Casper's mind. A large stuffed crocodile hung from the rafters above this table. Julie had affectionately named the thing Archimedes. His belly should have been pale, but was stained a dark colour from the fumes of the various liquids that had boiled beneath him.

Dr Mogfadian stood at the head of this table, a grim overseer, watching his niece manipulating bottles, filling tubes and measuring powders.

Casper shifted uncomfortably. He did not often come into the laboratory, even though this was where the doctor, or sometimes even Julie, prepared his medication. It was not a place he felt particularly safe. Things were prone to explode in this room, sending glass shrapnel and hot liquids flying about in random directions. It was an unpredictable place of cuts and burns.

Unfortunately, sometimes his duties called him to the room, often when there was heavy lifting to be done. There was a sudden hiss and a highly suspect rattle from one of the glass apparatus on the table where the doctor and Julie worked. Casper took a nervous step away, placing his back against a book-lined wall.

Dr Mogfadian looked over at him and laughed. "No need for nerves, my fine fellow, my apprentice is quite capable."

"I don't trust this witchery," Casper said suspiciously.

"Witchery. Witchery." Dr Mogfadian sounded greatly offended. Too late, Casper realised his mistake – he had provided an opportunity. A lecture was certain to ensue. The good doctor was not a man to leave such a tightly closed door unexplored.

"This, my foolish man, this is not witchery. Have I not told you a dozen times? It is Art. The Art. The Art Magick. I… we," he corrected himself, gesturing to Julie, "are not toothless crones, gibbering away in some backward country cottage over a cauldron of… of frogs' legs or bats' wings. No, my fine fellow, this is a higher skill – one practised by men of learning for thousands of years. It requires a fine intellect – rather like my own – to grasp the complex principles and formulae required to bring one's efforts to a successful conclusion. Mathematics," he added, with a flourish of his arm. "Mathematics is essential to the process –"

Julie looked up from her work, rolling her eyes and shaking her head before going back to her duties. The doctor did not notice, too caught up in his own monologue. "– an in-depth understanding of chemicals and formulae. This is not just the random throwing of garden herbs into a brass kettle, not the thoughtless mixing of mere homely substances. This requires precision. It requires…"

It was very likely that this lecture would have continued for a considerable time had not Casper and Julie been saved by a pounding at the front door.

"Allow me to get that," Casper said, and, not awaiting a reply, strode out of the room, up the steps from the cellar, into the hall, finally opening the front door.

A chill wind invited itself in, making itself at home, spreading to every corner, every nook and cranny, evicting the warmth. It had been a cold year, and a disappointing summer. Wendlelow had existed in one of two states: it was either raining or thinking of raining. Today it was thinking of raining, and it was thinking very hard. The skies outside were grey with clouds, and there was a damp taste in the air.

The man at the door was in his late middle age, his dark hair peppered with grey. His face was lined and weathered; he looked like someone who made his living outdoors and in all kinds of weather.

"I'm here to speak with your master," he said in a gruff voice.

Casper stiffened in annoyance. Though he worked for Dr Mogfadian, he would never have described him as his 'master.' He found the phrase very offensive.

"He's not my master. He's my employer," Casper grunted.

"Same thing," the man said, rudely trying to push his way past Casper.

Casper laid a large hand on the man's chest and stopped him.

"No. It isn't," he said firmly.

The man stopped, looking Casper up and down, and shifted uncomfortably. "Your employer, then?"

Casper stared at him.

"Very well. Would you be so good as to tell your employer that Mr Amos Lunkerton is here to see him? And that I have a problem – one I hold him responsible for."

*

"It was your idea, I hold you accountable, sir," Amos said. Despite his bold words, there was a nervous edge to the man's voice.

They were all gathered in the best room. Casper had taken up a position in front of the door. Julie was perched on the arm of a chair, in a most unladylike fashion, whilst Dr Mogfadian stood before the fireplace, one hand stroking his goatee, the other clutching the golden orb on his cane. Amos stood in the centre of the room.

"You, sir, suggested that I drain the land. You said it would be good for farming, very profitable. You came to me with the idea and even put up the money. I had hardly started the job when the troubles began," Amos complained.

"You put up the money?" Julie said, giving her uncle a questioning look. Casper understood why. The doctor was not known for his acts of charity.

"My good man, do stop this fretting. I am not an imbecile; I am very well aware I came to you, and I had good reasons for so doing, as well you know. That marshy land was wasted – no use to you, none at all. Even a duck wouldn't go near it. I put up the money, funded its drainage, and all the thanks I get for my investment is your complaining like an old woman on washing day. You haven't even told me what the problem is," the doctor said tersely.

"Well, it's like this," Amos explained, "everything was fine to begin with, just rosy. I'd been about the work for two days, and was settling down for the evening and a well-earned rest, when all of a sudden… well… I've had two nights of it, and I won't suffer another one."

"Two nights of what, Mr Lunkerton?" Julie asked.

"I'd tell you, but I don't think my legs are up to it. I'm too shaken."

"Then please sit," Dr Mogfadian said, "but pray do not delay your explanation a moment longer. I am a busy man." He gestured to a comfortable leather chair.

Gratefully, the man took the seat, and waited a moment to compose himself before proceeding. "It comes at dusk. First there is a mist–" at this Amos started to become agitated. "I never had this problem before, nothing like it. Then I started to drain that land, and now, now, now!"

"Mr Lunkerton, compose yourself, please." The doctor's voice was firm. "Where is your backbone, man?"

The next time Amos spoke, he directed his speech to Julie, possibly believing that a female ear would be a more sympathetic one.

"Twilight brings it out, drifting in with the mist, roaming about the place. It's as though it were looking for a way in. It rattles the door handle and scratches at the windows – most unnerving it is. And me, living alone, not a person to turn to."

Dr Mogfadian looked intrigued, his eyes gleaming. "And what, pray tell, is this thing? What does it look like?"

"Look like! How would I know? I certainly wasn't going to open the door to find out, and you can be certain sure I kept my shutters tightly closed. I never so much as touched them when it was a-wandering about – not once."

"Could it just be a tramp, or maybe some local boys trying to scare you?" suggested Julie reasonably.

"Tramp, she says. Tramp!" Amos scoffed, as though this were the most ridiculous thing that had ever been said to him. "Would a tramp leave long scratch marks down the length of my door? Scratches like those made by the claws of a beast? Would village boys, for that matter? This thing ain't natural. I should have listened to my instinct and not been tempted by your money."

For a moment Dr Mogfadian said nothing; he just stared into the ashy fire grate. When he eventually looked up, he wore a broad smile, as if he were having the most wonderful of mornings and wanted to share his good fortune with all he met. It was, Casper noticed, a smile that did not reach his eyes.

"Amos Lunkerton, my good farmer, my excellent landowner, please allow us to speak a moment in private." He took the man by the arm, drew him from his seat, wrapped a grandfatherly arm about his shoulder, and led him to the door. Casper dutifully stepped aside for them as they passed and made to follow, but the doctor laid a hand on his shoulder.

"There really is no need for you to come," he reassured, beaming like a Cheshire cat. "We shall not go far. If I have need of your… assistance, I will call. In the meantime, please keep my niece company."

So saying, he shut the door.

"I wonder what the old devil is up to now?" Julie said, dropping off the arm of the chair and onto the more comfortable padding of the seat.

Casper shrugged, but took care to move closer to the door, listening for anything that might be said. Unfortunately, the words of the two men were nothing more than indistinguishable whispers, their content muted by the painted wood. At one point Amos must have become agitated, for he could be clearly heard to say, "No, I didn't find anyth–" but he was cut off by a hush from the doctor.

For five more minutes the sound of muffled voices continued until eventually the door opened and both men re-entered the room.

Doctor Mogfadian retook his position by the fire, still wearing his large smile.

He turned and addressed Casper first. "Mr Trenchton, would you do me the great honour of accompanying Mr Lunkerton back to his steading and spending the evening in his company?"

"What? Babysit him? Why?"

"Because I asked, my fine fellow – and because Mr Lunkerton is a man with a fairly unique problem, and the presence of a gentleman such as yourself would go a long way to easing his nerves. I would ask you to remain observant. Please report to me exactly what you see during the night – if, indeed, you see anything."

The doctor rested his blackthorn cane against the side of a chair and walked to the window. He stared out into the street, clasped his hands behind his back, and continued talking without turning to face them.

"Julie, I will need you to look into the history of Mr Lunkerton's farm, and I would like it done today, please, my girl."

"I will see what I can do, but a day is not very long," Julie said doubtfully.

"Today is Wednesday, is it not?" the doctor asked. "So perhaps you could enlist the assistance of those scribblers?"

*

Every Wednesday, Julie attended a society meeting held in the hall attached to St Michael's Church. Here a group of like-minded individuals gathered to discuss local stories and customs. The group had been set up a few years ago by the librarian of Wendlelow University, as a sort of memorial to a missing friend who apparently had always had an interest in strange tales and traditions. The group called themselves The McGinnity Society for Lore and Mythos.

The doctor had a very low opinion of the group, whom he referred to as 'the Scribblers', or, if he was feeling generous, 'that bunch of old gasbags.' His personal belief – often stated whenever they came up in conversation – was that they did nothing practical to further develop a subject that he was greatly interested in, beyond writing notes and, as he put it, 'wittering on to each other.'

Julie thought he was wrong. Though she had only been a part of the group for a short time, she liked them. She had heard that they had helped local officials with a few unusual problems that had beset the town in the past – though when she had tried to explain this to Benedict, all he had said was, "Bunkum."

She had first seen the group advertised in that journalistic lighthouse, *The Wendlelow Tattler*. She had asked the doctor if they could go to a gathering, but had only been to one meeting together before he announced he would not lower himself by going to another. And because he was stiflingly protective of her, this meant she could not attend either. However, after he had employed Casper, she asked again, this time pointing out that the big man could accompany her.

To her surprise, the doctor agreed.

In fact, tonight was the first night that she would be going to a meeting alone. Casper never entered the church hall with her, simply depositing her at the gate, then wandering over to *The Waggoner's Arms*, a local public house, to await the end of the meeting. She had invited him to come in with her, thinking that he might gain some pleasure from the experience, but he had always declined. When she had further pressed him, he had said that he had personal reasons for not wishing to attend.

He was a quiet, lonely man, and Julie thought the company might be good for him. She knew he suffered terribly with his nerves – indeed, she had helped her uncle prepare the elixir used to stabilise his mood.

It was a good turnout. The bad weather had been keeping some of the members away recently, but tonight it was a little drier, and this was the busiest she had seen the church hall for a while.

All six members were present, including herself.

At a large table, stacked with papers, sitting in a comfortable chair, was the club founder and chairman, Nolan Perkins. Behind him were the seventh and eighth unofficial members of the group: Nolan's silent wife, Isobel, who was preparing drinks and laying out little cakes, prepared by her own hand; as well as their little son, Thomas, who spent his time toddling about, trying to purloin treats without anyone noticing.

If not tottering around, he could usually be found beneath a table, the remains of some sticky cake on his little fingers and smeared around his mouth.

Nolan was a man in early middle age, a few years older than herself, with spectacles, a hairline that was showing signs of receding, and the beginnings of a physique that showed evidence he was married to a more than competent cook, and one who was not sparing with the portions served. He wore a tweed jacket and sucked contentedly on a pipe.

The other members sat in seats arranged in a semi-circle before Nolan's table. There was Mrs Bannerman, a stern-looking old lady, clutching a pair of knitting needles as if they were made of gold. Occasionally, there was a rhythmic clicking as she set them about their business.

Mr and Mrs Potter sat next to each other, sucking on boiled sweets taken from a paper bag on Mrs Potter's lap. Many of these treats found their way to Thomas, who was a favourite of the pair. Mr Potter looked eager; Mrs Potter distant – present perhaps only in body, her mind on a flight of fancy elsewhere.

Finally, there was Roger Stopford, affectionately known as Young Roger. He was in his early twenties. He lived and worked with his aunt and uncle, who were local greengrocers. He was a pleasant-looking man with a mop of Auburn hair. At the moment, it looked neat, but Julie knew that, come the slightest breeze, it would gain a life of its own, its thick strands springing out in different directions.

Roger had saved her a seat next to him. He gave her a devoted, puppyish look, and she felt herself blush. He was younger than she was, but had few friends, and seemed to have lit a candle for her in his heart, despite being aware of her engagement.

Although she much preferred trousers, she was always careful to wear a dress in public. Benedict was willing to allow her these little outings but did not want her to draw any unwanted attention to herself.

That night they discussed a great many subjects, from ghostly apparitions to the odd, slightly worrying customs of a local village called Crowsmere. Each person got a chance to speak and told the group of a particular tradition or story they had researched that week.

Even Mrs Potter returned from her daydreams to tell them the story of the ghost of a local swineherd, said to wander the fields to the west of the town. He was apparently seen at twilight, often preceded by the sound of sobbing. Mrs Potter was attempting to locate the source of this legend, to see if she could discover who this poor soul was said to be and why he wept so.

Towards the end of the evening Nolan encouraged a session of open discussion; anyone was allowed to speak, so long as they were not impudent, and ask questions of their fellows. There was plenty of back and forth, much conjecture, and more than a little mutual backslapping, for all knew how much considerable time and effort the other had put into their research and wished to show their gratitude. Roger was always very complimentary of her own humble efforts.

It was during this section of the evening that they were allowed to suggest topics for further research.

"I have a question, perhaps one of you can answer," Julie said, rising from her seat.

All eyes turned upon her.

She paused for a moment to compose both herself and her query. "Today, I heard that there was a legend attached to Wych Hollow Farm, a holding not far from the town. I was told this by an old man at the market, though he could provide no more details." This was a lie. Benedict could be a private man, and though he wanted the information, he was not keen on having her discuss his personal affairs in public, so it was a necessary one. "He told me about the place, said he had heard about some kind of strange story attached to it. I wondered if anyone here knew what it may be."

There was a general murmuring about the room; people looked questioningly at each other, but no one stood up to answer her question.

Wonderful, she thought, *Benedict will be in a mood if I come back empty-handed. I shall be forced to spend the remainder of the evening listening to him go on about how hopeless this little society is.*

While this was going on Nolan had leaned over to consult a book that sat on one side of his table. It was one he brought to every meeting, entitled *Yesterday's Tales & Traditions of a Midland County*, written by an old friend of his – the very lady, in fact, that he had dedicated this society to. It was a book he claimed to have helped to edit.

He spent a few moments flicking through its pages, puffing thoughtfully on his pipe. Little clouds of smoke drifted into the air, errant grey phantoms, trying their hardest to take a recognisable shape. When he finally closed the book, he wore a satisfied smile.

"I might just be able to help you there," he announced.

*

Casper Trenchton sat in Amos' cart. A handsome, brown-and-white horse of mature years was leading it

127

down the winding country lanes. The weather had not improved as the day had progressed; it was still overcast. Icy fingers seemed to prod at any exposed area of flesh, and Casper was very glad to be wearing his heavy greatcoat.

Doctor Mogfadian had been very explicit in his instructions – he was to stay at Amos Lunkerton's farm this evening, to keep the man company, to protect him from any danger, and also to observe and then recount the nature of the threat.

Casper was not sure what form it would take, and from the way his employer had dispatched his niece to that silly society of hers on a fact-finding mission, it was clear to him that the he did not know either.

Doctor Mogfadian may have been unsure as to the nature of the danger he faced, but that had not stopped him expounding his knowledge on other aspects of the farm.

"The name Wych Hollow does not refer to a crone or hag," the doctor had explained, unnecessarily, "but rather to the wych elms that seem prevalent in the area. Now wych comes from the Old English word wiche, meaning a kind of elm, or wice, meaning a kind of tree. Compare, if you will, the word wicker, which of course…"

At this point Casper had switched off from what the doctor had been saying, and had turned his attention to more practical matters, such as which items he needed to pack for this particular outing, and whether he should prepare sandwiches or if he would be provided with a meal by his host.

The cart trundled onward.

"So, you don't know what sort of thing has been troubling your place?" Casper asked. His father's sword was clutched between his knees. It had seemed prudent to bring it. For the first time, he was beginning to regret disposing of the man's service revolver. "No stories or tales told by your family over the years?"

"Nah, they wouldn't know, would they? I've only owned the place five years – bought it from an old childless couple who couldn't work it no more. Got it for a good price too. But if they knew any stories about the place, they weren't tellin'."

Casper grunted, and for a while they sat in silence.

"And you'll feed me?" he eventually asked the farmer. This was an aspect of the arrangement that was of great concern to him. Doctor Mogfadian had assured him that he would get a good meal, but he'd heard nothing from the farmer about it and wanted to make sure that the man understood his obligations.

"Aye, you'll be fed," came the reply, followed by, "That's my place, down there." With one hand he pointed to Casper's right. Through a break in the trees he could see a small farmhouse, surrounded by a collection of barns and outbuildings that had a decidedly tired look about them.

Past the farthest building there was a number of trees – elms after which the farm was named. They had been bent and twisted in sinister ways by the wind; their leaves had started to fall early, skeletal fingers beginning to show through the foliage. They surrounded a damp parcel of land, the tools of drainage scattered all about it.

They turned a corner and the farm and its surroundings were obscured from view.

Eventually they turned onto a track, rutted and muddy. Casper found himself being bounced around uncomfortably on the wooden bench, in a tooth-jarring rhythm. After a short time, the track levelled out and Wych Hollow Farm once more came into view – a one-storey building, the once-whitewashed walls flaking paint like dead skin.

The farmer drove his cart into a barn and then stabled his horse, ensuring it had sufficient food and water. Only when this was done did he escort Casper into his home.

The farmhouse's front door opened into the main room, which served as a kitchen, dining room and general living area. The rear of the property was a collection of bedrooms. A small stone outhouse, which served as a latrine, sat some distance away at the rear of the property, like a lonely, disowned child.

The property smelled of damp and mildew, a scent that caused Casper to wrinkle his nose in distaste, but one that he adapted to very quickly. He strode about the place, carrying the sword by its sheath, testing doors, and ensuring that all the shuttered windows were secure, whilst his host set about preparing the promised meal. When he was satisfied that everything indoors was shipshape and Bristol fashion, he did a circle of the outside of the farm. Up close the outbuildings looked less tired and more exhausted, and much of the woodwork was in need of a loving hand.

Amos had at least made some attempts to tidy the main property, but still, there were some long unsightly scratch marks down the front door. These might have been made by a very large farm dog jumping up and asking to be let in, but when Casper was finally introduced to the farmer's best friend he noted that the beast was a collie, a breed of very average size.

The meal prepared by Amos was a simple one. The scent of fried sausages, bacon and eggs pervaded the kitchen, and Casper, a man with a healthy appetite, felt his stomach start to rumble. After they finished their meal, Amos set about cleaning the dishes, whilst Casper reclined in a chair before the fire, enjoying a cigarette.

"We need to get back out before dusk draws in," Amos said, coming over to stand by him. "Your mas… your employer wants me to drag the pond."

Casper groaned. He was full, he was warm, he was drowsy. The last thing he wanted was to don his greatcoat, pull on his shoes, and go traipsing about the cold, muddy farm.

"Can't it wait till the morning?" Casper asked.

"No!" came the reply. "The doctor's paid me good money to see it's done as early as possible – this very day were his words."

"Well go then," said Casper, waving his free hand, as if to dismiss the man. "I'm not stopping you, old chap."

"I'm not wandering about by that pond on my own, not after all that's happened. Your employer sent you here to watch over me, so you've got to come too. I ain't got nothing more to say on the matter."

With a reluctant sigh, Casper rose from his seat and pulled on his coat, but in a blatant show of defiance refused to take his sword, which he left leaning against the wall like a bored silent sentry.

He escorted Amos to one of the barns where the man collected what he needed: a large rake with a length of rope attached to it. Then they made their way to the marshy, elm-shrouded pool, where the farmer set about his business, throwing the rake into the water, and using the rope to drag it back.

Casper wondered how long it would take – surely not a lengthy amount of time. It was not a big body of water, and the sun was low in the sky. Surely the farmer would want to be back indoors and safely locked in before nightfall.

Amos worked as quickly as he could, in what seemed to Casper a slightly desperate manner. He was in a race against the setting sun. The action of the rake stirred the silt, turning the pool into a muddy cauldron and releasing pungent odours that would have been better left undisturbed.

Casper considered assisting the man in his job, but Amos had wandered quite deep into the marshy area; sludge had enveloped much of his boots. Casper looked down at his own relatively clean shoes and decided against it.

After what felt like forever, Amos let out a cry of satisfaction.

"I've got something!"

It took a couple more attempts, but eventually the rake brought something out of the dirty water. At this distance, and with the rapidly fading light, Casper could not be sure what it was. The farmer bent down, scooped it up, and put it in a bag that hung over his shoulder, then made his way back to drier footing. He looked back at the pool, a concerned expression etched onto his weather-beaten face. The light, already poor, was worsening, the air growing more chill as the sun dipped further below the horizon.

Night was drawing in fast.

Amos suddenly hurried back in the direction of his cottage, leaving the rake abandoned, and Casper, who had turned to watch the man's retreat, felt a cold sensation on his back, as if a clammy hand were running down the length of his spine. He was gripped by a sudden panic, and hurried after the man.

It was not until they were safely back inside Amos's warm little home, the door tightly shutting out the night, that Casper began to feel more relaxed. He settled himself back by the fire and lit another cigarette, while Amos carried his find into one of the bedrooms. Perhaps he should have been more inquisitive, and asked the farmer what he had discovered, but he found he did not really care. Maybe it was the effect of Dr Mogfadian's medication, but he found it difficult to become excited about things, difficult to raise his interest in events going on around him.

Amos offered him a glass of gin, but he had lost his taste for alcohol. When he went to the pub, he usually just had a coffee. He put this down to an unintended effect of the doctor's medication – and it was not the only one.

He also found that his interest in women and passion had waned. He knew he should feel lonely, and yet he just did not care. It was strange when he thought about it – he had never had a romance. True, he had greatly cared for the sister of a close friend. But he had failed her, and as a result she had died. He had never truly discovered how she felt about him. For some reason, that troubled him just as much as her death did.

Of course, there had been women in his life – he was no blushing bride. But these women had been the sort whose affections could be negotiated and purchased, and the 'fruity cuddles' that had ensued had taken place against walls in back alleys – hardly the stuff of great romantic novels.

Both men sat silently, Casper smoking like a factory chimney, Amos nursing a small glass of cheap gin. The farmer had set two apples on the fire grate, and these slowly roasted, spitting and releasing their sweet aroma about the room.

Outside, obscured by the heavy shutters, night had completed its transition, throwing its heavy veil about the farm and surrounding countryside.

Casper felt his eyes grow heavy; warmth, food, and the comfort of the chair taking him by the hand and leading him slowly down the path of slumber. He felt at peace. Indeed, he would have been little more relaxed if he were in his own bed.

But it was not a peace that was destined to last for long. There came a sudden, forceful rattling of the front doorknob.

Casper's eyes shot open, and Amos leapt up from his seat as if there were a cobra upon his lap.

He stared at the door as though Satan himself were on the other side of it, and slowly backed away.

The handle rattled again.

"Jumpy, aren't you?" said Casper with false bravado. "Probably just a neighbour wanting to borrow something."

But he was not sure if even he believed this explanation. If it were a neighbour, why not knock to announce their presence?

"That's no neighbour. It's here," Amos whispered, in a voice that quite unmanned Casper. He felt fear flood his being, an icy wave that threatened to drown him. He strode to the corner of the room and snatched up his sword, and there he stood for a while, unmoving, waiting.

Come on, you coward, seize the initiative, he chided himself. *Do something, like your father used to say – take action, be a man.*

"Answer the door," he snapped to the farmer.

"Are you mad?"

"Do it," demanded Casper. "Now."

"I'll not go near the bloody thing," the farmer said, pressing his back against the far wall.

"Then I will," Casper declared, taking a step forward.

At this move towards the door, the farmer cried out in terror and leapt upon him, knocking the sword from Casper's grip. The two men grappled, but it was a short-lived contest. The farmer was strong, but it was a wiry strength and no match for the bulk and power that Casper could call upon. He threw the man down, then turned once more, intent on flinging open the wooden obstacle and facing the formless horror that tormented them from without.

It was at that moment that a new sound arose – a chill-sending screech, which filled his ears and kept his feet glued to the spot. It was a sound that could only be that of nails biting into glass and slowly being drawn downward. It put his teeth on edge and played upon his nerves in a way that the rattling of the handle had not.

Taking a moment to compose himself, Casper rolled his shoulders, then, slowly approaching the shutters from behind which the sound was emanating, he raised his hand and made ready to pull them open.

"Please, don't." Amos's voice sounded pathetic – a man on the verge of tears, a man begging for his life.

Casper swallowed and stepped away. He looked towards a heavy Welsh dresser, which sat against one wall.

"Help me push that against the door."

A thankful Amos sprang up to obey.

*

Julie and Benedict were working hard in the laboratory, while above them, Archimedes viewed the proceedings with dusty eyes.

"It's a sort of elemental, an entity bound to the pool. In days gone by our forefathers would have ignored the place, keeping it at arm's length out of respect, or else they would have paid it tribute, throwing valuables into its depths," Julie was saying, whilst the doctor poured some clear liquid into a vial. "They knew that if enraged, such beings could be very dangerous."

"And few things would be better guaranteed to raise its ire than the destruction of its home," Benedict observed in a wry voice.

"Nolan said such places should be avoided, for who can know what will cause such things offence? You were right to let me consult him – he is an intelligent man."

At this, Benedict stiffened. "Never mistake education for intelligence, my dear," he said dryly. "With time and research, no doubt I would have reached the same conclusion – but this could well be an urgent matter. Time is of the essence. So, your scribbler friends have been a useful tool.

"If this really is some kind of elemental being, then there will be something I can do to assist good Farmer Lunkerton. But I am going to need your help."

He continued the mixing of various liquids and powders – drops of this, scoops of that – all swirling about, forming a murky-looking brew.

"What's in it?" Julie asked, intrigued by the work. A great many of the substances Benedict was adding were not labelled, and this was odd. He was usually very fastidious in the storage and labelling of his reagents.

"Primarily holy water – never underestimate the power of faith – sap from a rowan tree, salt and iron dust, with a few other special ingredients. You will need to pour the liquid into the pool, and invoke the Art, in order to seal the arcane pact and so settle the troubled waters."

"Me!" Julie exclaimed.

"Yes, you. Of course you. Who else? That oaf Trenchton? No, you alone I trust with this. You are not just my niece – you are my apprentice, and this situation provides a unique opportunity for you to put some of the skills I have taught you into practice."

"What, pouring a liquid into a dirty pond?" Julie sneered. "Oh yes, great skill required for that."

"No," Benedict said, an edge of annoyance in his tone. "Now come, my dear, you know better than that. Have I not schooled you?"

He put the flask down carefully, then made his way to the bookshelves, carefully studying the many bindings before him, before settling on one and pulling it out.

"The Art requires words of power. Words which must be uttered at the dispensing of the liquid, in order for it to achieve its fullest potential." He flicked through the book, his eyes quickly scanning the pages until he finally found the one he was looking for. "In this case, it is a single word – very potent, very dangerous."

He read the word aloud. (It has been omitted from this text by the author for the reader's safety.)

"Repeat it," he said. "Commit it to memory. Remember – it is a word of power. It wants to be forgotten. It detests being manipulated by mere mortals. It is a living force – no mere dictionary could contain it. It would burn the pages. It must dwell within a book that has been carefully prepared to hold it.

"It will dance about your brain, desperate to escape. You must fight to contain it there. Once used, it will flow free, to be forgotten – until once more it is committed to memory."

Julie repeated the word. It flitted about her mind like a caged bird desperate to escape, but with all her will she focused and held it in place, until eventually she sensed it settling, coming to rest. Part of her knew that it was merely waiting – waiting patiently for a chance to escape.

"Remember, when you invoke the Art, when you are ready to release the word, a potent force will use your body as a conduit. You will feel it – a build-up of energy in your very spine, a sensation that will make you want to shake your whole body to release it. This you must not do. Channel it – force it into the word of power as it is uttered, so the full potency can be delivered to the potion."

Julie was nervous, but she was also excited – like any apprentice the world over, when finally allowed to put theory into practice.

Benedict picked up the bottle containing the fluid and proceeded to carefully pour half into one bell-bottomed flask, before repeating the procedure with a second.

"Enough for a second dose. What is it I always say, my dear?" Julie did not reply, but the doctor did not seem to mind; he merely went on. "Care in all things – and always have a sufficient supply of the essentials. Better to have too much than too little, eh?"

*

Morning was announced by the crowing of a cockerel, but Casper needed no wake-up call. His eyes felt heavy, his mouth sour – he wanted nothing more than to lie down and rest. The strange noises – those terrible rattlings and scratchings that had so worked on both the men's nerves during the hours of darkness – had ended about an hour ago. However, it was a long time before either of them was prepared to consider opening the door.

Even then – when the Welsh dresser had been dragged away and returned to its original home – they did nothing more than listen carefully. But all they heard was the call of the skylark, and the voice of the wood pigeon.

Eventually, Casper directed Amos to open the door, whilst he stood with his sword, ready to split the skull of any potential intruder.

Outside, all was peaceful.

Whilst Amos prepared a breakfast of porridge and honey and a hot cup of coffee, Casper walked about the property. All he could find were drag marks frosted with a slivery slime, as if somebody had been pulling a heavy net of eels behind them. These circled the main cottage and seemed to lead away towards the grove of Wych Elms, soon becoming lost in the marshy ground.

It was an hour after breakfast when Doctor Mogfadian arrived with Julie, his Rolls-Royce Tourer smoothly drifting along the dirt track in the farmyard like an elegant black swan on a dirty river. The doctor bounded out of the vehicle, making his way to the farmhouse, blackthorn stick in hand, deftly avoiding puddles as he went. Casper understood the man to be in his early fifties, but he moved with the grace of someone twenty-five years younger. Behind him, Julie struggled with two bags.

"Well, go and help her then, Trenchton," his employer barked.

Casper made his way over to the woman and relieved her of the heavy burdens.

"Be careful with them, Casper, there are breakables in there," she warned.

He turned to see the doctor and Amos deep in conversation, a very weighty expression on the doctor's face. But after a few moments, he relaxed, and it was replaced by a broad smile. He gave Amos a friendly slap on the back and they both entered the farmhouse. By the time Casper reached the door, the doctor had re-emerged, carrying a familiar-looking bag. This he locked in his car's boot.

When they had all gathered in the cottage's living area, it was an enthusiastic Doctor Mogfadian who held court, his eyes sparkling like a child at a birthday feast. He talked about the pond, about something called an *Elemental*, and a strange potion he had concocted, of which he seemed very proud.

"It must be delivered directly into the pool of water," he said, then gestured to Julie. "My dear, if you would do the honours."

Julie went to where Casper had placed the bags and pulled out two bottles filled with a gloomy fluid. She handed one to the doctor, which he displayed as though he were a fisherman, and it a prize-winning trout.

"Of course, only one is needed, but it is always wise to bring a spare," he announced, nodding in the direction of the vial Julie still held. "Now, gentlemen, would one of you be so good as to describe any, err… interesting – shall we say – events that may have occurred last night?"

Casper went on to explain about the disturbances, how they had secured the door, and the restless night that had ensued. He also mentioned the unusual tracks he had discovered that morning.

"So, you didn't get a look at the thing?" The doctor sounded disappointed.

"No, Mr Lunkerton was not keen on me opening the shutters," Casper said.

The doctor gave the farmer a frustrated look. "Never mind," he sighed. "It would have been very interesting to have a description of the entity. Very interesting indeed. Still, beggars and all that. Now, Mr Lunkerton, perhaps you would be so good as to provide us with a warm drink, then we will proceed with this little escapade."

Amos obliged, and while they sat enjoying their drinks, the doctor explained his plan.

"Casper, you will escort Julie to the pond. There, she will introduce the liquid I have created into its troubled waters. I will stay a little way back with Mr Lunkerton to observe the proceedings."

"You won't be doing it yourself, then?" Casper asked.

"No need, my dear man," the doctor said reassuringly. "It is a very simple process, and Julie is more than capable of performing it. Besides, it shall be good practice for her."

"Then why do I need to go?" Casper asked. He remembered the muddy ground and the state of the farmer's boots yesterday. Whilst no one would describe him as precious about his clothing, he had no wish to soil them unnecessarily.

"The *why* is simple. You will be there to provide moral and physical support, should any be required. No more questions need be asked. From what Mr Lunkerton has told us, the thing in the pond is never active when the sun shines its golden rays upon the earth. But, just in case he has... *misjudged...* you shall be there," the doctor explained.

When they had finished their drinks, they went outside. The day was grey, and Casper was not reassured to see the sun hidden behind a fairly dense veil of cloud. A light mist was starting to form about the clustered elms.

"Should we wait for a sunnier day?" he asked. The presence of that mist made him oddly uneasy.

"Now's as good as ever, Trenchton," the doctor said.

He followed Julie into the boggy ground, whilst Amos and Doctor Mogfadian halted and observed their progress. The closer they drew to the pond, the worse the going became, and the heavier the mist. Gradually, shapes started to lose their colour, and the trunks of trees stood out like gothic columns on a grey canvas.

There was a horrible sucking sound, and an unpleasant cold, wet sensation on his right foot. He looked down to see that his shoe had vanished into the muck, dirty water soaking his trouser leg. He tried to lift his foot, which started to come free, but the mud retained its hold on his shoe, unwilling to give up this new possession. He stopped resisting – he had no desire to wander about in just a sock. He tried twisting his foot about, hoping to loosen the ground's filthy grip upon him. But it was to no avail.

He looked up. Julie was continuing to forge ahead, hopping from left to right, avoiding the worst of the ground. He was about to call out, to tell her to slow down and wait, when he saw it.

A shadow moving in the mist.

Moving towards them.

Its shape was hard to define, but it was getting larger. Soon it would move out of the greyness and reveal its true form. Julie, intent on watching her footing, seemed not to have noticed it, but Amos and the doctor had, and they both cried out in warning.

As Casper watched, it passed from the mist, revealing itself. The tatters of cloth the thing wore were not enough to disguise its hideousness. It bore the features of an old crone, with a cruel nose like the beak of a raven. A long bony protrusion sprouted from the left side of its head – a single horn that pointed skywards. Its parchment-like skin drew tightly about its bony frame. Its hands were too large, with knobbly fingers, from whose tips sprouted the curved claws of a raptor. It possessed no legs, seeming to glide across the ground with the grace of a figure skater. Through its torn, dirty dress he could make out a single slug-like muscle, greyish in colour, oozing a malodorous slime.

Julie looked up and cried out in alarm, which spurred the thing forward, drawn to her as a dog might be drawn to its master's whistle.

Casper swore and tore his foot free of the mud. His shoe was gone, lost forever, but he drove forward regardless, ploughing through the filth, pulling his sword free and throwing aside its useless sheath. He thrust Julie away just as the Thing's sharp talons reached for her, and tried to block the incoming blow with his weapon. But he was not fast enough, and a series of deep red lines scored his arm.

In desperation, he swung his blade wildly, but the thing slid backwards out of reach with a worrying ease.

Casper faced it, breathing raggedly, slowly feeling his feet once more dragged into the ground's sticky grip. He stared intently at the thing, and it looked back at him with eyes blacker than Satan's soul. Then it came forward, gliding on its powerful, slimy appendage. There was a flurry of movement. It lashed out at Casper, who was firmly in the grip of the mud.

He did his best to deflect the blows.

When it finally drifted back from the brief engagement, Casper found a ragged crimson tear on his shirt.

It's going to rip me apart, he thought.

He tried his best to dislodge his feet from the thick mud, looking about him for a dry bit of ground on which to make a stand.

"Throw the bottle, say the word!" shouted a well-spoken voice behind him.

The thing drifted left then right, a serpent awaiting the perfect time to strike. Then it lunged at him again.

"Casper, get down." It was Julie's voice.

He threw himself to the ground, just avoiding a clawed hand that should have taken off his head. He heard Julie cry out something – a word – but one that seemed to pass through his mind, slipping from his grasp before he could remember it. Then he was in a tempest of billowing darkness. A fetid taste clogged his mouth, and a smell like rotting compost invaded his nostrils. He coughed and wheezed, fearing for a second that he might choke to death, until moments later, he found he was tasting clean air.

Ahead, the dark cloud passed into the fog and soon was lost to sight.

*

Casper sat on a stool in Amos' cottage, shuddering partly from his cold damp clothes, partly from shock. Behind him, Doctor Mogfadian held court.

"Of course, I understood there was always a danger the being might sense our intentions and attempt to thwart us. I knew success in this endeavour would be greatly dependent on the conditions of the weather. I admit I was concerned – due to the inclement year we have had – that they might not favour us. That is why I wisely had Casper accompany Julie, and why I ensured we had two bottles of the elixir prepared."

You knew there was danger and yet you sent us anyway, you puffed-up old windbag, Casper thought, but he held his tongue and kept his face turned towards the fire so his employer could not see his enraged countenance.

After the attack, Julie had returned to the doctor to retrieve the second bottle. She spent a few moments looking at a book the doctor had produced from within the folds of his jacket, continuously mouthing one word, like a student trying to commit a Latin phrase to memory. While Casper, shoeless and muddy with bleeding gashes, awaited her return. Finally, she made her way back towards the pool. Casper dutifully followed her, heavy sword in hand.

Thankfully, they were not troubled by the thing from the mist again, and Julie made short work of emptying the potion into the fetid water, once more uttering that enigmatic word. That had been about half an hour ago.

Casper winced as Julie cleaned the wound on his arm, gently applying a bandage made from a clean shirt kindly provided by the farmer.

"You look like you wandered into the lion enclosure at the zoo," she smiled.

Casper grunted.

"My heroic knight, thank you for looking after me." She leaned forward, kissed him on the cheek, then stood up to examine her work. "Yes, I think you will live to fight another day, *Sir Casper*." She smiled.

Casper found himself smiling back, the hard knot of dislike he had always felt toward the woman beginning to loosen.

"Of course," the doctor was continuing his oration, "one cannot say for certain how long the effects of the *Art Magick* will last. There are a great many factors at play – it could be permanent, it could merely be transient, weakening after only a few years…"

Casper rose from his seat and made his way to the cottage window. He pressed his head against the glass and looked out past the tired-looking outbuildings and over the surrounding fields.

It had started to rain. A light drizzle.

"…my advice would be to leave that little body of water alone. I no longer consider it to be suitable for husbandry. No, not at all. Now, it goes without saying, that should you encounter any more problems, my fine fellow, you need only contact me, and I will come to your assistance – though of course, any future help I render will come with a little... err, fee."

Casper's gaze was drawn back to the Wych Elms gathered about the small body of water, as though they were a coven of hags around their cauldron. The downpour increased, becoming heavier and more incessant. The mist was lighter than it had been earlier in that place of marshy horror, but it was still there, swirling about like the fumes of a toxic brew, weaving between trunks, tendrils snaking up out of the hollow as if reaching out for him.

He shuddered.

Bright Young Things

January 1924

The crystal-clear liquid dripped, oh so slowly, into the container – a tiny box-shaped glass bottle, its walls so thick that the inner reservoir appeared almost non-existent.

Dr Mogfadian peered over Julie's shoulder, his eyes had an intense look – that of a man driven by genius or possibly madness.

"Careful, my dear. If just one drop were to so much as touch your skin, it would be fatal. Indeed, quite fatal," he said.

Even Casper, standing as he was a safe distance from the business in hand, found himself cringing inwardly.

"Careful, Julie," he whispered through gritted teeth.

"What is my mantra: care at all times, and in all things," the doctor said, but if Julie were listening, she made no comment – just stared with hawk-like intensity at the task before her.

Doctor Mogfadian wore thick protective gloves, but he had advised Julie not to do so – they were, he stated, too cumbersome. He held the opinion that if she were to be useful to himself and, eventually, to her future husband, she must learn to do these things in the proper way.

The last bead of liquid hung on the edge of its container, as if resisting all efforts to move it to its new home; finally, it gave up its hopeless fight.

146

"Well done, my dear – yes, well done," praised the doctor, clapping his thickly gloved hands together.

Carefully setting both containers down, the woman stepped backwards and wiped the perspiration from her brow.

Doctor Mogfadian leaned forward to examine her work, looking at it from different angles. "None of the fluid can have dripped over the edge. Just the slightest smear on the rim could be deadly."

"Doctor, surely if she had spilt some, she would be sick by now," Casper said. "Please, just stopper the damn bottle." Somehow, he did not feel that any of them would be safe until the vile fluid was properly sealed in its container.

"Sick, sick? Noooo… No, she would not. That is the genius of this tincture – not only is it untraceable, but it is slow-acting. It can take hours to affect the body." The doctor moved around the small container, continuing to examine it from different angles, letting the light catch it in different ways. He licked his dry lips. "Just a mere smear of it... yes, slow to act, but still fatal. To any doctor, it would appear that the victim had suffered a heart attack. It is the king of poisons!"

"A heart attack!" Julie took a step away from the tiny bottle.

Casper looked over at her – she was visibly shaken. Usually, she relished these episodes in the laboratory.

Today, she clearly did not.

There had been a time when Casper had disliked the woman. He had thought the doctor over-indulgent of her and her fancies. She dressed as a man most of the time – sometimes even in public, when working in the antiques shop.

But a recent event had caused this coldness to melt away and be replaced with a flickering flame. It was not, he knew, a flame that would ever grow into a bonfire of passion – but rather, it was the cosy flame of affection that one feels toward a cherished, but often annoying, younger sister.

When the doctor was finally satisfied, he placed the tiny cork stopper in the vial and carried it to a cupboard, setting it among a collection of different-shaped and coloured bottles.

"I still don't understand why you had her make it. What use could you possibly have for something like that?" Casper asked. But then, he often found himself saying this about a great many of the horrible things the doctor brewed down here.

"I don't want it, Trenchton. It is merely a part of Julie's training. Although…" a wicked smile passed over the man's face, "I could use it to keep the cats off the rose garden."

"Benedict," Julie said reproachfully.

He laughed. "Never fear – this poison is too fine a thing to waste on the local moggies. Still, I do wish they would stop…"

Casper tuned out the conversation. Doctor Mogfadian's complaints about the local feline population were well known to him. It was a subject on which the man frequently dwelt. He returned to reading *The Wendlelow Tattler,* that bold trafficker of local knowledge – or, as the doctor referred to it, 'that old rag.'

The front page was dominated by one story – the deaths of three socialites whose bodies had been found badly burned on the grounds of the old castle just outside town. It was a mystery as to what had happened, but these "bright young things," as the Tattler referred to them, were the sons and daughters of rich and influential families.

This trendy young set treated Wendlelow as their playground – drinking, carousing, and partaking in illicit substances at all hours of the day and night – but especially at night. Their favourite haunt was *The Steppin' Cat*, a jazz bar that had opened about six months previously. In Casper's opinion, these youthful jazz fans would have been better suited to a London nightlife rather than one in Wendlelow. They'd have been far happier – and less of a nuisance – in that great city. Still, the local paper seemed to love them and was always printing stories about their madcap antics.

"'Three dead,'" he read aloud. "'Osbert Townsend-Walker, Bryan Byron, and Charlotte Beauchamp.'"

"How terrible," Julie said, and she looked genuinely moved by what had happened. But then, she had known Charlotte. The woman and her friend were regular visitors to the antiques shop that she ran.

"There is, I detect, a mystery there," the doctor announced. "But one I fear that will not be solved by us. For now, we have a greater task to perform."

Both Casper and Julie looked at him questioningly.

"The preparation and devouring of an evening's repast," he stated.

*

Two days later, Julie and Casper walked towards the church hall where, once a week, Julie attended a meeting of The McGinnity Society for Lore and Mythos – or, as the group usually referred to themselves, The MSLM.

A damp fog clung to the town's streets and settled in the lungs of anyone unfortunate enough to be out and about. On many occasions during their walk, Julie heard some poor soul coughing. Even Casper was not immune to its effects.

She held onto his arm, drawing closer to his body for warmth. He was a great lump of a man – as dour as he was strong – but being by him made her feel safe. No footpad or drunk would ever dream of approaching her when in his company.

"Why don't you come in with me today?" she asked. "You never know – you might enjoy it."

Casper did not immediately reply. His eyes were on a parked car on the other side of the street. As he watched, its door opened and Nolan Perkins – the society's founder and chairman – his wife, Isobel, and his young son, Thomas, emerged.

Casper's eyes narrowed.

"Casper, come in with me?"

As Casper looked at her, his features softened. "No, I will wait for you in *The Waggoner's*," he nodded in the direction of a public house not far from where they stood. "Take your time, enjoy yourself with your friends."

The inside of the church hall seemed every bit as cold as the outside. Whilst she and Nolan arranged chairs and set up a table, Isobel set about preparing cups of tea and arranging an assortment of fine-looking biscuits on a large plate.

The rest of the group arrived together not long after.

There was Mrs Bannerman – back straight as a rod, steel hair pulled into a tight bun, wearing a grey dress and a severe look upon her face. She seemed, for all the world, like the headmistress of a Victorian girls' school. She carried a bag under one arm, from which protruded two knitting needles.

She was followed by a couple in their mid-forties, Mr and Mrs Potter. He wore the excited look of a boy turned loose for his summer holidays; she the resigned appearance of a convicted felon.

Finally, young Roger Stopford entered, bounding into the room with an enthusiasm that – if it were an illness – he might very well have contracted from Mr Potter. He looked about him, and upon spotting Julie, hurried over, a broad smile on his face.

"How are you today?" he asked eagerly, his sharp eyes twinkling in a lively manner, his thick Auburn hair catching the light. He was a most pleasing man to look upon.

"I am very well, thank you, Roger," she replied, careful to keep her voice as neutral as possible. Roger did little to hide the infatuation he had for her – always doing things he thought, or hoped, might please her. It was touching, but also a little embarrassing, given her status as an engaged woman.

"Shall I fetch you a cup of tea, and maybe some biscuits?" he offered.

"Roger, you shouldn't feel that you need to keep doing things for me. I am more than capable of fetching my own tea," she chastised gently.

Roger smiled. "I don't mind. I want to do it," he said, and quickly strode off to collect the essential supplies.

It was an interesting night, though she had little to contribute herself, having been kept too busy in the shop during the day, and helping mix the doctor's oft-times noxious elixirs in the evening.

Perhaps the most interesting speaker was Roger. He had spent the week looking into the story of a grey boy, said to haunt the very pub where Casper was currently supping. He was supposed to be the spirit of a homeless child, who had come begging for food and shelter one cold winter night but was turned away by the establishment's heartless owner. His frozen body was found curled up on the steps to the building entrance the following morning. Ever after, on snowy nights, it was believed you could hear his pitiful sobs coming from the street or, looking out, see his grey form drifting by the window.

It was as Roger was finishing off his tale – and explaining his intention to do more research into the story, hopefully to get a more accurate date for the event, and maybe even to find out the identity of the unfortunate boy and the mean landlord – that a man entered.

He was greying at the temples, with crow's feet deep at the corners of his eyes. Julie smiled. It was Father Barnabus, the priest of St Michael's – the church next door to which their meeting room was attached.

He stood silently during the final minutes of the club meeting, then walked over, shook Nolan's hand, and joined him in conversation. Intrigued, she watched the two men but was unable to make out what they were saying. After a short time, they turned and walked in her direction, and it was then that Julie picked up the tail end of their conversation.

"…Of course, with most of us investigating the hound thing, we won't have the time. But it's possible Ms Mogfadian may be able to help you. Her uncle is known to have an interest in such matters," Nolan said. "Julie, I believe you and Father Barnabus have met before."

She and the priest exchanged greetings.

After the introduction, Nolan continued, "He has come here looking for assistance. Perhaps you and your uncle would be willing to help him?"

Julie did not immediately respond. She was wondering what 'the hound thing' was, and why she had never heard anything about it before. Could it be that members of the group did not trust her with all matters? If so, that hurt – and the only reason she could think of for their treating her that way was her connection to Benedict. She knew that he and Nolan did not see eye to eye.

"Do you think your uncle would consider assisting?" Father Barnabus queried. "I do not ask for myself, but on behalf of one of my parishioners."

"Help with what?" she asked, quickly surfacing from her own swirling self-concerns.

"Why, with those terrible deaths! The burned bodies that have been the talk of the town. There have been two more!"

*

It was early the next morning that Julie and Dr Mogfadian sat in the best room with Father Barnabus. Casper was not present, having been dispatched to watch over the antiques shop. Julie knew her guardian would not be interested in assisting Father Barnabus for any altruistic reason, but he might lend a hand if he believed he was being given an opportunity to show off what he judged to be his considerable talents – particularly if he believed there might be some financial remuneration.

"You are, of course, aware of the terrible deaths at the castle – those poor young people," Father Barnabus said.

Julie knew Benedict was not a man who generally kept up to date with current affairs, being far more concerned with his studies and the dustier events of the past. But he was well aware of the burnings at the castle, largely due to Casper's talking about them.

"Yes, of course," the doctor replied.

"And have you heard that more people have been killed since, in a similar way?"

"No, I have not."

"Olivia Waugh. A close friend of the group, found burned to death in her bedroom. The strange thing was, the fire was completely confined to her. It did not spread to the rest of the house. In truth, it did little damage to the room she was found in – just some burn marks on the floor, as well as a melted window pane and a dark smoky stain on the ceiling above her body."

"I see," the doctor said, his interest made clear by the set of his eyes. "I have heard rumours of such things happening before. Please, go on."

"What you will certainly not know is of the death that occurred last night. I only found out about it this morning from my parishioner; the police are attempting to keep it quiet."

"Was the victim connected to the others in any way?" the doctor asked.

"Not directly, but he was a witness to a strange occurrence – one that happened not far from Olivia Waugh's home. She lived on the edge of town, on a little street, Pickering Way – so popular with the well-to-do."

"And what did he claim to have witnessed?" the doctor asked.

"I don't know. The police are keeping that information out of the public eye."

"Why do they believe his death is connected?" Julie asked.

"He was found in his home the following morning, burned to death, exactly like the previous victims. The fire was confined to just his body. Again, one window was discovered with a glass pane gone – as though it had been exposed to the focused heat of a flamethrower. But again, there was little to no other damage elsewhere, as though the heat had been concentrated in just one small area."

"I think, hmmm… what do I think, I wonder," Doctor Mogfadian mused, stroking his goatee with a thoughtful hand. "Julie, be a dear, go to my study and fetch the map of the town that hangs on the wall over my desk."

Julie left the room.

"If you have come to me, then you must suspect something… unusual is afoot. Pray, speak your mind," Doctor Mogfadian said.

"I suspect…" Father Barnabus paused, as if a little embarrassed by what he was about to say. "I suspect deviltry. Do not mock me, sir. I have encountered many odd things in my life."

But the doctor's look was not one of disbelief or ridicule – it was merely thoughtful. "A devil… ehh… ahh… but which one? There are so many, and only one God. He is quite… beset." A tiny smile creased the corners of his mouth.

The priest made no reply, just watched the doctor, and for a short while an awkward silence hung in the room, only broken by the return of Julie carrying a framed picture, which she set down on a chair.

"Show me on the map where the deaths occurred," the doctor said, reaching into his pocket and withdrawing a handful of farthings, which he then gave to Father Barnabus.

The man placed three of them on the area of the map that depicted the castle. "Townsend-Walker, Beauchamp and Byron were killed here." Then he placed a coin on a street at the edge of town. "Olivia Waugh was killed in her home, here."

"And the latest victim?" the doctor asked.

"I have only the sketchiest of ideas, but I think he lived in a cottage just outside town. He was a farm labourer – probably around here." He placed another marker so close to Olivia Waugh's that they almost touched.

"And the member of your congregation – the one who sought your help – were they a friend of this little group too?" Julie asked.

"No, but his daughter is, and she was with them the night they died, as was another – a young man called Anthony Ponsonby."

"And where does he currently live?" the doctor asked. Another coin was placed, this one farther down Pickering Way. "And where does your parishioner's daughter reside?"

The final coin was placed close to the centre of the town.

"I will need all their names if I am to be of assistance," the doctor said. His voice had an urgent edge to it.

"Along with Mr Ponsonby, the other person involved is Daphne Galthorpe-Harding. She is my parishioner's daughter."

"I know her," Julie said. "She comes by the antiques shop with Charlotte. I am quite friendly with her."

"How convenient," the doctor said. "And you say Ponsonby, Galthorpe-Harding, and Waugh were all with the group on the night of the original deaths?"

"Yes. Mr Galthorpe-Harding stated that his daughter was badly shaken when she returned that night. She seldom leaves her own room – much less the house – since the incident, such is the extent of the shock to her nervous system."

As Doctor Mogfadian stared at the town map and its collection of little markers, he paid particular attention to the lonely coin at the centre of town.

"What are you thinking?" Julie asked.

"I am thinking I need to speak to Anthony Ponsonby and then visit the castle ruins and the site of the original tragedy. I am thinking you," he pointed at Julie, "need to visit the library and find out what you can about the castle and its more… *picturesque* historical occupants."

"But first go close up the shop and send Casper back here. He can help me with my investigations."

"Casper!" Julie said doubtfully.

"Let us say that I will feel happier knowing that the stout young fellow is at my elbow." The doctor turned to Father Barnabus. "You are in luck, my God-bothering fellow. I will look into this. Normally, I would charge for this service."

"I have no money. I was hoping, as a good citizen of the town, you would want to help."

"My fine man, I am neither good, nor do I consider myself to be a citizen of this frightful town. I am merely a temporary resident, here out of necessity. However, fortunately for you, I am sufficiently intrigued by this little mystery to want to assist." A concerned crease furrowed the doctor's brow. "In fact, it may be in my best interests to do so."

*

Casper meandered down Pickering Way. In the summer, this street would be alive with greenery, its trees casting a pleasing shade over anyone walking this way. The front gardens of the large houses would be filled with a kaleidoscope of colour from the flowerbeds.

But in winter, it was very different. The trees were mere skeletons and the cold weather had reduced the gardens to patches of barren wasteland, with just last year's dried stems as a reminder of what had gone before.

Doctor Mogfadian walked at Casper's side. To say he was offended would have been an understatement.

They had been turned away from the Ponsonby home by a servant, who had said that no member of the household was available to speak with them.

Casper knew when to shut his mouth. The doctor's complexion had turned a vivid red, making his anger both visible and audible.

"The only purpose of my visit was to try to render aid to their foolish son. Ungrateful! Stubborn!"

"They don't have to speak to you," Casper finally said, a little concerned that the man would continue to wax lyrical on this subject for some time. "Besides, you mentioned a Daphne whatnot – surely she will see Julie if they really are on friendly terms."

"That, Trenchton, is beside the point, as you well know. A man of my position does not appreciate being turned away from the door like a common tradesman."

They stopped outside what had been Olivia Waugh's home. It was like all the properties on this street – a townhouse of Georgian design. Three storeys high, with four large white windows on every floor, each made up of many small panes of glass. One of these had been partially boarded up – it was one of the central windows on the first floor. Its woodwork, not obscured by the temporary repairs, was blackened and the paint bubbled.

Both men gazed up at the house. Casper knew there was no point in knocking – the newspapers had said that the family had retreated to a place in the country to mourn privately.

"Must have been hot, to melt that glass, and how come only one pane was affected?" Casper asked.

But the doctor did not reply. Instead, he continued to stare upward, an unsettled look having replaced his usual confident expression. When he finally spoke, it was only to say, "Onward, Trenchton, to the castle."

A small, poorly maintained road snaked toward the remains of Wendlelow Castle. What once had been a fine building was now a romantic ruin, the bare bones of a thing that would once have dominated the skyline. Grass and moss had grown up all around, and ivy had invaded portions of the stone structure, so that in places it more resembled a thing of nature rather than something constructed by man.

"Apparently they were found in what used to be the Great Hall," the doctor said as he led Casper through a maze of crumbling stone walls. He finally halted in what, centuries ago, would have been the Great Chamber – but no longer. Only in places did the stones rise up to hint at the former boundaries of a grand room such as this. Now, at its centre, was nothing but an area of black, charred stonework, which might have been the scars of a bonfire, but both men knew better.

"Fortunately, we have had no heavy rain. So, if I am correct, and I usually am, Trenchton, then what I am looking for should still be here."

He scanned the ground, looking around the area of charred stonework. Occasionally, an old flagstone could be seen poking through the greenery, and these he paid particular attention to.

"Nothing." He sounded frustrated. "Where did you put it, you fools?"

"What's that?" Casper pointed to an area of wall, free of ivy. Upon it had been chalked strange symbols.

"Well done, that man." Doctor Mogfadian gave him a slap on the shoulder before walking over to get a closer look at the discovery.

He stared for some time at the markings, lips moving silently, as if in prayer. Slowly, his expression changed... becoming darker and almost fearful.

"The Art has been practised here," he stated.

"You mean magic and all that hocus pocus?" Casper asked.

"Hocus pocus, tontus talontus, vade celeriter jubeo," the doctor replied. "A pseudo-Latin phrase used by false conjurors in the seventeenth century. It is not connected to the true Art Magick, Trenchton."

"It's all Greek to me," Casper replied.

"Of course it is," Doctor Mogfadian said. "But then, I suspect a good part of the English language is, as you say, 'all Greek to you.'"

Casper cast his employer a cold glance, but did not reply.

"Truth be told, I wish it were mere hocus pocus," the doctor said, sounding regretful, even a little agitated. "I wish it were six young fools playing at wizardry one drunken winter's night, before staggering home to their warm beds. Sadly, though, it is not. Whoever led this group had just enough knowledge to endanger both themselves and the whole town, but not enough sense to employ the necessary protections."

"What do you mean?" Casper asked. Some of the doctor's agitation was rubbing off on him; he was feeling on edge, and vulnerable, but to what? What threatened them? He wished his employer would be more forthcoming, rather than just continuing to beat around the bush.

"I mean, our bright young fools employed the Art to cry out into the void but did not like that which answered their call!"

*

Julie was just shutting the antiques shop when she heard a familiar shout.

It was Roger, just up the road. His aunt and uncle had a grocery shop where he helped out. It was only a street away, and he visited her whenever he could find the time.

"Closing up already, has it been that slow today?" he asked, a jolly smile splitting his face.

"Not slow, no, but Benedict has given me a task and it must take precedence. I have to go to the University library and look up something for him."

"I thought your uncle had a library of his own you could use."

"He does, but it is very… err… specialised, and may not contain the information needed. Besides, at the University library, I can pick Nolan's brains."

"Well, I find myself with a spare hour. Perhaps you would allow me to accompany you. An extra pair of eyes is often helpful," he said, offering her his arm.

Julie slid her arm through his. "Why, thank you, Roger. That would be most helpful."

After a brisk walk, they arrived at the University. Along the way, Julie outlined what she was looking for.

Benedict wanted the history of the castle – anything unique or supernatural.

It was, she thought, very different to walk arm-in-arm with Roger – so unlike walking with Casper. When strolling with the large man, she felt safe, as though nothing could possibly harm her; whilst walking with Roger left her with a sense of pride to be escorted by such a young, good-looking man.

Nolan was very accommodating, guiding them through the relevant sections of the library where all the books on local history were to be found, even going so far as to suggest a couple of likely volumes.

It was Roger who struck gold, wrapping his knuckles sharply on the desk and pushing a book across the table in her direction, index finger tapping the relevant spot on the page.

The text he'd found dealt with the legends and tales about the castle, and there were quite a few. On spring evenings, observers could see the White Lady looking out over the town from the top of the north tower. Another tale told of a blood-curdling scream issuing from the open steps to the undercroft. No one had ever been brave enough to try to pinpoint its source.

But the most promising tale was that of The Dreaded Earl – a black-hearted, 14th Century practitioner of the Dark Arts, who had summoned up some terrible thing – the book didn't make clear what it was. Around that time, women and children started disappearing from the town. This usually happened around Midsummer's Eve or Halloween and the townspeople blamed the owner of the castle for the disappearances.

The Earl was said to have decorated the trees about the castle with red rags, supposedly dyed with the blood of his victims. The priests of that day believed he had abandoned God, giving his devotions to something far more terrible.

It was said that when younger, he had travelled to many far-off places and had returned with a knowledge of things that were best left alone.

The reward for these evil dedications was supposed to be the promise of a long life, and shadowy advisers, who brought him wealth and good fortune. But old age has a way of inducing regret, and in later years he stopped these evil practices, instead turning to the church, regularly attending services, donating great sums of money to it, in the hope that God would intercede and spare him some terrible fate that awaited him after death.

There are some deeds, however, that are so dark – some pacts so binding – that no amount of prayer or charity can wash away their stain, or open their padlock. So, when that terrible man finally passed on, folk whispered that he had been carried away to do the bidding of that entity with which he had so unwisely cast his lot.

Eventually, after his allotted hour expired, Roger was forced to make his apologies and return to his aunt and uncle's shop.

Julie stayed on till the light started to fade and the glow of the library lamps replaced that of the winter sun. But though she read many more stories associated with the castle and the surrounding area, she did not feel that any of them fit as well as those of The Dreaded Earl.

*

"I have a terrible suspicion I know what this thing is," Doctor Mogfadian announced. "Of course, I have always had an inkling as to the identity of the perpetrator of these horrific events, but after what I have seen today, combined with what Julie has told me... Well, it is looking like, yet again, I am correct in my initial hypothesis, and tonight, I intend to obtain cast-iron confirmation."

They had gathered together in the best room of the doctor's house, Julie perched in her usual place, cross-legged on the arm of a chair, the doctor, back to them, looking out of the window.

"What is it?" Julie asked.

"Not yet, my dear. I never reveal mere speculation. I will tell you more tomorrow, when I am absolutely certain I am correct."

Casper remained silent – his normal stance when others were talking rot, as the doctor most certainly was. He was a man of endless speculation, who would never shut up until he or the unfortunate person he was bloviating at died.

"The sooner you tell us what you know, the sooner we can help you find a solution to this threat," Julie said.

"There is nothing that either of you could, or would be willing to do, to combat this particular danger. Save this." He raised one finger in the air. "You, Julie, must arrange for us to visit your friend, Daphne Galthorpe-Harding. I need to see her if I am to stop this."

"I can try, but I cannot promise she will want to talk to us."

"You must do more than try, my dear, you must succeed. Failure to do so will mean the destruction of all my carefully laid plans. You must do this, and do it now. Casper and I must pay the Ponsonby home one last visit, and we all must pray that Wendlelow's streets will be quiet tonight."

"Do I need to bring my sword?" Casper asked.

"It would be pointless. If you had to use it, you would already be a walking dead man."

*

Casper found himself crouched in a field behind a hedge, Doctor Mogfadian at his side. A pale full moon shone down on them. Both men carried field glasses.

The lane they were hunkered down beside eventually ended at the remains of the castle, which was visible in the moonlight, reminding Casper of the bones of some great prehistoric beast rising from the hilltop.

"You must be silent, you must stay hidden, whatever you see, whatever may happen. Both our lives depend upon it," the doctor said for what Casper thought must be the thirtieth time.

"Yes, I know," he hissed back.

It was after ten, they had been hiding for over an hour, it was cold, and a light rain did nothing to improve their discomfort.

From somewhere nearby, an owl gave voice, a hooting which carried on the chill breeze and played a merry jig with his nerves.

"There. On the track," the doctor whispered, pointing in the direction of the castle, the fear in his voice causing a wave of ice to surge through Casper's veins.

He stared in the direction his employer was pointing, but the man must have had the eyes of a hawk, for he could make out nothing. He continued peering at the shadowy track, squinting in frustration.

Then he spied it.

A shape, with no identifying characteristics, moved with slow purpose, emitting a reddish-orange glow one usually associates with the embers of a dying fire. It turned a corner and disappeared from view, reappearing a few minutes later on a straight section of track.

Now Casper could discern the nature of the thing.

It was a wagon – or, to be more accurate, it resembled an old hay wain, the sort prevalent about farms when Casper was young.

With it came a reverential silence; even the wind in the trees seemed to die down in its presence. Silent were its wheels upon the rutted track, and silent the two great oxen that drew it. These beasts were as black as pitch, with sickly yellow eyes flecked with orange, and sturdy horns riddled with subtle veins of fire. A putrid yellow bile dripped from the mouths of these monstrosities, vanishing before making contact with the earth. Not a mark did it leave upon the ground – not the track of a wheel, nor the scar of a hoof.

The wain itself was empty – no driver sat upon its bench, no cargo lay in its bed – but it emitted an autumnal glow, as if it had once carried a great fire which had died to little more than hot embers.

A haze of heat hung over the cart, and occasionally this would intensify, seeming to take the shape of a man: arms pinned to his sides, head thrown back, screaming out in silent agony – only to fade away again, making Casper question whether this was merely his mind deceiving him.

Following the lane, the wagon went right past their hiding place and headed toward town.

"We must trail it – but at a safe distance. It. Must. Not. Detect. Us," Doctor Mogfadian punctuated.

"I think we could outrun it," Casper said, trying to make light of the situation, though in truth he was badly frightened.

The doctor looked shocked at this comment. "Listen to me: neither the beasts of burden, nor the damned thing they pull, can be allowed to become aware of you. Do you understand? Say no and you shall stay here on your own, shivering in this field. I won't take any risks, Trenchton."

The stress was so evident in his employer's voice, and so out of character, that Casper stiffened.

"All right," he said. "I will be guided by you."

By now, the unearthly vehicle had turned a corner and was obscured by field boundaries, with only the forge-like glow revealing its location.

"Now we follow – and, *bade me*, for this is essential, watch for any people – on the road, down a side street, in an alley, looking out from windows of their homes. Tell me if you see anyone, or even suspect seeing someone."

"I will," Casper replied. "But wha…"

"It is late," Doctor Mogfadian said, cutting Casper off mid-word. "That is in our favour. The weather is poor. That will keep people off the streets. Let us hope fate is with us – it only needs to venture two streets into the town to reach the Ponsonbys' home."

"But what if I see someone? What does it mean?" Casper asked.

"If it is merely one person, maybe…" The doctor looked unsure. "More than one… we pack our bags and leave town tomorrow."

Quietly they followed the lane, always keeping their quarry out of sight, looking for nocturnal wanderers. They saw none.

They concealed themselves in a bush in a garden at the entrance to Pickering Way. Ahead of them, the diabolic wain had drawn to a halt outside the home of the Ponsonby family. It was lit up by a street lamp, and seemed to have taken on a misty, insubstantial quality, as though the illumination were imposing upon it a reality in which it struggled to exist.

"The little snob will wish he took the time to see me now," Doctor Mogfadian muttered, putting the field glasses to his eyes. After a moment's hesitation, Casper did likewise, curiosity overcoming fear.

Above the wagon, the heat haze had, once again, intensified. It drifted upward, a shapeless, scalding mass, moving toward the second floor of the house, coming to a stop at the window farthest from them.

Then an arm-like appendage reached forward and touched the glass. Almost immediately, the pane melted, dripping over the window ledge, molten droplets falling into the garden like a burning rain. Yet strangely, no other part of the frame was damaged by the supernatural heat, save for a slight blistering of the paintwork.

Then the thing drifted in through the window.

"Remember, watch the street, check the windows," the doctor said.

Both men set aside their field glasses, eyes now scouting buildings, doors, and pavements.

Then the screaming started.

Both Casper and the doctor jumped at the noise; it was a sound so intense, so filled with agony, that Casper felt physically sick.

"Come on. Hurry up!" the doctor hissed.

Lights started to appear in the Ponsonby family home.

"Come on, for the sake of my Lord, die, die quickly," the doctor said.

More lights appeared in houses up and down the street.

A thick, oily smoke billowed out of the damaged window.

The screaming spluttered down to a pathetic sob, then silence.

Gradually, the black vehicle and its oxen faded, until after a few moments, nothing of it remained. Seconds later, Casper saw curtains pulled aside, in windows all about the street, faces peering out into the dark.

Then the doctor was pulling him, drawing him away into the night.

*

The following morning, Julie and Doctor Mogfadian found themselves staring at the immaculate front door of socialite Daphne Galthorpe-Harding.

"We are lucky she agreed to see us. By all accounts, she is quite badly shaken," Julie stated.

But then, you aren't looking so composed yourself, Benedict, she thought.

Indeed, though smartly dressed in his top hat, dark suit and cape, he had the bearing of a man bedevilled with torments.

A servant opened the door, and after a brief explanation of their presence, guided them to a finely decorated room, within which sat their hostess – a woman in her early twenties, with hair of a golden hue, and eyes like the waters of the Caribbean Sea.

Doctor Mogfadian sat in silence, whilst Julie and their hostess engaged in small talk. It was clear that Daphne was troubled. The woman was usually incredibly friendly, carrying herself with an airy grace which she wore like a fine gown.

But this was all gone. The person before her bore no resemblance to the talkative woman she had conversed with so many times in the little antiques shop. Instead, before them sat a drained, lethargic individual, her clothes slightly rumpled and her hair untended. She responded to questions slowly, never trying to lead the conversation in that confident way she usually did.

"Daphne, I have brought my guardian, Doctor Benedict Mogfadian. He is keen to talk with you. It may be that he can be of service to you, helping to ease your troubles."

Daphne turned a hopeful gaze upon the doctor.

"Miss Galthorpe-Harding," he leaned forward as he spoke. "I am here to ask questions. There are things I must know, so I beg of you – please, be candid with me."

Daphne looked over at Julie uncertainly.

"You can trust Benedict," she reassured the woman. "However strange your story, he will listen and not judge."

Daphne licked her lips nervously, looked the doctor up and down, before nodding her agreement.

"I will tell what I know, which is little. I only hope you will be able to help me," Daphne said. "But first I will call

Steedings and have him serve us some whisky. A stiff drink is just what I need." She reached for the bell on the small table nearby.

"There is no need. Allow me." Doctor Mogfadian walked over to the sideboard displaying a selection of cut-glass decanters and set to work. Julie deemed it a clear sign of the woman's distress that she would allow a guest to serve her in her own home. This went against many rules of etiquette that would have been ingrained in her from an early age.

"It has been terrible," Daphne said. "Since that night I have had no peace of mind."

Doctor Mogfadian returned, handing her a small glass, which she took with a shaking hand.

"Go on, please," he said, passing a drink to Julie before resuming his seat.

"Are you sure you won't have a drink, doctor?" Daphne asked.

"No, I am fine. Pray continue."

And so she did.

"Osbert Townsend-Warner had made the suggestion. It had been a quiet night at *The Steppin' Cat* and he had seemed restless, as if there was something on his mind that he wanted to share. Finally, he told us about a perfectly spiffing thing he had discovered in his father's library... a book of spells!

"'It's the sort of thing one of those wizardly characters from The Arabian Nights might own,' he had said, then added, 'Wouldn't it be wonderful to try out a few of the magic tricks in it?' He said he'd read most of the thing, and it was the most fantastic nonsense ever committed to paper. He loved it and said we would, too. We could pop by his parents' place, grab the book, and some chalk and candles. What a larks!"

Daphne went silent for a time, just staring into her glass of whisky, lost in thought. Finally, she gave her slender body a small shake and continued. "So we did. Of course, no one – not even Ossy – wanted to do the rituals in their homes. The thought of being caught in the act, for one thing. But worse than that, the idea that something might actually be drawn to us and take up residence, so to speak. Then Olivia said she had heard that the castle ruins were supposed to be haunted, and wouldn't it be terribly romantic to try it there?"

According to Daphne, they had made their way to the ruins, sipping champagne from a bottle and singing at the tops of their voices. It had not taken long for Osbert to chalk the markings onto a wall, whilst Bryan had set about lighting candles. There had been a lot of laughter. Olivia was probably the drunkest of the group and could barely stop giggling. They only quietened down when Osbert had finished drawing and was standing, old book in one hand, his other arm raised up like a Shakespearian performer, preparing to deliver a show-stopping speech.

"He started to read the text; it was in a language I had never heard before – words that made my stomach turn. After a while, there was a strange blur that distorted the marking. That was enough for me; I had no problem watching Ossy make a perfect fool of himself, but I had never thought anything would actually happen. I slowly backed away, so did Anthony and Olivia. The others were rooted to the spot. Even Ossy had stopped his chanting. Fiery smoke started billowing out of the chalked circle on the wall, and I turned and ran, followed by the more sensible members of the group. I did not look back, even when I heard the screaming. The rest you must surely know from the papers. Olivia died, and then some other poor fellow, so now there is only myself and Anthony left."

Julie did not speak; news of the Ponsonby tragedy was not yet common knowledge and she had no wish to be the one to break it to her friend.

"Something is coming for me, I know it. Whatever killed the others is coming for me. You have to help me," Daphne implored the doctor. "Julie has told me what a clever fellow you are, particularly in these sorts of matters."

"Help you?" Doctor Mogfadian leaned forward and gently patted the woman's hand, giving her a reassuring smile. "My dear, I already have."

*

Doctor Mogfadian seemed greatly relaxed. It had been three days since he and Julie had visited Daphne Galthorpe-Harding. Every morning since that day, the clearly agitated doctor had dispatched Casper to collect copies of the local newspaper. And they had spent a great deal of time scouring it for any articles relating to unusual deaths by fire. But no more stories had circulated, and today he did not read much further than *The Tattler's* third page before he set down those virtuous, printed sheets and allowed a smile of relief to lighten his hitherto troubled face.

"I can now say, with some confidence, and also, I think, a little self-satisfaction, that I have laid the town's recent problem to rest." He allowed himself a tiny bow, as if acknowledging the applause of an appreciative audience. Casper watched Julie walk over to the discarded newspaper and start to peruse it.

"But what was that thing we saw?" he asked. This was a question he had posed continuously over the past few days, but his employer had always declined to reply. "Perhaps, now that the issue is settled, you will be more inclined to tell us. I mean, for goodness' sake, you had us packing our bags to flee at a moment's notice!"

The doctor nodded, then spoke. "It was a Hell Wain."

"A what?" Casper asked.

"A terrible thing, Trenchton, drawn from the darkest pit. Once unleashed, it is like a contagion, spreading throughout the population, seeking and killing every person it encounters. I suspect – though of course one can never be certain – that it was the soul of that blighted Earl, bound in torment by the very thing he had made a pact with in life. So very… Faustian."

"That was why you had me looking out for passers-by that night."

"Very astute, my lumbering fellow. Had it so much as encountered just one person that night, it would have returned, tracking that poor soul to their home and killing them as it did the rest, no doubt travelling deeper into Wendlelow and meeting even more people on the way. It would have ravaged the town, people would have fled, and the nocturnal streets would be unsafe to walk. Eventually, someone would be seen escaping from town, and it would pursue them, unleashing its terror upon an unsuspecting nation."

"So, we were fortunate to meet no one that night," Casper said, "and not to be seen ourselves."

"Very fortunate," Doctor Mogfadian agreed. "Of course, I suspected what it was early on. I was aware of a similar case in Egypt in the middle of the last century. Two men of vision and courage were able to put a stop to it before it spread from the village it had... infected."

Julie gasped. She had thrown the newspaper to the floor, and tears welled up and spilled over her eyes. "Daphne Galthorpe-Harding is dead. She died two nights ago of heart failure." She stood uncertainly, looking at the doctor, then purposefully strode to the cabinet and pulled out a familiar bottle, tiny, square, its little reservoir completely empty.

"Benedict, what did you do?" she demanded, her misery morphing into anger.

"My dear, I protected the community, in the only way I could," the doctor said, almost airily.

Casper leaned forward, watching the exchange, intrigued, his mind slowly piecing the puzzle together.

"Bloody well tell me. What did you do?" Julie said, a dangerous edge in her voice. She slammed the tiny bottle on the table between them.

The doctor smiled. "I saved the town, protected my – no, our – interests," he said, waving a hand as if to swat away her concerns.

Julie leaned towards him, eyes filled with hatred.

"What. Did. You. Do?"

The Reaping

Taken from the notes of Roger Stopford
August 1924

There are a great many tales in this world: tales of love, tales of daring, innocent tales designed to enchant the young and the young at heart, and, of course, those tales designed to tingle the spine, chill the heart, and unnerve the bravest of souls.

We seek out these latter tales, these deliciously terrifying stories, we know not why; perhaps it is to satisfy a hidden, morbid craving, one we are not even aware that we possess. Perhaps it is so that, on the completion of a particularly nasty story, we can look about at our cosy abodes, draw nearer to the roaring fire, and really appreciate what it is to have safe, ordinary lives.

But I digress. I will leave it to better-educated men than I to decide why we should seek such grim stories. My job, dear reader, is not to philosophise about why – we leave that to others – mine is simply to tell.

Writers seek inspiration in a great many ways and from a great many sources. Sometimes a writer is lucky enough to stumble on the fragments of a true story. If he is clever and worthy of his craft, he will twist it and retell it in his own words, adding new flourishes and changing the characters and their motivations to suit his personal tastes. Some writers may try to keep as close as possible to the original source material, hoping the readers are titillated enough by its supposedly truthful origins.

This story I will tell is, I think, best presented in the latter way. I first stumbled on it when looking at an old edition of *The Wendlelow Tattler*, that most supreme and noble publisher of local Shropshire news. It attracted my attention in a way only the strange and macabre can do, for I have ever been an odd fellow with odd tastes.

I sensed that there was a good deal more meat to the tale than even the esteemed Tattler had laid on the platter, and as it happened, I was right. But more about that later. First, I will present you with a copy of the newspaper article that I read – that so drew me in.

Shropshire's Own Ghost Town

Two nights ago, Carchar Haearn, a bustling, historical village, became a ghost town. The population, estimated at three hundred souls, disappeared from that healthy, thriving village, and no one knows where they went.

Carchar Haearn is, or was, a village between places, sitting on the Shropshire–Powys border. Over the centuries, the little settlement had been ruled by both English and Welsh lords, and as such its folk were touched with a little bit of both the Anglo-Saxon and Celtic cultures. They wore their mixed heritage with pride, and though somewhat reserved in their attitude, neighbouring villages always spoke of them in a positive way, telling of their honesty and good humour on market days. But all this was to change.

Ghost towns are usually associated with the American West – old mining towns in some far-flung location, abandoned since the veins of precious metal that first drew settlers to that place ran dry. But ghost towns are not unique to the New World; indeed, they can be located throughout the globe, even here, in sleepy Shropshire.

Most British ghost towns are old plague villages, abandoned long ago, when the residents either died or fled from that catastrophic contagion. They are usually little more than ruins buried within woodlands or under farmers' fields, with only a few mossy, lichen-covered stones to show that they were ever living, breathing communities of people with hopes and dreams of their own.

Many of these places are largely forgotten. But there are some examples to be found; these include Ambion in the county of Leicestershire and Tusmore in Oxfordshire. Such villages are nearly always medieval, and modern examples of British ghost towns are rare, but not unknown.

This reporter was able to locate a few of Carchar Haearn's ex-residents.

Bryn Chapper, who ran the village store, moved to Dudley, and though happy to discuss his life in the village, refused to discuss the cause of the mass exodus.

This was also true of most of the former villagers interviewed.

Despite this reporter's best efforts, I was only able to speak to one resident who would, in any way, allude to that strange September when a village died!

Mrs Beanbody left Carchar Haearn on the advice of her employer, as he and a great many others were concerned by some building work being done in the area. "I left on February 20th," she said. "The day before everyone else did."

So, what happened to the other residents? Many theories exist, from the extreme: the locals fell victim to an age-old curse, placed by a witch; to the religious: the hand of God swept them off the face of the earth for unnameable sins; to the more prosaic: a downturn in local prosperity caused the good people of Carchar Haearn to migrate to more prosperous areas of the country.

Whatever it was that caused the people of Carchar Haearn to leave their homes, this reporter has, to date, been able to trace a mere five of the three hundred residents of that most mysterious of villages!

As a piece of news, this story, whilst intriguing and offering an entertaining read for a rainy Sunday afternoon, does little to explain what happened, only hinting in the vaguest of ways at the strange and the mysterious.

But I was fortunate to be able to uncover a little more of Carchar Haearn's story, albeit by mere chance. I bumped into an old chum of mine, Richard Fredricks. We had been friends in our younger days at Toadstone boarding school. Though neither of us looked back on our days at the grim old pile with any great affection, we were still happy to chat over a pint in the Badger and Buck – one of Wendlelow's better pubs.

Conversation strayed, as it is wont to do, and I found myself talking with my friend about this most unusual of news articles. To my surprise, he said he thought he might have something connected to the story back at his flat. He asked me if I might be interested in seeing it.

I didn't need to be asked a second time!

At his flat, he handed me a notebook once belonging to an uncle of his who was a police officer. This uncle had interviewed James Pendle, who, though not a resident of Carchar Haearn, had worked as a site manager. In this capacity, he oversaw the construction of some new buildings at the outskirts of the village. It was he who had notified the authorities about the fate of the doomed settlement.

It was my friend's uncle, along with another officer, who was given the task of interviewing this gentleman.

The notes were quite extensive, since it appeared that equipment on the site had been damaged, and the investors had requested a copy of the interview for insurance purposes.

In defiance of police protocol, my friend's uncle had shared the notepad with him. He found the tale unusual and wanted to share it with his nephew to solicit his valued opinion.

Richard, seeing my interest in it, allowed me to borrow the notepad.

At home, I spent much time poring over the pad, intrigued by what the words implied but never came right out and said. Anxious to return my borrowed property, I made a copy of it, which follows:

Interview with James Pendle

Date: 26th April 1924

Interviewing Officer: PC Alfred Fredricks

Also Present: PC Cyril Atherton

PC Fredricks: You understand why you have been asked to attend this interview, Mr Pendle?

Mr Pendle: I do.

PC Fredricks: And you understand your rights? And can confirm that at this time you have agreed to waive legal assistance?

Mr Pendle: Yes, but I really don't see what more I can tell you, I…

PC Fredricks: I am aware that you have already given a statement to your employers, but they have asked that we interview you and send a copy of that interview to them to forward to their insurers. It seems they need it to proceed with their claim. Also, as the only traceable person from Carchar Haearn, we'd like to get a better understanding of what happened there on the night of the 21st of February.

Mr Pendle: But I wasn't there that night. I told you.

PC Fredricks: Nevertheless, you were there during the day and many days beforehand. You are our best and only witness to events leading up to that night. Anything you can tell us, no matter how trivial it may seem, could be of help.

Mr Pendle: All right.

PC Fredricks: Fine. What were your responsibilities as the site manager in Carchar Haearn?

Mr Pendle: I oversaw the day-to-day running of the site, managed the mountain of paperwork that always seems to build up around these jobs, and provided the shareholders with regular updates.

PC Fredricks: I imagine you were kept very busy then?

Mr Pendle: Yes, you could say that. I was run off my feet. I think it was the worst job I have ever worked on. It was plagued with problems from the beginning – and don't get me started on the locals!

PC Fredricks: We can come to that in good order, Mr Pendle; for now, can you describe your first impressions of the village and its people?

Mr Pendle: Quaint, that's what I would say about the place, like something out of one of those Thomas Hardy novels my wife talks about so much. The cottages and the local pub were huddled about a village green. In the middle of this grass was a great, rectangular granite slab sunk into the ground, like one of those flagstones you see in old churches. It had four cup marks in each corner.
And as I say, the locals, funny lot, rum, insular, isolated like their bloody village, they were a problem from the start, didn't want us there you see and made it quite clear as well.

PC Fredricks: In what way did they make it clear?

Mr Pendle: Threats, acts of vandalism. It's too much, really. I'm just trying to earn a living, you know? I've a wife and three kids at home. I don't see them for weeks at a time, because the chances of landing a contract that's on my doorstep is non-existent. I'm forced to live out of a suitcase, sleeping in hostels or the spare rooms in pubs and then to top it all off, I have to put up with silly buggers.

Sometimes, when I come home after a long job, I feel like a stranger in the house – a part-time intruder in the lives of my family, throwing their normal routines into disarray. I worry sometimes, do they really need me? I mean, except for the money I bring in, if I'd been one of the ones to vanish, would they really even miss me?

PC Fredricks: What exactly was the nature of the villagers' complaint against you and your fellow workers?

Mr Pendle: Well, that's easy enough to answer; you've been to that village haven't you?

PC Fredricks: I have in the course of my investigation, yes.

Mr Pendle: So you'll have seen the iron.

PC Fredricks: You mean the iron poles?

Mr Pendle: Yes, the poles... the great iron rods, tall as a man, thick as his arm, thrust into the ground all about the village perimeter. There were hundreds of them, like a small forest circling the place. Well, the locals were obsessed with them, like they were an important local landmark or something. Eyesore, I say. The problem was, they were pretty close to the existing cottages, and we needed to dig some up in order to have the space to build the new houses... it had all been agreed and signed off – legal-like.

PC Fredricks: And it was this that instigated the bad feeling?

Mr Pendle: Yeah... I couldn't see what the problem was, it wasn't like we were digging them all up, I reckon we needed to grub up about a quarter of them, so there were still plenty left. I tried to explain this to Mr Chapper, but he weren't interested.

PC Fredricks: Mr Chapper?

Mr Pendle: He ran some shop in the village. Acted like a spokesman for the villagers. To me, he was a nuisance who wouldn't let us be and I reckon he was behind that bout of vandalism. If you want to interview anyone, it would be him, ringleader and nasty piece of work he was. If you can ever find him, that is.
I explained it was all above board and legal, but he just kept on saying we'd no right to take them down, that we didn't know what they were for, bein' outsiders and such. So, I tells him, tell me what they're for, then, because I can't see no rhyme or reason to them.

PC Fredricks: And what did he say to that?

Mr Pendle: Not much, just grumbled on about us not understanding. Anyroad, this went on for a while, us working, them complaining, until one evening things got a bit heated. That would have been around February 16th if I remember rightly. Young Wallace and a few of the lads had gone to drink in the village, against my advice. I could see the way things were headed.

PC Fredricks: Young Wallace… that will be… James Wallace correct?

Mr Pendle: Yes, Jim Wallace. He weren't the oldest member of my crew, but he had the sort of strength of personality that the others looked up to and respected. He was their unofficial leader, when I weren't about that is. He was a good lad at heart; his father was a widower, crippled in the Great War, relied on his son to provide a roof for him. God knows who will care for him now!

PC Fredricks: And they had a run-in with the locals?

Mr Pendle: You could say that. There's only one pub in the village – *The Elder Earl*, small place, these village inns sometimes are, and I should know, I stayed in a few! I'd visited this one myself before relations with the locals deteriorated, all old beams and sour ale.

It had a pretty odd sign outside too, showing a cruel-looking hound, an ugly beastie, with an obscene hoggish quality to its face. I always thought it must have been part of a pack, cause the huntsman could be seen on a hill silhouetted in the background, blowing on a horn, a creepy looking primitive, wearing antlers on his head! Very unpleasant, give me a *Woolpack* or *Wheatsheaf* any day.

I'd spoke with Wallace and his friends, told them to get along with the locals, buy them a few drinks, get them on our side, make our job easier. Well, the way they told it, things started off a bit shaky, the locals were suspicious of them and more than a little angry about what we were doing, but my boys bought a few drinks for the regulars, and this seemed to bring them round. It wasn't long before they were laughing and joking together.

PC Fredricks: But something went wrong?

Mr Pendle: Aye, sure enough the conversation turned to those iron poles. Wallace said he tried to steer the chit chat away from it, knowing it was a touchy subject, but, those local lads kept bringing it up, saying how important it was to the village. They seemed to think of it as… well not so much a wall as, well, a shield or talisman against something… something unpleasant.

Now my crew is city through and through, they've no time for silly local superstitions, and, I'm afraid, they laughed right in the locals' faces, called them every kind of fool they could bring to mind. Well, you can imagine how that went down, all the goodwill flew right out the window, faster than a magpie with a shiny bauble and before you know it fists are flying all over the place.

The lads came back in a very sorry state, accompanied by the town constable and a couple of the older, more level-headed of the villagers and didn't they give me a roasting! Can't keep control of my workforce, my men are no better than hired thugs, says they, like their lads never threw a punch and anyone could see they had. They'd done quite a job too, bruises and bloody lips wherever I looked. Yes, my workers had taken a good beating. I can still see Wallace now – a shiner on his right eye and a lip split right down the middle. Nothing that would kill him, mind, but nevertheless...

Well, it took all my self-control, but I gritted my teeth and apologised. I ask you, what more could I do? Things were strained enough already; I had to do something to try to limit the damage. I promised to keep an eye on the boys and not let them go drinking again, to make sure they went straight back to their lodgings after work.

PC Fredricks: Was that the same night the vandalism occurred?

Mr Pendle: No, that was the following night. In spite of nursing some pretty nasty bruises after that beating, the boys were productive the following day, ripping up those iron poles with surprising vigour. Perhaps it was their way of getting their own back on the locals – hurting them the only way they legally could.

We must have pulled about forty of the bloody things out. It was hard graft too; they were planted deep – very deep. Anyroad, by the end of that day when they had retired to the caravans the company had given us for accommodation, they were ready to collapse. It was that night the vandalism occurred, and we were all so tired we slept straight through it, like babes through a thunderstorm!

PC Fredricks: And just for the record, can you give some examples of the damage done to your equipment?

The following section of the interview was merely a list given by Mr Pendle of all the broken and damaged equipment, punctuated with his occasional exclamation of discontent and annoyance at what had been done to his worksite and the apparatus located there; it is not particularly relevant to the overall tale, so it shall be passed over here. It is sufficient to say that the damage was extensive and clearly of a vindictive nature, committed by a group of very angry and frustrated people.

PC Fredricks: Did you speak to the locals about this damage, perhaps to see if they knew who was responsible?

Mr Pendle: Well, the lads were all for marching into the village and banging some heads together till they got some information on who was responsible. But I was able to calm 'em down; the last thing I wanted was more of 'em getting into scraps.

Instead, I decided it was best to keep our distance and just get on with the job of plucking out more of that iron.

To be honest, I'd have been glad never to have laid eyes on any of 'em again and I reckoned us just getting on with our work would wind 'em up far more than a face-to-face and I was right. That night, while the crew were eating, I went for a walk about the site alone, just to make sure all was in order, and who should come storming over to me? Mr Chapper, and wasn't he in a foul mood? Cussing and waving his arms around like a mad prophet.

PC Fredricks: Did you feel threatened by Mr Chapper?

Mr Pendle: Did I say I felt threatened? I most certainly wasn't! And here's why. It didn't take me long to realise that the fella wasn't just angry; he was scared. There was something in his eyes that said the slightest thing might send him scampering back home. I was tempted to put on my best front, give him a scare and send him running like a rabbit with a fox on his arse.

PC Fredricks: So, why didn't you?

Mr Pendle: Simple, it weren't me he was scared of.

PC Fredricks: So if not you, who? Your men? You think he was worried about them being close at hand and... how shall I put it... lending you moral support?

Mr Pendle: No, no, it weren't that either, it was that mound, the one to the west of the village, just over the Welsh border, kept looking at it like Old Nick himself might pop out and start chasing him around the fields.

Well, anyway, I told him to calm down, said he wasn't being reasonable. And, to be fair, the mad old badger did attempt to compose himself. Went silent for a few seconds, closed his eyes, and I don't know, I suppose he must have counted to ten or something. I've heard that does the trick, but whatever he did, when he opened his eyes again he seemed a little more relaxed.

He told me a rum tale then. Apparently, a little girl had vanished around those parts about two years ago. She'd gone wandering one night in the fields and never came home. I said I was very sorry to hear that, but wasn't sure what it had to do with me or my work. At this, he started to become agitated again, and I said I didn't understand. He said, over the years, a lot of people have vanished in the local countryside.

Well, I can spot a veiled threat as well as the next man, and I didn't appreciate it, not coming from that pot of boiled cabbage and I told him as much! Said he'd be best to pop off before I did something I regretted.

Again, he said I didn't understand.

I said I understood perfectly and he should think himself lucky I wasn't reporting his threats to the police.

He paused, closed his eyes, once more composing himself, then told me to listen carefully, as what he had to say was important for the well-being of all the folk at Carchar Haearn.

PC Fredricks: And what was that?

Mr Pendle: Never found out.

PC Fredricks: You never found out?

Mr Pendle: That's right, something happened, you see, something odd! It was a relatively clear night, the moon wasn't quite full, but it was close. Anyroad it chose that moment to come out from hiding behind the clouds and it lit up the surrounding area like some weird nocturnal sun.

I've never seen the moon so bright, I could make out the old scarecrow flapping about in the field to the west. I could clearly see the outlines of the trees in the patch of woodland bordering the meadow – and that mound, well I'd never taken much notice of it before, bless me I can see it now, it seemed more like an ancient fortress than a burial mound. The old standing stones on the summit were like primitive crenellations.

A howling rose up on the wind, like a pack of mad dogs, and I thought my ears detected a horn, somewhere distant, barely audible. The effect on Mr Chapper was almost instantaneous; he turned tail and ran! And I very nearly followed straight on his heels.

At this point, at Mr Pendle's request, I asked PC Atherton to fetch him a drink of water, he knocked it back in two good gulps, I could tell he was a little shaken. We let him have a few moments to collect his thoughts before continuing with the interview:

PC Fredricks: Can you tell me what happened on the 21st September, please?

Mr Pendle: That was my last day on the site, though I was only there in the morning. That afternoon, I had a meeting with the investors to provide an update on the build and discuss the ongoing problems with vandalism and such.

PC Fredricks: And this kept you away from the site for the remainder of the day?

Mr Pendle: Yes, I was supposed to return later that day, but the meeting overran and I was tired, so I booked into a hotel and decided to return to Carchar Haearn the following morning. I remember being pretty annoyed at having to stay over, frustrated with the investors for keeping me so long. But now, well, I probably owe them my life!

PC Fredricks: You think the rest of your work crew are dead, then?

Mr Pendle: I dunno, perhaps… I ain't got a clue what happened to them, but since none of their families has seen hide nor hair of them, well, it don't look good, does it?

PC Fredricks: Tell me what happened when you returned to Carchar Haearn the following day?

Mr Pendle: Must have arrived there about, I dunno, one in the afternoon. The site was empty, the tools still packed neatly away in the work shed. I was pretty annoyed. I'd been put over the coals the day before – those investors blamed me for all the problems on the site, and then I come back to find my guys taking the day off. I was fair fuming, I'll tell you. With no sign of 'em on the site, I figured they'd wandered into the village for a pint…you know, while the cat's away, and all that.

I went straight to *The Elder Earl;* to my surprise, it was closed. It was then I noticed how dead the village was, not a soul in sight. In the cottages, all the curtains were still drawn; it was as though the whole village had overslept. As my annoyance started to give way to concern, the silence of the place started to bear down on me, an unease drifted on the wind, an unease that settled into the marrow of my bones. I wanted nothing more than to get away from Carchar Haearn, as far away as I could and if I never saw or heard of the place again, well, that was fine by me!

But, of course, I couldn't. I had my responsibility to the men under me. I tried knocking on the Inn door, but there was no answer. The handle was unlocked, though, so steadying myself, I entered, calling out continuously to the owner, making him aware of my presence.

The Taproom was empty; the smell of last night's tobacco and ale still ripe in the air. Nothing seemed amiss. The bar stools and chairs were neatly in their allotted place, the tables wiped clean, the glasses stacked on the shelves behind the bar, like crystal sentries awaiting their duties.

Still calling out, I made my way upstairs. Ahead of me on the landing, a door stood open. Instinct told me this was the Innkeeper's room. In contrast to the Taproom, it was in complete disarray!

A bedside table had been overturned, its contents scattered across the floor. It was as though a gale had found its way down the chimney, played merry havoc with the bedclothes, curtains, and furniture, then fled back out the way it had come, ignoring the rest of the property, for reasons only it knew.

I raced out into the street shouting at the top of my voice, it was a mercy none were there to see me, for I must have looked like a man who had lost his mind. Perhaps I had!

I ran to the cottage next door. Like the Inn, its front door was unlocked, and like the Inn, only one room was in disarray. This time, it was the parlour. The table and chairs were scattered and broken, and a shattered mug lay on the floor in a puddle of cold tea. I knew the owner of this cottage – Percy Wingham – an old man who kept odd hours.

I checked the third and fourth cottages; each time it was the same – the doors unbarred, the rooms within untouched, except for the bedrooms, which, like the Inn, were a chaos of broken furniture and discarded bed sheets. With the exception of old Percy, whatever had found these people, had found them sleeping!

I wandered the streets, I can't say for how long, calling out, at a loss for what to do. Gradually a dark cloud drew itself curtain-like over the sun, rain accompanying it, a perpetual drizzle that slowly soaked into my clothes. A wind rose from the direction of the mound and was accompanied by a howl, like the call of the leader of a mad pack. There was something unearthly about it, and something familiar too.

I fled Carchar Haearn, and I will never return.

There is little more of interest in the police report, and in truth, little more in the way of documentation that could help me to understand the fate of the folk of that tragic village and the workmen who laboured there in those final weeks. Indeed, I might have had little more to add at this point, if it were not for a visit to a rural inn some weeks ago.

Whilst I was there enjoying a refreshing pint with an old friend, one of the old timers at the bar broke into song. I was told by some of the regulars that, when plied with enough of the favoured local brew, he was wont to sing some of the older folk songs, those that were not much remembered by others.

His voice was not great, but good enough; and before long, some of the regulars who remembered the old ditties joined in with him. But there was one song in particular that stood out – at least, to me. It seemed a companion to the narrative that I have set before you on these pages. If you do not agree, well, I am not quite sure of what more to say on the matter.

A Lord of the ancient mound,
His folk fair but never tame,
In the wilds he could be found,
And The Rowan King was his name.

A peaceful realm for his kith,
Then came the children of men,
Driving his folk into myth,
Never to see them again!

Ride up the mound,

Ride round,
You'll see him on a moonlit night,
Ride up the mound,
Ride round.

Tall was he with horns and hood,
Riding the land unimpaired,
By green hills and darkened wood,
No man or child was spared.

Ride up the mound,
Ride round,
You'll see him on a moonlit night,
Ride up the mound,
Ride round.

Crafty were the mortal men,
Their homes they would not depart,
Iron Staves about their den,
To drive away the grim Svart.

But The Rowan King, he knew all,
And cried out when he saw man's keep,
"When your Iron Stalks do fall,
A grim harvest shall I reap."

Ride up the mound,
Ride round,
Ride up the mound,
Ride round,
You'll see him on a moonlit night,
Ride up the mound,
Ride round.

Threads of Shadow

October 1924

1.
Benedict's Story

Doctor Benedict Mogfadian thinks back – back over the river of his life – back over the events that led him to this moment. His moment of ultimate success.

He was born Benedict Weathers in 1826, on Magpie Lane in the little university town of Wendlelow. His mother, Ivy Weathers, a young seamstress, was unmarried, and he had never known who his father was. But this was one of the lesser scandals that surrounded the boy's youth.

He lived most of his early life in the house of his married aunt, Abigail Baker, just three doors down from his mother's home. It was an unusual arrangement, but at that age, Benedict had not thought it so – it was all he had ever known. There had been a time when his mother had lived with them, but that was when he was too young to remember.

It is not to be supposed that Ivy Weathers had abandoned her son, or even that she did not care for him. The truth was that the woman doted on the child, visiting her sister every day and spending many hours in the company of her little prince.

It was not until he was old enough to play out in the street with other children that he learned his situation was considered unconventional.

He made friends with a neighbour's daughter, Sybil, an energetic, imaginative girl and the de facto leader of a small group of children, who ran, screamed and charged about Magpie Lane as though it were their private playground.

Sybil had taken him under her wing the first day his aunt had led him out onto the street, telling him he was "old enough to be out getting fresh air, and not under my feet when I've jobs that need seeing to".

He had stood alone outside the front door, uncertain of what to do. His mother had made little attempt to socialise with the other neighbours, considering them her inferiors; so, as a result, Benedict knew no one his age and had no playmates. If it were left to her, Ivy Weathers would never have allowed her son to play with this "riff-raff" at all. She would have been delighted to have kept Benedict confined to her sister's home.

But as he got older, she had to work more, and so he had spent more time in just his aunt's company – and that lady was not inclined to isolate him.

He remembered that day so well: standing there, the hot sun on his face, people walking past, and horse and carts rumbling down the cobbled street. Women sat on the front steps of their homes, scrubbing dirty clothes on washboards, whilst shouting and laughing with each other. Farther down the street, a group of larger boys were kicking a tightly wadded ball of cloth about, yelling and pushing, fighting over the dirty bundle as if it contained a treasure beyond value.

That day, no one was at his side. There was no one to hold his hand or tell him what to do. It was his first real taste of freedom, and it was terrifying.

One of his aunt's instructions to him had been, "Go out and make friends." The other had been, "Keep an eye out when crossing the street." This latter was a task he'd been set before and he was proud of the fact that he was very good at it.

But the 'make friends' part was confusing. Who should he make friends with? Those larger boys with the raggedy ball? Surely not. The old woman sitting on a stool by her front door, smoking a clay pipe and messing with a basket of wool? No, not her, either.

And how did one 'make friends' anyway?

It is possible he might have spent all day there, watching the goings-on and trying to build up the courage to take a few faltering steps away from the supposed security of the front door. Fortunately, someone came over and spoke to him.

"You're Benedict, ain't ya?" The person addressing him was about his height; she wore a white cotton bonnet, and a dress which, like his own clothes, was clean but much patched and mended.

"Yes," Benedict said uncertainly. Behind her, a group of children, both boys and girls, watched the exchange with clear interest.

"I'm Sybil." The little girl put out her hand in a formal manner. Benedict shook it, feeling frightfully grown-up.

"Do you want to come and play with us?" she asked.

Benedict nodded shyly, so Sybil grabbed him by the wrist and marched him over to the crowd of small, curious faces.

And so it was that Benedict had friendship thrust upon him, and he was most glad of it.

It had been a wonderful day – once his initial nervousness had died down – they had chased one another and played at being the King's soldiers. In fact, Benedict could not remember ever being so happy before in all his life.

He later learned that Sybil lived two doors up on the other side of the street. Her mother was friends with his aunt, who had asked Sybil to look out for him.

At first, their play was restricted. They were not allowed to wander out of sight of their front doors; but slowly the group of children – who numbered five in total and consisted of two girls and three boys – had learned that they could stray farther than that, even going as far as to wander into the neighbouring street. Their families were either at work or too busy about the home to keep a constant eye on them.

They made a sort of base – or headquarters, as Sybil called it – in a little alcove in an alley. They piled up wooden crates to hide the area away from prying eyes. Here they told each other wonderful stories and laid out exciting plans for the day.

They went to war with the children from a neighbouring street. Each side stole rotten eggs and threw them at each other until some nosy adult had forced a truce by chasing the warring factions away.

Sybil and Benedict became very close. She said they were best friends. But Benedict had been told repeatedly by his mother that she was his best friend, so he was careful never to refer to his little chum that way.

"Why do you live with your aunty and not your mam?" Sybil asked one day. They were all sitting together in a circle in their little den in the alley. One of their group, Bobby, had found a way to attach some old sacking to some rusted nails sticking out of the wall, draping the other end over the crates and resting old house bricks on them to keep them in place, creating a sort of shelter.

"I always have," said Benedict. "Why'd you wanna know?"

"It's odd, is all," Sybil said. "We all live with our mams and dads. I asked me ma, but she didn't know."

"Bobby don't. He lives with his grandma," Benedict replied, pleased to have spotted a hole in his friend's argument.

"Yeah, but Bobby's parents are dead. His grandma's all he's got," Sybil replied. "I've never even seen ya visit ya mam's house. Have ya ever even stepped inside it?"

Benedict didn't reply immediately, mainly because he did not know the answer. It had always been that way. At first, he had assumed that this was how all families lived. It was only when he got some friends that he realised his situation was far from usual.

It was also true that he never entered his mother's home. Again, he did not know the reason for this, except that the few times he had come close to the house, he had felt extremely unsteady and just a little sick – like he did when he spent too long spinning around in one place.

"I'm not sure, but whenever I go near it I feel bad," Benedict explained.

"Ain't nothing wrong with your ma's house. I walk past it every day," Bobby said.

"Well, if I go near it, I get sick."

"What rot! My grandma says your mam's just sick of the sight of you," Bobby sneered, in a tone that said he was spoiling for a fight.

Benedict was a little shocked to find that other people had been talking about him and his mother and saying such nasty things.

"She don't want ya in the house. Ya mam never wanted ya at all, 'cause ya da' were a wrong'un," Bobby baited. Over the last few days, the larger boy had started to exert his influence over the group of friends, using his size and forceful personality to threaten Sybil's leadership.

"Liar!" Benedict lunged at Bobby, and a struggle ensued. Bobby, however, was easily the strongest, and he soon had Benedict in a painful armlock. He pushed Benedict out of the gang's den into the alley, with the rest of the group following behind.

"Bobby, stop it," Sybil snapped, trying to impose her authority, but Bobby was not intimidated. Ignoring the girl, he marched his small captive, who was struggling like a fish on a line, out of the alley and into Magpie Lane.

"I'll prove ya lying," Bobby said, pushing Benedict in the direction of his mother's house.

"Ger off," Benedict increased his struggles as he saw the direction his captor was pushing him. He was genuinely anxious, and slightly ashamed that Sybil and the others should see him like this. Tears stung the corners of his eyes.

His mother's front door loomed before him, like a waiting beast. Step by step they drew closer. It was not long before he could make out the strange mark burned into the doors – a Witch-brand, his aunt called it.

Benedict tried to comprehend what was happening. He and Bobby had never been exactly close, but he had never believed the boy disliked him. He did not understand that he was merely a victim of Bobby's power play – a way for him to undermine Sybil without directly confronting the girl.

"Maybe it ain't the fact your mam's disowned you, maybe it's the magic mark you don't like. Is that it? You really some kind o' monster?"

Benedict was feeling worse by the minute.

"Granma says witches and warlocks can't abide the touch of a Witch-brand," Bobby snarled, fighting to keep hold of a now desperate Benedict. "So I reckon I can prove ya a bad'un."

By now they were almost touching the door. Sybil was shouting at Bobby to stop. Some grown-ups were making their way over to see what the fuss was about. Rough hands pushed his face towards the charred wood. Waves of nausea passed over him. There was a burning sensation where his cheek nearly touched the door.

"Oi, leave that boy be," came a man's voice from somewhere behind them.

Then there was darkness.

When he came to, he was in the middle of the street. He rolled over. Bobby was crouched a few feet away, a shocked look on his face, a bloody scratch running down his left cheek.

"Did you see his eyes? His face?" someone in the crowd asked.

"He ain't right." Another voice.

"Freak!" Bobby said, scrabbling to his feet, pointing an accusing finger at Benedict.

The general murmuring of the crowd was grim. Benedict looked about and caught Sybil's eye, and held out a hand to his friend, but the girl looked at him as though he both horrified and repulsed her, then turned and ran away.

It was a tearful, scared Benedict that banged on the door to his aunt's house, and when she finally answered, he threw himself into the woman's arms.

*

Benedict's friends did not call for him again, and he did not leave the house over the coming days. Folks banged on the door, or shouted insults from the street. There was much discussion between his aunt and his mother, and finally, his mam came to speak to him, tears in her eyes.

"Benedict, your father is a very powerful man with lots of friends. One of those friends is rich, and he will be coming in a few days to take you to his big house. You'll like it there."

"Will you be coming too?" came the sniffled reply.

His mother shook her head sadly.

It was a few days later that an elegant carriage pulled up outside his aunt's house. A tall man emerged, dressed in fine black clothes, carrying a dark stick with a golden orb on top. Benedict was not good with ages, but he could tell that the man was older than his mother by the flecks of grey in his hair.

The stranger knocked on the front door and was admitted and introduced to Benedict as Sir Charles Mogfadian. Within the hour, Benedict's few belongings were stowed in a trunk on the back of the carriage, his goodbyes were said, and he was trundling away, out of Wendlelow along the country roads, all the time sobbing bitterly.

His new guardian sat silently beside him.

He was taken south to live in the Cotswolds, in a place called Puddlebury Manor – a grand house on a large estate.

He went from spending days in idle play to long hours of work. He was educated. First, he was taught to speak properly, though he had never known there was an improper way to talk. He spent long hours trying to shed his Shropshire accent and adopt the more refined speech of his guardian. When he achieved this, he was taught to read and write. Then he was taught the principles of mathematics and something Sir Charles referred to as The Art. This seemed to involve a lot of chanting and the mixing of noxious brews in vast arrays of complicated glass structures.

Years passed at Puddlebury Manor and he grew older; secrets were divulged to him, the greatest of which was the identity of his father.

He was the son of Alberic, The Rowan King, Lord of all the Fair Folk – his lineage was both feared and revered.

"You are a young man of two worlds – your father's and mother's," Sir Charles had said, rolling his r's in that way that so fascinated the boy. "One of the gifts of your heritage will be a long life; you will not age as others do. This will be both an advantage and an occasional call to despair. From your mother, you inherited her freedom. You will not be bound like those from your father's side, but free to walk about this world, free to perform a great duty – one that lies outside even my ability."

Years passed, and Benedict still retained his boyish looks. Whenever his aunt or mother visited, he was astounded to see how much older they looked. He learned to gauge the true passage of time this way.

Sir Charles was a great swordsman and taught the boy to fence in order to keep him fit and sharp, and give him a way to defend himself.

He also divulged the secret of the blackthorn cane he carried everywhere with him.

Finally, in 1856, after many years, his guardian announced that he was ready to attend university.

"You look old enough, just about," the man declared one fine summer's day as they walked about the grounds of Puddlebury Manor. "You are certainly clever enough. There are a great many places you might go to be educated, but I have settled upon Cambridge. Though Wendlelow is closer, you have history in that town, so yes, I think Cambridge the safer option."

So it was that Benedict found himself at that great institution at the start of the autumn term.

That first year was a golden period in his life. He made friends. He excelled in his lessons. He fell in love.

Her name was Margaret. She was the chestnut-haired daughter of a local innkeeper – a pretty girl; she might have had the choice of a dozen young suitors, but she had chosen him. They would walk arm in arm along the river – on those days when his lessons permitted – watching the boats glide by, or go picnicking in the fields outside the town. Benedict's allowance was considerable, and he was more than happy to spoil the girl.

He began to imagine a life with her at Puddlebury Manor, of which the childless Sir Charles had made him an heir. Margaret was an intelligent girl; she could aid him in his great work – that sombre duty laid upon him by dint of his birth.

So he decided to ask Margaret to wed. He invested a large portion of his money in a ring – a fine object, topped with a single jewel, dazzling, like a tiny star plucked from the night's sky and set in a band of gold. He would propose the following week, when there was to be a break in tuition; it gave him the perfect opportunity to plan something special.

He would never forget that day.

He had told Margaret that he would be travelling out of town for the half-term, back to Puddlebury Manor to see his guardian.

Boldly, he made his way to Margaret's home, the precious ring carefully concealed in his pocket, walking with a light step. He had hired a boat, stowed a hamper of food and wine aboard it. He would row them down the river, out of the town, find some secluded inlet, where they could go ashore and dine in a meadow, beneath the sky's blue roof, accompanied by an orchestra of birdsong. Then, as they lay in each other's arms, he would produce the ring and prove his devotion to her.

It was a busy day at her father's inn, filled with the many students celebrating the end of term. He could not see Margaret at the bar but was certain that she would be working that day. He looked about the room, almost missing her at first.

When he finally spotted her, his heart plummeted. He felt as though he had been punched in the stomach by a champion pugilist.

Margaret was in the corner of the inn, close to the fireplace. She was sitting on another man's knee, arms wrapped about his neck and kissing him.

At first she did not notice his presence, so captivated was she with her new beau. But when she finally separated from the embrace and turned and caught sight of him, a look of shock quickly replaced the contented smile she had been wearing.

Benedict realised that the young man upon whose knee she was perched, whose lips she had been kissing, and whose arms were holding her as possessively as he might a chest of gold, was a certain Percy Pulverton – the rich, handsome son of a lord from the county of Sussex, and a notorious rake. Percy clearly saw him and smirked. Margaret made to rise, but the young noble held her in place.

Benedict turned, red-faced, devastated, and staggered out into the street, vaguely aware of laughter behind him.

No one could have possibly felt sorrier for Benedict than he did, being shamed in public like that. Fighting tears, he dashed to the small boat he'd hired and rowed off down the river and out of that cursed town. In his misery, he might have rowed forever – rowed until the river met the sea, and then continued out into the dark ocean, to be dragged away from it all on uncaring currents.

But he did not.

He stayed out on the water until he exhausted himself, both physically and emotionally, and finally, returning to shore, he curled up in a broken-hearted heap on the grass.

There he lay for hours, eyes closed, feeling the kiss of the sun on his skin and the gentle tickle of insects wandering across his hands and face, never caring enough to brush them away.

Eventually, the hurt gave way to anger. He stood, squared his shoulders. A cold bitterness took hold of his innermost self. He took the expensive engagement ring and threw it out into the swirling waters. Then he boarded the small boat and made his way back to the set of rooms he rented above a chandler's shop.

From that point onwards, he threw himself into his work. He had been a fool to put something so precious as his heart in the hands of another, and he would never do so again. Instead, let him focus on making a success of his life; let Margaret see what a dynamic individual she had so foolishly cast aside.

Let her regret. Not him.

As his time at Cambridge progressed, he became less sociable with his peers, spending more time on his own, striving for his qualifications. Regular correspondence with his benefactor at Puddlebury Manor had led him to the conclusion that he was far above the Margarets of this world. Indeed, he was the son of a great being, so even the likes of Percy Pulverton were lesser than he. What had he been thinking? He did not need the love or even the friendship of these people.

One day, he learned that Margaret had been abandoned by Percy Pulverton after she had fallen pregnant, and was sent to live with an aunt up north. That was the last he ever heard of her.

In 1859, he finally finished his time within Cambridge University's age-worn halls, leaving with a doctorate and returning to Puddlebury Manor. Years passed. In 1871, his mother died, followed shortly after by his aunt; he lost contact with the remainder of his relatives in Wendlelow. Sir Charles continued to school him in The Art Magick, preparing him for the great task that lay before him. It would not be easy; not only must his skills in the Art be exemplary, but he must locate two items, both very ancient, both very powerful. One lost to history, the other locked away in a place he could not go.

The two men turned their attention to trying to locate the item that had been lost, and slowly, like hounds tracking some elusive prey, they began to pick up its scent, uncovering, through much research, tempting clues as to its whereabouts.

By then, Sir Charles was a very old man, and his health was failing.

He reminded Benedict that he had named him his heir, and as such, all his property, land, and wealth would be passed to him. This he was to use in the pursuit of the great cause. He would also come into possession of Puddlebury Manor's great library, with its many esoteric books, and old stuffed crocodile, which hung from the ceiling in the centre of the room – an item the old man seemed to have genuine affection for and had always referred to as his Little Dragon.

Sir Charles passed in the winter of 1876, at the grand old age of ninety-four, his only regret not seeing the task he had laboured so long towards completed.

The old man had been a great force in Benedict's life, rewarding him with not only an education, but also an estate.

And yet, something was still lacking, and he knew what it was. 'Weathers' was, he felt, a peasant's name. The Weathers of this world were common labourers – they were men who were mocked by ladies, or else discarded in favour of more affluent individuals.

So, he took his benefactor's full name and thus became Benedict Mogfadian, and adopted his impressive and mysterious style. He wore the dark suit and the short cape, carried the blackthorn walking stick, and donned the stovepipe hat whenever he was out and about.

He thought back to the first day of his transition, admiring himself before the mirror. Apprentice no longer, he was now the master.

But there was still something missing. It was the gravitas that came with age. He still looked quite young. He decided that what he needed was a beard to command respect, and so he grew and sculpted his facial hair into a short, pointed goatee.

Over the years, he took lovers and made acquaintances, but never for long. Well aware that he was ageing at a much slower rate than those around him, he was forced to frequently cut ties with people, lest they start to ask uncomfortable questions.

As the decades receded, and he continued his work towards his ultimate goal, he learned that more than just two items would be required for its attainment, and other conditions must also be satisfied.

By 1906 he had moved back to Wendlelow, using his substantial capital to buy a lavishly appointed home in Witchley Street, near the centre of town.

Now he faced another problem. When his mother passed away, she should have arranged for his father's gift to be returned. Unfortunately, his father had abandoned her as she aged, and the bitter woman had taken up with a drayman. Though they had never wed, they had children together – and these brats had held on to the precious item, naming it a family heirloom. It remained locked in the family home, sealed behind a Witch-brand-marked door that he could not even knock upon, let alone enter.

The object was Olwyn-Cysgod – a spell-wrought spinning wheel – so tantalisingly close, yet just out of his reach.

To solve this problem, he hired a servant – a large former soldier by the name of Jenkins. The year was 1908, and he had been in the process of planning an audacious robbery when that red-headed busybody, Elspeth Mc-something-or-other, and her skinny assistant stuck their noses in. They had been hanging around his mother's old home, asking questions about the heirloom.

He feared their intentions.

Did they plan to snatch the spinning wheel from under his nose?

He had Jenkins keep the house under surveillance.

That first night, his servant rushed home with a fantastic story: the Witch-brand was gone, scoured from the door by the scrawny young man. The woman and the decrepit old crone had fled the property, rightly fearing the wrath of his father's agents.

Certain this was a precursor to an attempt on the spinning wheel, he had acted quickly, hurrying to Magpie Lane. By the time they arrived, all was quiet – the excitement had died down and the good folk of Wendlelow had found their beds. The locked door proved no obstacle to a man of Jenkins' talents, who, prior to his time in the military, had led a colourful life.

Once open, it was a simple matter to locate the spinning wheel. It was too large an item to hide away, and sat in the corner of a room, a strange prize, there for the taking – but heavy, too heavy for even Jenkins to move on his own, being a substantial thing of bronze. Fortunately, with the Witch-brand gone, Dr Mogfadian could enter the property without suffering any ill effects. Between them, the two men were able to get the thing out of the house and load it onto a waiting cart.

Securely locked away in a cupboard beneath the stairs at Witchley Street, Dr Mogfadian finally felt he had taken the first of many steps on the road to success.

Then Jenkins died. The man had been a great asset to him and, better still, had been a good friend to his young niece Julie – watching the girl and treating her like a daughter. But he had been foolish, and worse, inquisitive – a trait carried over from his colourful life before the military – always messing with things, always poking his nose into places it did not belong, always wanting to know why, never taking him at his word. One morning a distraught Julie had discovered him dead on the floor of his laboratory.

He could not risk an investigation into the man's death, nor did he want the authorities snooping around his property, so, securing Julie's silence on the matter with an effective combination of threats and promises, he had secretly buried the man's body in the back garden. Then he had given the little plot to his niece to turn into a rose garden. The roses that grew there were some of the finest in the neighbourhood, and it amused him to think of the buried thing that helped sustain them – the finest compost ever to be put to use.

For the next few years, he did not hire another man, his only servants being two disagreeable old women who cooked and cleaned for him.

He remembered when he had first hired Casper Trenchton – the year had been 1921. He had learned of a young man residing in the town with all the necessary traits he could desire in a manservant: an individual slow of wit, one over whom he could lord his intellect – a man dependent on him for his peace of mind.

He had sought him out and made him an offer that he could not turn down.

He was aware that Casper did not necessarily like him, or, for that matter, even his niece. But that did not bother him. What mattered was the man's reliance upon him for the medication which eased his melancholic mood. This made him compliant. In fact, the man's dislike of Julie could be seen as an advantage; it meant that he personally remained the greatest influence in the big fellow's life.

Eventually, he had managed to pick up the trail of the last item he required: a torc – very ancient, very powerful, and very dangerous.

A year after he had employed Casper, he learned of a Mr Todhumer, who worked at Wendlelow University and had a strange tale to tell. He was able to contact him and listened to the man's intriguing story.

According to Todhumer, some years ago there had been a frightful disturbance at that noble centre of learning, followed by the death of his employer, a man by the name of Professor Wainwright. These events seemed to have been prompted by the discovery of a golden torc, found locked away in a box in the bowels of that ancient institution.

Better still, Mr Todhumer claimed he knew what had happened to the torc. According to him, it had been carried out of the university by a group of fearful academics, taken from the town and thrown into a small pool by a farm, just a short journey away.

Obtaining the name of the farm and its location from the willing contact was the work of a moment, and before the week was out, he was able to visit there – a place called Wych Hollow. He had managed to convince the owner, a certain Amos Lunkerton that the land beneath the pool could be put to good use and had offered to bankroll its drainage in exchange for the first claim on any items the farmer uncovered during the work.

There had been problems. It was some sort of universal law that, no matter how simple a project seemed, unforeseen problems must always arise. But Dr Mogfadian was resourceful, and these difficulties were of little concern to him. Soon, he had the torc in his possession and could prepare the final stages of his plan.

He approached a group of investors and building contractors in 1924 and offered to put the lion's share of the capital into the housing project at the edge of a little village called Carchar Haearn. This would see the construction of new affordable housing built for labourers and their families.

The project had eventually fallen through, and both he and the other investors had lost a packet. Outwardly, he was devastated at the financial disaster; inwardly, he was over the moon. For him, at least, the whole thing had been a roaring success.

For his true aim had never been to create and sell homes, but to remove a portion of the iron staves that surrounded the village – and which local folklore said protected it from dark magic and dangerous entities.

His father was imprisoned, contained in a hidden realm, by an ancient magic, woven by men who were wise in such things, at the behest of the Saxon Lord Wendle, many centuries ago, after years of harassing the lord and his subjects.

But at certain times, the power of these binding enchantments would weaken – usually when the moon was fat, or on nights of great power, such as Midsummer and Halloween. Then he and his minions might ride forth.

One of the entrances to his enchanted prison was located in a mound close to Carchar Haearn. Knowing the danger their community faced, the local people had surrounded their village with iron staves, for none of the fair folk can abide the touch of iron. So he was prevented from entering the little village, and from harming or enslaving the poor folk who lived there.

But now, his father was free to ride into Carchar Haearn and do as he wished, and Doctor Mogfadian could go there himself, unhindered by nosy locals, to access the village green and the ancient granite slab at its centre – an ancient, sacred place essential to the success of his plan.

He had waited patiently for the night of Halloween – that potent date in the magician's calendar.

And now that day had come, this very evening, his great task would be completed. He would use the torc and the bronze spinning wheel, along with carefully selected spells, to break the bindings that kept his father imprisoned in the hidden realm. Finally released, his father would once more be free to roam the world, to enact revenge on the people of Wendlelow, whose lord had confined him so many years ago.

There was only one thing he had not accounted for.

Casper and Julie had become friends.

2.
Casper's Story

It was the afternoon of the 31st October 1924. Casper was finally satisfied with his lot in life. He had, a long time ago, come to terms with the fact that he would not marry, and would sire no children, at least not in wedlock. He would live a life untrumpeted in the pages of history, without even a footnote in its book to record his name.

He did not care.

He had found peace; yes, it was a chemical peace, brought on by the potions of Doctor Mogfadian, but he would gladly take that over the gut-twisting attacks of nerves and the seemingly never-ending sleepless nights. He even felt like he had a family of sorts, as in Julie he had found someone he looked on as a sister, someone to watch out for, someone who gave him a sense of purpose.

He escorted her about town and helped with her daily duties at the antiques shop she ran. In fact, he probably spent more time in her company than he did his employer's.

As he walked down the street, towards Doctor Mogfadian's home – where he lived in a room on the upper floor – he thought back, back to that fateful night years before, the night he had first met the doctor, the night his life had finally changed for the better.

It had been a week after the demise of his father, and Casper's mood had sunk to a dramatic all-time low – quite an achievement, even for him. It wasn't that he had been particularly close to his father; the man was a bully, and after that fateful night at his boarding school, which had left his nerves shattered like glass, he had only grown more distant – seemingly adding embarrassment to the list of grievances he held towards his son.

So it had surprised him just how hard he had taken his father's passing. Perhaps it was the loss of a connection; Casper's father had been his last living relative. Combined with the removal of his final safety net – though a cold man, he had never left his son wanting, providing small amounts of money for the frequently unemployed Casper.

He had now taken up residence in Wendlelow, a small university town in Shropshire. A place he had enjoyed visiting with his mother when he was younger, and she was still alive – a place he held affection for.

He had been leaning against a wall, drunk. Alcohol had a way of easing his melancholy state – at least for a short time. When the realisation struck him: he would never speak to his father again. Never have the chance to settle their differences. But what bothered him most was the idea that he would never have the opportunity to make him proud.

His back slid down the rough brickwork until he was hunched over on his knees, letting out a cannonade of pitiful sobs, clutching at his hair with his fists.

"You look to me like a fellow who is down on his luck."

Casper looked up, suddenly embarrassed and angry at being discovered in this state. He resisted the urge to scramble to his feet and punch the individual on the nose – the last thing he needed was to be arrested for being drunk and disorderly. He had no job at the moment, and few funds; if he were forced to pay bail, it would leave him with insufficient money for this month's rent.

"What do you care?" he muttered instead.

The man ignored his question. "I would say that you are a fellow with few disposable funds, very probably no job, and a mind greatly troubled by sorrows – possibly regrets."

Casper just stared at him. The man was dressed as though he were returning from dinner at a fashionable gentleman's club, replete with top hat and cane.

"I'm looking to hire a man. I've been asking around town – your name was mentioned a few times as a chap possessing all the necessary talents I require."

"Really," Casper said dryly.

"In short," the man added, "a strong, capable fellow, and just the sort of individual who could use my help. In fact, you might say I am in a unique position to provide all you need. My name is Doctor Benedict Mogfadian."

He thrust a white-gloved hand forward. Curious by now, Casper grabbed the man's hand. But instead of shaking it in greeting, he used it to pull himself to his feet, nearly toppling the smaller man over in the process.

"I have just the thing for a man with an unsettled mind," Doctor Mogfadian declared, letting go of Casper's hand and wiping his own on his trouser leg.

Drunk, desperate, and more than a little tempted, he agreed to follow the man to his home, where the doctor had provided him with what he had referred to as a potion. A milky liquid in a thin glass bottle, with a chalky taste that was unpleasant on the tongue.

That little flask changed the course of his life forever. After feeling its effects, it had taken little convincing for him to accept a position in the doctor's home.

His role was difficult to describe. The doctor saw him as a helper. Casper saw himself more as hired muscle, and general dogsbody. His father would have been ashamed of the job, but Casper, now free of that 'gentleman's' judgement, decided that he couldn't care less. The doctor fed him, gave him a roof over his head, and most important of all, supplied him with that mind-easing tonic that had finally made his life bearable.

One of his many duties was to escort the man's niece Julie about town or stay with her whilst she worked at the antiques shop – which her uncle had bought on her behalf, a project intended to keep her occupied and out of trouble.

For the longest time, the woman had grated on his nerves with her boyish affectations and the way she was protected from life's many trials by her wealthy guardian. She had no idea how fortunate she was.

She was engaged to a fairly powerful man, though Casper had never met him. He was, by all accounts, away in some far-off land, going about his business – though what that business was, Casper had yet to learn.

The doctor had explained that one of his roles, when accompanying Julie, was to keep any potential suitors away. He had done this on more than one occasion, always without her realising it. Usually, just having a quiet word with the gentleman in question down an alley and out of sight and earshot of Wendlelow's general population.

Gradually, his dislike for Julie had lessened, until finally they had become friends, and he had started to regard her with a sort of brotherly affection.

In fact, she might be one of the few friends he had left. He seldom saw Ewan Baughan, now Lord Baughan – a title he had inherited following the death of his older brother. The man was simply too busy with his estate these days.

He found himself talking with Julie in a way he could not remember having done with anyone else. She was one of the few people who saw him as more than just a hired thug.

When he arrived at the house on Witchley Street, he was surprised by how quiet it seemed. Both Julie and her uncle should have been about, since the night before,

Doctor Mogfadian had dramatically announced that this day would be a day of great importance. Julie need not open the antiques shop, and he had several errands, of a most vital nature, for Casper to complete.

However, when his tasks were explained, they proved to be yawningly mundane, and worse still, extremely time-consuming.

Casper knocked on the door of the doctor's study. There was no answer. Trying the latch, it proved to be unlocked, so he opened it and peered inside.

No one was there.

He decided to check the doctor's laboratory in the basement, but aside from Archimedes, the stuffed crocodile suspended from the ceiling, the room was vacant.

Casper became concerned, though he couldn't put his finger on exactly why he should feel that way. He had, after all, returned to unoccupied houses before without worry about those who lived there. But there was something about the doctor's manner that morning – a shiftiness, a restlessness. And Julie's demeanour over the past couple of weeks, a certain fatalism, that portended trouble.

He knew that the relationship between herself and her uncle had become strained lately. Julie held the man responsible for the death of her friend, something Casper felt she might very well be justified in doing. Though the doctor had not directly confessed to anything, neither had he made any serious attempt to deny it.

The nature of the mundane tasks Doctor Mogfadian had laid out for him that morning were also of concern, since they had not seemed urgent at the time, and could have waited a day or two. Usually, when he had been assigned such tasks in the past and dispatched in such a hurried fashion, it was because the doctor wished him out of the way for some reason.

Casper checked all the lower rooms before bounding upstairs and rapping urgently on Julie's door.

There was no reply.

He knocked a second time, but still, nothing.

Carefully, he turned the handle and peered inside.

No one was there, save for a small rag doll that lay propped on the pillow of the woman's bed, a tatty, much-loved thing; he knew she called it Molly.

Closing the door, he made his way about the upper floor, looking in every room. And though he understood that no one was there, the knocking and the opening and closing of doors became a ritual, a series of manoeuvres to be performed before any serious decisions needed to be considered.

When he entered his room he noticed a letter had been pushed beneath the door. Casper had a vision of desperate hands, so scared of discovery that they dared not even risk the noise of the ancient hinges.

He sat on the bed, gazing at the envelope and recognised the handwriting.

Dear Casper,

Help me, please. I have wanted to write this letter for so long, for surely you are one of the few people whom I can trust and who is capable of opposing his plan. I must be swift, for I do not know how long I will have to write this missive.

The day has come, the day I am to be taken to wed my fiancé, a day I have dreaded all my life. For my betrothed is no mortal man, but a being of dark origins.

Benedict promised me to this terrifying entity when I was just a girl, using eldritch forces to bind me to him – the same forces that have bound me all these many years to Benedict, never allowing me to stray too far from him. A sinister power that has held my tongue firm, preventing me from speaking of these things. But I can write, just – though it is hard, so hard to put pen to paper, to denounce that old badger. Like trying to write when your hand is being held firmly by another.

It did indeed seem to Casper that the writing was forced. Julie's penmanship – normally so precise and neat – was very poor, as if she were fighting against something that sought to restrain her. In places, she had scratched so deeply into the paper that it was nearly ripped.

I could have sent this letter to Nolan or any other member of the MSLM, but I have delayed too long; only now have I built up the reserves of strength required to do this, and now it is nearly too late. You are my only hope, the one person I can get a letter to. One of the few people who might actually believe what I am about to tell you.

Benedict is not any normal human, not like you or me; he is the son of an ancient Fairy Lord, called The Rowan King.

The very being to whom I am engaged.

And today, this very Halloween, he seeks to release this terrible king from his centuries-old imprisonment. For years he has been researching and gathering all the things he needs in order to achieve this task. A golden torc, a bronze spinning wheel called Olwyn Cysgod – The Shadow Wheel – as well as various spells and rites that must be performed in order to weaken the bonds that bind his father.

The final piece in this supernatural jigsaw puzzle was put in place when he gained access to the area where the ritual must be performed: a stone slab – on which the old spinning wheel must be positioned – located in an abandoned village called Carchar Haearn. This little hamlet sits by an old mound crowned by standing stones, one of the main entrances to his father's prison. He contrived a way to remove some of the iron poles that surround the village, fortifying it from The Rowan King and his minions. Now the village is abandoned; I do not know the fate of its poor occupants, but I fear not all fled in time to avoid the wrath of the unseelie lord.

Beware of Benedict. He is older than he looks – perhaps nearly a century old. He is cunning too; but worse, he has proved himself willing to commit murder in order to see his task completed. I am essential to his plan, and as he has bound my mind with chains of enchantment, there is little I can do to disobey him. Thank God he is so distracted with preparations; else I would never have time to craft this letter.

Go to my friend, Nolan Perkins, at the university library. Get his help. He is clever and may well know a way to free me from my bonds and prevent Benedict from releasing this terrible being on an unsuspecting world. For I must tell you, I fear what The Rowan King will do when freed. I have no doubt that vengeance is foremost in his mind – vengeance against mankind for the imprisonment of him and his people. I dread to imagine what havoc he will wreak upon the land.

Find me at Carchar Haearn.

Your friend,
Julie.

Casper stared at the letter in his hand, his mind whirling. Life with Doctor Mogfadian had been strange; he had experienced many odd things during his time in the man's service and so, however much he wanted to, he could not believe that this was some Halloween trick being perpetrated upon him.

This meant he had a decision to make.

If he opposed the doctor, it would mean an end to their relationship. He would be denied access to the doctor's potions – the one that kept his pensive unhappiness at bay. He would return to the way he had been all those years ago. The dark moods, the terrible thoughts. A fine cowardice gripped him.

No, I have already failed one woman I cared for. I will not fail another, he thought.

He walked over to the fireplace and snatched up his military sabre. Concealing the weapon beneath his greatcoat, he strode from the room.

Wendlelow University was quiet as he approached its iron-studded doors. He stopped before them, willing himself to enter, but pride chained him to the spot. He had not spoken to that little prig, Perkins, in over two decades.

He was aware that the man lived and worked in the same town as he; it was one of those strange twists of fate that had seen them drawn within each other's orbits, and a constant act of will on his part to ensure that their paths never crossed.

He had never gone to any of the meetings the man held – and that Julie attended – always brushing off any attempts by her to entice him in, instead spending the night drinking coffee or tea in the public house over the road. He had long ago sworn off alcohol, as Doctor Mogfadian believed the stuff would dilute his medication's effectiveness.

He knew something of Nolan's personal life. He was married to a mute woman from town, and they had one child named Thomas.

As boys, he and Nolan had never really got on. They had been too different. Casper was strong, interested in sports, and – at least during their time at Toadstone School – had plenty of friends.

Nolan, for his part, had been quiet, studious, and a little distant. He had been one of the boys present on the night Casper had experienced his fit – the one that had broken his mind and left him the ragged, tatter of a man he was today. Nolan had been there when the doctors carried him off. He had borne witness to his moment of greatest shame, and now Casper had to ask for his help.

The day after that dreadful night, he had been taken home, but neither his father nor the servants knew how to help the distressed boy. A doctor had been called for and diagnosed a fever of the brain, possibly brought on by overwork, but when, after several weeks of rest, he still hadn't recovered, that same doctor recommended the boy be confined to an asylum.

This had brought on the darkest period of his life – an era spent in and out of such grim institutions, hauling with him the weights of shame and hopelessness that he'd continued to bear throughout his life.

Finally, he had been released for the last time and sent to stay with Ewan Baughan, at his family seat.

He had learned one valuable lesson in all those horrible years.

Hide your feelings.

Bury them deep; only exhibit distress when alone, and behind closed doors. Do not draw attention to yourself – attention was dangerous, and likely to see a resumption of his forced care. And so, he had lived a miserable, lonely existence, until he had met Doctor Mogfadian. Until he had met Julie.

He gritted his teeth; a muscle pulsed in his jaw. Taking one deep breath, he proceeded to bound up the steps to the university entrance, taking them two at a time. He must set pride aside, for Julie's sake. He wanted to help her, but he was out of his depth. He did not even know where the village of Carchar Haearn was located.

The university library was quiet. A few people were reading at desks or walking the aisles of book-lined shelves. The room had an earthy smell that brought back memories of his father's study, as well as sitting with Ewan in Toadstone school library, worrying over a project set for him by one of his tutors – men who seemed to take pleasure in filling boys' time with that most un-boyish of activities: sitting and reading in thoughtful silence.

It also reminded him of another library, in a large house deep in the Welsh countryside – of sitting in it with a beautiful young woman he desperately wanted to please. A woman who had made him want to be a better man. A woman long dead, and dead because of him.

Despite its windows, the university library was dark, as though the books had the power to absorb light, drawing it in, leaving the place in a perpetual twilight, only broken here and there by lamps producing little pools of gold upon the tables.

He found Nolan easily. The man stood at a desk, arranging books into different piles.

"Mr Perkins," he said with little warmth.

Nolan looked up, his surprised expression at first defensive, then becoming as cold as the late autumn winds. And to think he had wondered if the man would recognise him.

"Mr Trenchton." He seemed to speak with great care. "How may I help you?"

"I'm not the one who needs help. Julie Mogfadian does – she's in trouble." Casper thrust Julie's letter at Nolan as if he were a ticket collector on a train, and it the only form of communication that was needed between them.

"Julie's in trouble?" The voice came from a table not far from where they stood. Until that moment, both men had been speaking quietly, but this new voice spoke so loudly that it earned an intolerant 'Shhhh' from someone nearby.

Casper recognised the fellow – Robert... no, Roger, that was it. At the doctor's request, he had had a little chat with the man a few weeks ago, encouraging him to think again about his familiar friendship with Julie. Casper had agreed with the doctor and had already decided to have a word with him even before he was instructed to do so.

The confrontation had taken place in a quiet side street, and had involved him pushing Roger to the floor and applying his trusty boot to the young man's side a few times. Followed by a firm warning.

Afterwards, Julie had commented on the man's absence from her life – she now only saw him at Nolan's folklore meetings. It was clear from her confusion that Roger had wisely chosen to stay silent on the subject of their private meeting.

Roger paused when he saw that it was Casper who had been speaking. After a brief period, where he seemed to wrestle with indecision, he rose from his seat and made his way over to the two men.

"It's all right, Roger. Go back to your book. I'm dealing with this," Nolan said, never taking his gaze off Casper.

"No, please, if Julie's in trouble I want to help," Roger said; this was directed at Casper and said in the soothing tone of a man trying to keep a volatile hound at ease.

Casper did not reply to him, but once more thrust Julie's letter at the head librarian, who eventually took it and read it through.

"Olwyn Cysgod, I thought that thing long gone," Nolan said. "Have you seen it?"

"No. He kept it hidden from me. Julie's letter was the first time I've heard of it," replied Casper.

"I see."

"This place, Carchar Haearn, do you know where it is?" Casper asked.

"I do." It was Roger who interjected. "I read a newspaper article about it, and I even visited the place, though it is abandoned now."

"That's right," Nolan said, "I thought I recognised the name."

"So, you will help Julie?"

"Of course we will." The question had been directed at Nolan, but it was Roger who answered. The librarian continued to look uncertain, glancing from the letter he held to Casper, as though they were back at school and this were a bully's trick designed to lure him away, out of sight of tutors and friends.

"For God's sake, Perkins, play the man," Casper hissed.

Pride stung; Nolan gave him a cold look. "I never fully trusted Julie," he admitted. "But that was not due to anything she had done. My suspicion of her always stemmed from her association with that man. I am sure he's a meddler in the black arts. She never did anything to earn that distrust."

"Then help her," Roger said.

"It would be dangerous. There is more at stake here than a woman's safety. If Julie's letter is true, then Mogfadian is seeking to release an ancient evil from imprisonment. It might be better to try to involve the police, but experience tells me that they would either not listen or be too slow to act."

Nolan scanned the letter again, finally saying, "No, there is only us… I will do what I can."

Casper felt a knot inside him unclench.

"Do what?" he asked, aware that when dealing with the unusual, it was seldom advisable to simply charge in, which would have been his preferred tactic.

"From what Julie says, it seems she has been bound by some enchantment, meaning the doctor is able to exert a certain amount of control over her. Before we do anything, we must find a way to release her from this. Wait here." So saying, Nolan strode off, vanishing into the stacks.

For ten minutes, Casper and Roger stood in awkward silence, barely acknowledging each other's existence.

When he finally returned, Nolan was carrying a large book, much worn, bound in soft, brown leather, embossed with the title, *Principales Magicae Humilis*. Sitting down, he began perusing the tome.

"A book of folk magic," he explained, then added, "I've been polishing my Latin these last few years. It helps with cataloguing some of the older books."

Casper merely grunted impatiently, mentally urging the man to hurry up, as if he could speed him in this task through willpower alone.

After what felt like an eternity, Nolan looked up.

"I think I have it," he said.

"Think?" Casper said. "Is that the best you can do?"

"I can't be certain of anything, I'm no magician. But if you know one who can help us, by all means…"

"Is there anything we can do?" Roger interjected.

"You, Roger, can go to the baker's and buy a loaf of bread. You, Casper, can add more wood to the fire and heat up a poker. I must finish reading this."

When Roger returned, Casper and Nolan were waiting for him by the fire. He walked over to the nearest table and dumped the warm loaf of bread on top of it.

Nolan produced a pocket knife and made a mess of cutting a single slice of the bread, but seemed happy enough with the result. He then cut the slice into quarters and carefully selected the best piece, which he turned over to expose the crusty side. He gestured to Casper, who walked over to the fire and drew out the poker heating there. It glowed like some torturous device from the depths of hell. Carefully, he handed it to Nolan.

By now, a great many of the library's silent readers had set aside their books and were looking over, intrigued by the trio's actions.

He looked at Roger. "Pick up that piece of bread and hold it still." Roger did so, wincing as Nolan lowered the glowing poker. There was a look of distaste on the head librarian's face, as if he had been asked to unblock a clogged sewer with his bare hands.

As Casper watched, Nolan muttered something under his breath. He did not recognise the language employed by his old school peer.

It certainly wasn't the Latin of the book he had been consulting – the language which Doctor Mogfadian employed in his rituals. It was gruffer; its jagged, craggy syllables left him with the impression that it was something ancient, something that would have been best forgotten.

Nolan wielded the poker like some huge writing instrument, burning a mark into the bread that resembled a blackened spiral with a line through it.

When he had finished, Nolan put the poker safely back into its holder and returned to the table. He knelt down to carefully examine his handiwork, peering at it with the critical eye of an artist appraising the quality of his latest creation.

"Good," he declared, sounding pleased. "Yes, very good."

He proceeded to wrap the item in a clean handkerchief.

"The magic symbol should be baked into a cake, but at a pinch this should work, though it may not be as effective." He handed the little wrapped parcel to Casper. "You must remove it from the handkerchief and put it in her mouth; it will weaken Mogfadian's grip on her. Then you should be able to lead her away, with little or no resistance."

"Does she need to swallow it, or just hold it in her mouth?" Casper asked.

"Just hold it in her mouth. Although if you can get her to swallow it, all the better."

Casper looked at the packaged thing doubtfully. "You're sure this will work, Perkins?"

"It will work for a short time," Nolan said. He sounded confident, but it was a confidence that failed to reach his eyes, which were twin pools of doubt. "I have a car. If Roger is willing to navigate, I will drive us to Carchar Haearn."

*

By the time the three men climbed into Nolan's green Morris Cowley, dusk was settling over the town. Roger sat in the back, peering between the two older men in the front seats, occasionally calling out directions.

Casper had hoped that when they left Wendlelow, Nolan would apply a turn of speed, driving in the same frantic fashion he was used to the doctor employing. But Nolan drove like a man taking his grandmother for an afternoon tour of the countryside.

"Can't you go faster?" Casper snapped, his frustration finally getting the better of him.

"It's slippery, the roads are full of wet leaves. We will be of no use to Julie if I run the car into a tree."

Casper snorted, and turned to peer out the window, grinding his teeth. An uncomfortable silence settled over the vehicle, broken only occasionally by Roger giving directions. Trees, whose leaves had been pinched into reds, browns, and oranges by the cold autumn breeze, swept past them.

Casper's sheathed sword was clasped between his knees, its tip resting on the floor. Both of his companions had paused when they had seen him pull the weapon from under his greatcoat. Roger, a recent victim of his violent outbursts, had chosen to say nothing. But Nolan had challenged him. "Casper, we are only going to bring Julie back, then we will contact the police; she can give her story to them, let them deal with her uncle. I won't be party to violence."

Casper looked the shorter man up and down, as if he were a hunting dog he was appraising for purchase. "No, I don't expect you would, would you?"

Carchar Haearn lay to the north of Wendlelow. Like the university town, it was nestled close to the Welsh border.

The car's headlights illuminated the shadowy, rolling landscape.

"We're getting closer," Roger said, sounding anxious.

"How can you tell? All these dark, hilly country roads look the same," Casper muttered.

Nolan spared Casper an awkward glance. "Do you remember?" he asked. "What happened? The last night you were at Toadstone school."

"No," Casper replied, never looking over at Nolan; he merely stared out the side window, into an area of agricultural land they were passing through.

"I was awake," Nolan said tentatively, "I saw it all."

Casper remained silent for a few seconds, a muscle in his jaw tensing and un-tensing. Finally, he replied, his voice firm. "I. Don't. Want. To. Know."

There was a peace to be found in ignorance.

They took one more turn, and the village of Carchar Haearn appeared. It was a collection of grey stone cottages, partially obscured by a thicket of metal rods the height of a man. From their present distance, they looked like toothpicks thrust into the ground. The section that had been dug up was stacked, log-like, into a large pile. To the west, there was a mound, an ancient structure, topped by primitive standing stones that resembled a crude crown.

A strange rope of light undulated from the village through the section of excavated staves, a ghostly umbilical cord, connecting the little settlement to the earthwork.

The three men looked on in silent wonder at the sight before them; an unsettling ambience hung in the air.

Once they reached the edge of the village, Nolan pulled his car over to the side of the road. Casper and Roger leapt out of the vehicle, but when Nolan made to follow, Casper leaned in the passenger door. "You stay here. Keep the engine running." His voice brooked no argument.

Nolan nodded his acceptance. "Casper, please bring her back safely."

For a moment, the two men regarded each other. Finally, the larger nodded. "I will."

*

Roger followed a few feet behind Casper as they crept down an abandoned street. Somewhere ahead of them, a voice was calling out to the night in a language that neither man recognised.

"You're sure you have that burnt bread?" Casper asked, for what might have been the third time.

"Yes." Roger put his hand into his pocket as if to reassure himself of the thing's presence.

"Then listen to me. When we find them, I want you to go to Julie, get her away from here as quickly as you can. Carry her if you must. I will deal with the doctor," Casper said.

"I will," Roger replied. Casper thought he sounded nervous, though he himself felt perfectly calm, almost unnaturally so.

"Don't wait for me," he continued. "Get her to the car, drive away. Understand?"

Casper had stopped walking; he gave the younger man a firm look while he awaited confirmation that his instructions had been understood.

Roger nodded.

At the end of the street, they turned left, clinging to the walls of an old inn; the weather-worn sign announced the place to be *The Elder Earl.*

Before them was a village green. A large packing crate had been dismantled on one side of it, and Doctor Mogfadian's Rolls-Royce Tourer was pulled up on the other.

At the centre of the grass was a granite slab, upon which Olwyn Cysgod had been placed, each of its four legs resting in cup-like divots carved into the rock. Doctor Mogfadian stood before the old bronze construction, foot slowly pumping the treadle, which in turn spun the wheel. His right hand was raised, and he was chanting in a strange-sounding language. Gossamer shadows drifted toward him. Where they touched his body, they became like dark ink, running down his left arm, becoming thinner, cloudy strings that then entwined themselves slowly around the rotating metal wheel, making it appear as though he were spinning darkness.

Finally, from this darkness floated a thin thread of shadow; it crept along the grass until it made contact with a bare, feminine foot.

Julie stood silently, her back to her uncle. She wore only a white shift that barely reached her knees; her arms were completely bare. A cold wind pressed the pale fabric close, revealing the outline of her body. About one arm was attached a golden torc. Like the fingers of a miserly man, the dark threads were drawn up her body towards this precious jewellery. Where the thin shadows made contact with it, they changed – becoming grey, then white – as if some part of the woman's purity were filtering away the blackness, until finally a glowing white strand left her body, drifting away in the direction of the mound.

Both men stared at the ancient earthwork in amazement. The glowing white cord had woven itself between the standing stones, giving its summit an eerie moon-like glow.

"Get her," Casper ordered, then shouted at the top of his voice. "MOGFADIAN."

The doctor glanced briefly in his direction but did not cease his weird craft. He had set torches about the village green, but with the illumination of the spectral cord, they were hardly needed.

"Go home, Trenchton. There is nothing here to interest you. You cannot aid me, and your presence would merely serve as a distraction from my work."

"I'm going," Casper said firmly, "but I'm taking Julie with me."

"And deprive her of her wedding day? I think not. Yonder, her future husband waits," he nodded in the direction of the mound. "Long have they waited to meet."

"I'm not going to let you hand her to anyone against her will." It was Roger who spoke.

For the first time, the doctor seemed to notice him. "Ahhh… the love-sick puppy." He chuckled. "You poor fool, do you really think she could ever truly care for you? Her husband is to be a lord, a great king, one who will wreak havoc upon this fallen land. She will be a queen, mother to princes, with the riches of his ancient court at her disposal. What can you offer her, boy? A grocery shop and a life of common toil? See? She does not even acknowledge you; she awaits the arrival of her master. My father."

It was true. Julie stared forward. Gone was her usual puckish smile, replaced instead with the haunted, slack-jawed, dream-like gaze of an opium addict. Even as they watched, part of the luminous cord just a few feet before her started to billow out, taking on a vaguely human shape.

"No. This is over, Mogfadian," Casper said, pulling his sword free and dropping its sheath to the ground. "Whatever the hell you are doing, it stops now. Roger, get Julie away from here."

Roger hurried over to the woman. The doctor growled in frustration and ceased his spinning. Almost immediately the dark strands fell away, followed by the white cord of light, then the humanoid shape faded to nothing. Darkness fell over the ancient earthwork; shadows drew in about the village green with only a few burning torches to keep them at bay.

Never taking his eyes off Casper, Doctor Mogfadian moved away from the bronze spinning wheel and bent down to retrieve his blackthorn cane from where it lay in the grass.

"This is a mistake, Trenchton. You have been a loyal servant to me. I was going to save you a place at my father's court. You would have been one of the few privileged humans." So saying, he twisted the end of the cane closest to the gold orb and pulled forth a long, thin blade. He moved to intercept Roger before the young man could reach Julie's side, but Casper put himself between the older man and the couple, giving his blade a menacing swing.

"Think twice about this. I've seen you fight. You have no finesse. You are no match for me, and I have no wish to kill you. Leave now and take the foolish boy with you," the doctor said, nodding in the direction of Roger, who was in the process of putting the branded bread in Julie's mouth.

"I don't think so," Casper said.

"No. You don't think, do you? That was always your problem. So be it." The doctor sounded almost regretful as he dropped into a fencing stance, putting his left arm behind his back.

Nolan's bread clearly had some effect, as a glance over his shoulder showed Casper that Julie had collapsed senseless into Roger's arms.

"Get her to the car. Don't wait for me," Casper said, shifting his gaze back to his opponent. Roger lifted the unconscious woman up and edged away from the green and back in the direction they had come.

With a shout, Casper rushed forward, his powerful arms swinging the sword in a great arc, like a man intent on harvesting a field of wheat. At first his smaller opponent gave ground, deftly knocking aside blows that would otherwise have split him in twain, then with cat-like quickness he counter-attacked, side-stepping a clumsy swing, flicking his thin blade toward Casper's face, his arms, his chest – each time leaving behind a thin red line of pain.

Casper dropped back, a little shocked at the man's speed. The doctor claimed to be in his fifties but moved with a youthful grace.

Allowing a brief glance behind him, he was agitated to see that Roger, laden with the unresponsive Julie, had not put as much ground between them as he would have liked.

He turned back in time to see the doctor lunging at him again. Casper fell back, desperately deflecting the carefully delivered blows, his thin curve of metal the only thing preserving his life. He felt another pain, this time in his leg, and saw a deep bloody gash had opened up there.

"Fifty my arse," Casper muttered.

If he could just get close enough to the man, get a good grip on him, he'd throttle the old weasel – or better yet, bash his brains out on the ground – but the doctor was too much the fox to be drawn nearer to his stronger, more powerfully built opponent, using the length of his swordstick to its full advantage.

Once more, they closed with each other, blades clashing. When they parted, Casper was relieved to see that he bore no additional wounds, but it had been a near engagement. He had felt the kiss of the wind from the tip of the doctor's sword just below his left eye.

"You would not oppose me if you understood the alternative. Better to be ruled by my father than the Crooked One – or worse still, the Maiden of Change," Doctor Mogfadian said, then quickly lunged at Casper again. There was another brief exchange of blows. This time, to his despair, Casper came away with a slash along his ribs. The doctor was, once again, frustratingly unharmed.

"I could take you apart, bit by bit. What is it they say – death by a thousand cuts?" the man sneered. "But I'm afraid I simply do not have the time, my good fellow."

Angered by the man's casual, cocky tone, Casper drove forward, going on the offensive, delivering blows that would have downed a shire horse, but that his opponent was too skilful to allow to land – side-stepping here, parrying there, and grinning as if he were taking part in nothing so terrible as a schoolyard game. Casper did not care. Keep that thin sliver of metal busy, close the gap, just get one hand on the man, throw him to the ground, stamp on him, the trusty old boot. He lunged again, intent on grabbing hold of the doctor's collar, but the older man danced away; at the same time his sword flashed, and Casper felt a pain in his side – another laceration to add to his bloody tattoos.

"Oh, no, you don't," Doctor Mogfadian said. He was looking past Casper, watching Roger turn a corner and disappear from view.

Realising the man was distracted, albeit briefly, Casper swiftly pressed home a desperate attack, swinging with every bit of strength his beefy arm could manage. It was a blow that he felt sure would shatter the doctor's slender blade, passing through it as though it were not there and felling its wielder instantly.

But it was not to be.

With relative ease, Doctor Mogfadian parried this mighty blow, allowing Casper's heavier blade to slide down the length of his own, then – in the very same motion – lunged forward and drove his own weapon through Casper's chest.

"I suppose I'm going to need to find a new man." He smiled a little sadly. "Now it is time to deal with your young friend and return my niece to her betrothed," he pulled his blade free and took a step backward.

At least, he tried to.

But Casper had wrapped one of his arms around the man's waist, holding him close – as close as a lover. Through his slowly greying vision, he saw the doctor's features contort in anger; his eyes morphed, becoming cat-like, the pupils dark slits of ebony, his nose and ears altering, seeming to sharpen, giving his face a cruel, demonic cast.

The older man let go of his swordstick and tried to push Casper away, but his grip was firm – his arm a band of steel, binding them together, immovable, even now, as the last of his life force seeped from his body. Doctor Mogfadian's features changed; now fear gripped his countenance.

Casper Trenchton raised his father's sword.

3.
Julie's Story

Threads of shadow, weaving their way through my life, binding me to that man – the man I hated. The man who defined me, who made me who I am. Threads that reach back in time, back to my childhood, back to that day when I was young, when he first came to the rectory.

Benedict – I shall never refer to him as uncle – is dead, and I thank the Good Lord that this is so.

Poor Casper Trenchton is also dead, and it is for him – my friend – that I weep.

Never again shall I be known as Julie Mogfadian. I am Julie Harrington, the daughter of the Reverend James

Harrington, my beloved father, murdered by that monster when I was still a child.

He had arrived at the rectory, all smiles and polite conversation, oozing charm as a snail oozes mucus – even while the blood of my father dried on his soul. He then took Miss Preece from me, murdering my tutor and nurse, and ill-using her body in some frightful nocturnal ritual, dedicated to a being I now know to be his father.

Lovely Miss Preece, who never harmed a soul, who loved me like a daughter, who – I later learned from her diary – was in love with my father. They had even been discussing marriage, and how best to let me know of their romance.

That promising future, the rector's daughter, the wonderful mother, all stolen from me by him. Of course, I nearly escaped the man's clutches. Brave Ned, our handyman, saw through the fellow. Realising that he wasn't my uncle, he tried to take me back to the safety of the local village, and there notify the authorities.

But Benedict dispatched some monstrosity to intercept us. It murdered Ned, herding me back toward the rectory, as a sheepdog might a stray lamb.

I was young then, too young to fight back, too young and too scared to use teeth and nails to defend myself. Benedict was simply too strong for me. He struck me, the only time in all the years I was with him that he did so, and that evening, as I cowered in my bedroom, cuddling my faithful doll Molly, he came for me.

It was Halloween, a night important to him and the thing he called 'father'. Before the ancient, symbol-marked oak tree that dominated the grounds of the rectory, he bound my mind and tongue with a craft he called The Art. It was a form of magic he had been taught by his own guardian, and of which he was so very proud. He offered me to The Rowan King, a future bride, burying a dowry of ancient, yellow gold beneath the roots of the tree.

The shade of my betrothed appeared in the night, so terrible I could not look upon him. He accepted me, and increased the potency of the magic which enveloped my mind, binding me even more closely to Benedict, so that – should I ever stray too far from him – I would fall into an enchanted sleep, only to awaken when he returned to my presence.

I could neither speak of the terrible fate that awaited me, nor flee the man who called me 'niece', though I did try once or twice in my teenage years.

He took me to live at Puddlebury Manor, and was good to me, seeming to show genuine affection for his future mother-in-law. I received fine clothes, was educated by the best tutors, and genuinely loved by his servants, who were very kind, becoming a second family to me.

He never again harmed me in any way. Slowly, as the years went by, I convinced myself that my future marriage would never happen. I understood that many things had to be put into place in order for the ritual that would release The Rowan King to be successful. I knew Benedict was missing many of these ingredients. The bronze spinning wheel – a gift to his mother from my future husband – had not been returned upon her death. Instead, her greedy family kept it, and due to the potent symbol of power on their door, neither Benedict nor any of his father's minions could gain access to it.

An ancient torc, once the property of The Rowan King's greatest champion, had been lost, and for all his research, Benedict could not locate its whereabouts. Finally, the village where the ritual must take place was locked away behind a hedge of iron, through which none of the Fae magic required to open the gateway could pass.

As I grew up, Benedict took me on as an apprentice, teaching me much about The Art, and allowing me to read some of the ancient grimoires he kept in Puddlebury Manor's library. I devoured them eagerly, foolishly supposing that within their timeworn pages I might find a way to release myself from the witchery that bound me to him. But every time I attempted a ritual that might see me emancipated from him and his master, I simply fell asleep, only to awaken in my comfortable bed. Benedict was always there when I woke, laughing and gently rebuking me for my folly.

My purity was of the utmost importance. I must be a maid on the day of the ritual, unsullied. To this end, I was kept away from other men. The only male servants allowed were old fellows, those totally loyal to my guardian.

As I grew up, I tried to fight back. My mind was always slightly befogged beneath a haze of sorcery, but I still found ways to rebel, ways to express myself. I chose to wear men's clothes when about the house. Benedict liked my hair long, to my waist, as the women of old might wear it. I had it cut to shoulder length. He liked to see me in fancy hats, the sort worn by women in high society. I wore an old Breton fiddler's cap that I found at the top of a cupboard. They were small things, but ones I hoped would irk him.

Slowly, I grew into womanhood. Benedict bought a property in Wendlelow so as to be closer to his mother's old home, waiting, with the patience of a predator stalking his prey, for the opportunity to seize Olwyn Cysgod.

He hired a new servant, a man called Jenkins, to help him. All his other servants had remained at Puddlebury Manor. He was an ex-military man, not young, but neither was he as old as my guardian would have liked. He did possess two qualities that my uncle valued above all others: he was strong, and his mind had been scarred by war. The doctor was quick to provide him with what he called 'one of his special potions', a concoction carefully created by himself that would ease the man's troubles and dampen his romantic ardour, thus making him a perfect companion, someone to protect me and warn off any potential suitors. A man dependent upon him for his peace of mind.

I should have hated him.

And yet Jenkins became like a second father to me. He was kind, helpful, giving me advice. We became very good friends. I confided in him, as much as my spell-fuddled brain would allow, hinting at how unhappy I was, at my desire to escape the doctor's clutches. Jenkins was an astute man. He decoded my hinted half-messages, understood my desire to escape, and tried to do what Benedict's magic had always ensured I could not. He started looking for ways to break the powers that bound me.

I remember the night Benedict laid claim to Olwyn Cysgod, the sickening feeling that he had finally made a big step towards his goal. Jenkins had been watching the house at Magpie Lane, awaiting an opportunity to break in, but an old sharp-tongued woman was always in residence. So, my guardian remained frustrated.

Finally, Jenkins returned one night telling the doctor that the old woman and her granddaughter had fled town, and better yet, that the marking on her door, the very sigil that had always barred my guardian's entrance, was gone, removed by hammer and chisel.

Benedict wasted no time. Within the hour, the ugly old spinning wheel was brooding in the cupboard beneath our stairs, firmly secured within by the best lock money could buy.

Not long after that, Jenkins died. At the time, I believed the local doctor's opinion: that my friend and co-conspirator's passing was the result of some fatal weakness of the heart. I was devastated, having lost my closest friend, the only person who understood my peril and had been quietly working away on my behalf.

I had lost my hope.

Of course, now I better understand the poisons at Benedict's disposal. I have also learned of the effects of one particularly baleful toxin, and I find myself wondering. Did Benedict guess at Jenkins' intentions? Did he come to realise that the depth of the man's loyalty to me surpassed his desire for the potions that had made him so compliant a servant?

Of course, I can never truly know. Men's hearts do fail them, and yet…

The loss of Jenkins was a blow to both of us, for if I had lost a friend, Benedict had lost a vital servant. He was forced to bring in women from the town to cook and clean for him, duties that had previously fallen to my deceased friend. Sadly, this caused a lot of disruption in the house; Benedict did not like women. I always imagined he had been hurt by one in his younger days and carried this injury about with him, nursing it bitterly. He was good to me, but then I was essential, and for a larger part of the time cowed by the grim spells cast upon me.

However, the women he brought in were strong-minded, and though they were careful not to declare outright war upon him – he was, after all, paying their wages – they had ways and means of letting their displeasure be known, and Benedict often found himself at odds with them.

I must confess to receiving some pleasure when seeing him stomp about the house, muttering under his breath after some altercation with one of these formidable ladies. There were few other things during that time of my life that made me smile, for with Jenkins gone I had lost my chaperone and could only leave the house in Benedict's company.

Eventually, he discovered Casper. He had been on the lookout for someone to replace Jenkins for a long time, and this man possessed most of the qualities he sought, with just one exception: he was too young. Too close to my own age. Still, he needed a man, and with Casper present to cook – the dear fellow was a dreadful cook – Benedict was able to reduce the female staff to one old lady who cleaned for him. His mood started to improve.

I know that Casper was given a larger dose of the potion than Jenkins was, just to be certain, to ensure compliance and to deaden any romantic urges.

I am sorry to say that, to begin with, we did not get on.

I viewed Casper as little more than an oaf, even though his arrival had signalled a new period of freedom for me. I, once again, had someone other than Benedict to escort me about town.

I had, for the longest time, expressed a need to have some hobby or pastime that took me away from the townhouse. I felt like a caged bird, wanting only to stretch my wings, to fly unhindered.

Well aware of my frustrations, Doctor Mogfadian purchased a disused property close to Wendlelow's market, and we began to build up a business selling antique goods to the town's more well-to-do folk. Benedict had inherited many old things which sat disused in Puddlebury Manor, and he stocked the shop with these items, as well as other things we collected on our travels. He also had many contacts from whom he could purchase items for resale in the shop.

It became quite profitable, although this was of little interest to Benedict, who had a seemingly endless reserve of funds. He provided me with what I considered to be a king's ransom, stored in a safe in the flat above the shop, so I might always be able to cover any expenses that occurred, no matter how large they might be.

I have always been interested in history and folk tales and had been aware of a little group that gathered in a church hall – not far from where we lived – to discuss such things. It was run by the university librarian, Mr Nolan Perkins, and they met once a week. I had been badgering

Benedict to take me to one of these meetings, genuinely believing he too would gain some pleasure from them.

To his credit, he did take me, but only the once. He quarrelled with various members of the group over the value of a long-lost book entitled *Hunllefau*, and was so disgusted with what he referred to as 'their cowardly attitude toward the item and how it might aid The Art', that he refused to ever again be in the same room as 'that group of small-minded scribblers.'

It was all terribly embarrassing, and I did not attend another meeting with them for a long time.

But the arrival of Casper changed that situation. Once more I could go to the little society meetings, sitting amongst friends – real friends, not people employed by my guardian – talking over matters that interested me. Better still, for reasons I did not fully understand, Casper refused to attend, directly defying his employer's instructions to keep me constantly under his scrutiny. Instead, he would retire to a public house while I enjoyed a few hours without any oversight. I cannot tell you how liberating that felt, how I used to long for those evenings to come, counting the days like a child awaiting Christmas.

Though I can never know for certain, I like to think that Casper sensed my frustration and retired to that public house to give me a precious evening alone, that brief moment of independence.

Slowly, his blunt ways, his unimaginative, dull outlook on life ceased to grate on me, and I grew to value him. If he could defy Benedict in this small manner, was it not possible he could do so in other ways too? Could he be an ally, as Jenkins had been?

Benedict's discovery of the lost torc was another great blow. He never told me exactly how he had come to learn of its location, but he was a persistent man, and learn it he did.

He paid a local farmer to drain a pool on his land, pretending to want to invest in the man's business; but Benedict had no interest in agriculture, and no need to make such a small, unrewarding investment. Eventually, I learned that the precious torc had been discarded in that small body of water.

When the terrible events at that farm were over, Benedict privately showed me the item he had recovered. The torc was beautiful. It had been stored in a water-damaged box, marked with a symbol I knew to be a Witch-brand. As dismayed as I was at its discovery, I was not totally forlorn, for I could not believe he would ever breach Carchar Haearn's formidable supernatural defences.

In this, I underestimated him.

I remember him showing me the torc in his study. It was a finely crafted thing, made of the purest gold I had ever seen, fine strands of precious metal twisted together in a pleasing way, one end capped off with a boar's head, the other with a stag's, each facing the other, as though poised to kiss.

Tiny flecks of metal – iron filings – had become lodged in its interwoven metal. I had suggested we clean them away, but Benedict was adamant that we not touch them, and that the thing should be stored in its wooden box.

"My dear," he had said, in that condescending tone he always liked to adopt, and that so irked me. "The only things keeping us safe from a very vengeful and angry spirit are those filings and that box. The filings must never be removed, and the torc never – and my dear I do mean never – removed from the box at night. Fortunately, I do not think that tiny quantity of iron will be enough to warp the effects of any magic I need to wield through it."

My friendship with Casper had grown since that morning at Wych Hollow Farm and the terrible confrontation with the thing from the pool. Casper's

242

bravery at stepping in to defend me from the horror that had attacked us greatly impressed me. Something within him seemed to have changed too; the ice about his soul seemed to melt, enough for me to see the real person within. We would talk occasionally. I wanted nothing more than to share my plight with my new friend, but the doctor's dark spells continued to silence my tongue.

This growing friendship occurred at a time when Benedict was becoming more distracted than ever. Much of his time was spent obsessing over a building project he had invested in.

I started experimenting in his laboratory. Rather than use The Art to break the spells woven about me – an endeavour doomed to failure – I tried something more subtle. Whilst he was away at shareholder meetings, I brewed tonics that might weaken the hold he had over me. None was very successful. But one afternoon I distilled a concoction of sage, meadowsweet, camomile, and an opiate – which was kept for use in Casper's medication. I found this made me drowsy, and whilst still unable to speak about my situation, with a little trial and error I discovered I could write more than I had previously been able to. Finally, I had a way to communicate with Casper, maybe even with Nolan and sweet Roger.

But the supply of the opiate was low. If I were to make any more, I would have to wait till Benedict restocked the ingredients, for I had no wish to draw his suspicions.

After the death of Daphne Galthorpe-Harding, our relationship deteriorated terribly. I could barely speak to him. I knew he was responsible for the woman's death, but could think of no way to prove it.

Benedict's building investment was a ploy, simply a means by which he could remove some of the iron staves that protected Carchar Haearn. Not long after the work had started, some terrible event occurred at the village, leaving it abandoned, with the construction team and many of the occupants missing. All the other people involved in the project dropped out, unwilling to sink any more money into it. Benedict did not care; he had what he needed from the venture.

He spent more time at home again, working in the laboratory or reading mouldering old tomes in his study. Months passed, but still I had no privacy, no opportunity to create the elixir that I so needed. The 31st of October was bearing down on me – the date on which the ritual must be performed.

At the last possible moment, I got my chance. On the 30th of October, Benedict announced that he was going to accompany the bronze spinning wheel on its journey to Carchar Haearn. He had hired some men to deliver it there, but, distrusting as he was, he would not let them go unsupervised, intending to follow them in his car. This gave me the precious time I needed alone in the laboratory. I worked swiftly. When the distance between myself and Benedict became too great, I would drift off into that mystical sleep, only awakening on his return. Fortunately, he had some business which held him in town for an hour before he and the workmen could transport the crate containing the spinning wheel.

It was time I put to good use. I found myself constantly looking at the carriage clock, wondering how much longer I would have to work, terrified that at any moment I would feel the mists of sleep drift over my eyes. Finally, I finished my task, and was even able to tidy the laboratory, falling asleep on the hallway floor moments after closing the cellar door behind me, the little potion hidden in my pocket.

When Benedict returned later that day, he found me asleep and gently awoke me, chastising me for refusing to accompany him on his journey. As soon as I was able, I concealed the little bottle of fluid in my room. I knew I must time its use with the greatest care. I needed long enough to write my letter and pass it on to Casper. I no longer held out any hope of getting it to any member of the MSLM.

But once again I was foiled. Though I had awakened early and had the letter written and in my pocket by the time I came downstairs, I discovered Benedict had dispatched Casper on an errand, and that he would not be coming with us to Carchar Haearn.

I had waited too long.

Worse still, I began to realise that Benedict had drugged my breakfast tea and this, combined with my potion, was making me drowsier than I wanted to be. I managed to stagger up the stairs and push my note under Casper's door. The last thing I remember was hearing Benedict chanting from his study, working The Art.

Working The Art on me.

I tried to resist, but slowly I drifted away from myself, carried off by the melodious tones of my guardian, firmly in the grip of his magic.

I became caught up in a dream. I found myself standing alone on a village green beneath a bright autumnal moon. A greyish, ghostly figure approached me – a man, powerfully built – but no... this was no man, for he bore a crown of antlers that sprouted directly from his skull. He came to stand before me and I found myself unable to move, held in place by the force of his presence.

Slowly, by degrees, he lost his misty, ghost-like appearance, starting to solidify, to take on colour. His eyes were brown orbs, pupil less, glittering as if a dozen tiny stars were trapped within them. His chin and nose were strong; his face looked as though Mother Nature herself had chiselled it from a mighty oak. It was cruel but handsome at the same time. He smelt of the forest in springtime, a smell that was quite intoxicating. His leggings were of animal hide, held in place by a black leather belt with a large, ornate, golden buckle. His muscular chest was bare.

The look this entity gave me was one of a man who had finally taken possession of a much-desired item – one he intended to hold on to for all eternity.

I should have been terrified. This was no dream, but a nightmare. Yet all I felt was a longing to be swept up in this terrible being's arms.

His spectral appearance was almost gone, now just the edge of his body seemed vague and ghostly. Slowly, he raised his arms to me and took a step forward.

Then he stopped.

A look of anger distorted his face. He looked to the left, and a guttural growl rumbled in his throat.

Then he faded away.

I awoke with a start.

I was in the back seat of Nolan's car, my head resting on Roger's lap, he gently stroking my hair. A strange sense of relief passed over me, for if I was here, like this, then something must have happened to doom Benedict's plans. I was safe, and the fog had lifted from my mind. I had no wish to speak at that moment, but knew I could now do so freely when I wanted to.

I stayed with Nolan and Isobel for a few days, resting, waiting, but neither Casper nor Benedict made an appearance, and with growing concern, we notified the police.

They were found lying next to each other, both quite dead. Benedict's head was split in two, he had died instantly. Casper's wound was more insidious, and the coroner suspected that it may have taken him some time to pass. I often wonder what he thought of in those last moments. I hope it was something peaceful. Though troubled, he was also an undeniably good man.

He was my friend.

I shall miss him.

Olwyn Cysgod was gone, though who took it I do not know. Nolan suspects there may be agents of my ex-fiancé who are capable of leaving his realm for brief periods, and that it is they who carried it away.

The golden torc was returned to its box as soon as we arrived back in Wendlelow. Nolan has taken it to the university. I have no wish to know what happened to it after that – let it pass from my life, its story unknown.

Sadly, it has left its mark on my body: a black stain that circles my upper arm where it touched my skin, like a bruise that can never fade.

Benedict's will did not name me as his heir. I am not sure who inherited his properties or his vast resources, as it was kept secret.

I am not destitute, though. I have the antiques shop with its little flat, and a safe full of money, which was never mentioned in the will. I have told no one of it either. It shall be my nest egg against hard times.

I did not attend Benedict's funeral; I had no wish to. He was buried in the grounds of Puddlebury Manor, as requested in his will.

I did attend Casper's, though, as did Nolan, and even Roger – though I think he came mainly for my sake, for he was never far from my side all that day, and very attentive to my needs.

So, I suddenly find myself free, something I never believed would happen. Free to pursue my life as I wish. Roger visits me almost daily, and now it is he who walks me to the weekly meetings of the MSLM. I know he cares for me, and I like that, but he is younger than I, and, well, I do not yet know how I feel.

With Benedict gone, I find Nolan seems more open with me. He and Isobel have become quite protective, like a kindly older brother and sister. At their suggestion, I have taken on Martha, an older woman who will do for me and see to the cooking, which was never my strength. This will allow me to spend more time at the shop.

I have moved a small part of Benedict's laboratory and equipment into my cellar, along with some of his choicer books. Archimedes, the stuffed crocodile, has also moved there, hanging from the ceiling, as is his wont, overseeing his little subterranean kingdom – my dusty old friend.

As yet, I have told no one about this room or its contents. I do not think they would understand, particularly Nolan, who has an aversion to any kind of spellcraft.

Roger told me about the little folk magic the head librarian had performed on the bread – magic that briefly broke Benedict's hold on me, allowing me to be brought to safety. I can only imagine what it took the man to discard his scruples and work that little enchantment. I am grateful he did.

Nolan has spoken to me of an old friend of his – a woman, some relative – who used to live in Wendlelow, and after whom he named the little folklore society he runs. Apparently, she was a very brave soul, having been called upon in the past to help the town with some of its more unusual problems.

Maybe I could use the arcane skills I have learned to do something similar.

Maybe I could be a source of good in this town.

Maybe…

Author's Note

Firstly, I would like to thank anyone and everyone who took the time to purchase and read this book. I hope it gave you many hours of pleasure and transported your imagination on many wonderful, chilling adventures.

Secondly, if you would be so kind, I would be very grateful for a short review on Amazon and Goodreads. It really helps.

A special thanks goes to my editor, Carson Buckingham, for making such wonderful suggestions and for being so patient and kind when checking my work.

I would like to offer a huge thanks to the members of the M. R. James Appreciation Society – Steve Howard, Caroline Moseley, Tim Shewan, Dawn Hinselwood, John Nickson – as well as Ehson Roudini, for their advanced reviews and for bravely setting forth on a quest to hunt down any renegade goblins hiding in the text.

Finally, a big thank to my wonderful wife Karen and to my family and friends who have supported me over the years. None of this would have been possible without you.

Also Available on Amazon & Audible.

Fireside Horror
By P. A. Sheldon

In the quiet lanes and mist-laced woods of Edwardian Shropshire lies the university town of Wendlelow – a place steeped in folklore, and shadowed by things far older than memory.

Elspeth McGinnity, a young widow with a keen eye for old tales and older truths, serves as both folklorist and investigator of the inexplicable. With the help of her steadfast cousin and assistant, Nolan Perkins, she delves into mysteries that defy science and reason – from prehistoric devils lurking beneath the hills, to restless spirits that whisper by lonely lakes, and creatures that should not walk where men tread.

For this is witch-haunted, boggart-cursed Wendlelow, hearth and home to the strange.

Pity those who dwell here.

Curl up by the fire, dim the lights, and prepare to be horrified.

Also Available on Amazon.

Pocket Horror
Classic Tales of Terror
Selected By P. A. Sheldon

This is a collection of some of the finest horror stories ever set down on paper. Classic tales to chill your blood from the likes of M. R. James, E. Nesbit, Washington Irving, F. J. Loring, Amelia B. Edwards and Saki, all bound up in a handy pocket–sized book.

Now you can enjoy a pleasing shiver wherever you go.

Stories in this book Include:

Oh, Whistle, and I'll Come to you, My Lad. By M. R. James.
Man–sized in Marble. By E. Nesbit.
The Ghost Coach. By Amelia B. Edwards.
The Open Window. By Saki.
The Tomb of Sarah. By F. J. Loring.
Uncle Abraham's Romance. By E. Nesbit.
The Legend of Sleepy Hollow. By Washington Irving.

Also Available on Amazon & Audible.

Noble Rot
By Carson Buckingham

What would you pay for half a huge duplex, ideally located and completely furnished with beautiful antiques that you could take with you, free of charge, if you ever move? The answer is – next to nothing. But why? Allison Pilch discovers that what initially seems idyllic carries a horrific hidden cost. Allison will have her sanity stretched to the limit by neighbours she hears, but never sees; a creepy room that she keeps locked, and a new boss with a disturbing affliction. Oh, and let's not forget the steadily growing dread and inexplicable fear of the dark that arrives out of nowhere…

Printed in Great Britain
by Amazon

3cca3fb7-55f8-47e5-9571-eca4048fe667R01